HOME IS WHERE THE COWBOY IS

O'SULLIVAN SISTERS BOOK 6

SOPHIA QUINN

———

ISBN: 978-1-99-103430-4 (Paperback)
ISBN: 978-1-99-103429-8 (Kindle)

Forever Love Publishing Ltd

www.foreverlovepublishing.com
2022 - USA

CHAPTER 1

Sierra McNeal stared at the empty space on the fireplace mantel where her favorite photo used to sit. She frowned as she moved toward it, the place now a gaping hole between a lineup of framed photos—Sierra with pigtails and ice cream smeared across her face, Sierra hugging her patient pet cat while her mother laughed in the background, Sierra holding up her trophy for first place in the middle school long-distance run with her grandparents beaming on either side of her, Sierra decked out in her hiking gear and standing proudly on top of a rock, a stunning vista view behind her. Snapshots of her life, lined up along the mantelpiece…and one of the most important ones was missing.

Sierra in a Christmas hat, her grandparents and mother squishing into the selfie shot. They were all laughing, all oblivious to the fact that it was the last Christmas they'd share with Grandpa Luke. All that remained of the memory now was a dust-free mark in the shiny mahogany.

Sierra's mother walked into the room carrying an empty box.

"Ma, what happened to the family photo? The one with all of us."

Her mother dropped the box with a sigh and swiped a hand over her forehead to push back a lock of hair that Sierra had been surprised to see now held more than a hint of gray. "Gran wanted it next to her bed in the hospital when she…" Her mother's lips pinched, and she blinked, then huffed. "Well, you know."

Sierra's throat grew tight, and she started to reach out to draw her mother into an embrace, but then her mother clipped, "You would have known that if you'd come back in time."

Sierra stiffened, and her arms dropped. She bit the inside of her cheek to keep from snapping back. Her mother was an orphan now. It didn't matter how old someone got, that sense of loss had to be overwhelming.

She was grieving.

They both were.

And if there was one thing Sierra had come to know well since she'd moved out of the house she'd shared with her mother until she'd graduated from high school, it was that her mother's guilt trips were almost always followed by instant regret.

Three, two…

"Oh, honey, I'm sorry," her mother said with a loud exhale. She moved to Sierra with her arms open wide. "I know you did everything you could to get back here before she passed."

Sierra's smile was forced as she wrapped her arms around her mother to console her. She had done everything she could. And she wasn't sure she'd ever forgive herself for not getting back to San Francisco in time.

But traveling home from Venezuela was a trek at the best of times, and getting from the remote village where she'd been stationed to Caracas had taken more buses and puddle jumpers than she cared to recall. Then the flight had been canceled and…

Well, what was the use in rehashing it all? What mattered was she hadn't been here when her mother had needed her.

She patted her mother's back and then gingerly tried to extricate herself from the bear hug. Glancing at the empty boxes, she arched her brows. "How about I tackle the attic?"

Her mother nodded. "I'll finish up down here."

Sierra winked. "Meet you in the kitchen in an hour for lunch."

Her mother chuckled, and Sierra was relieved to see her faint smile. "Deal."

Sierra grabbed a box and headed to the stairs as her mother said, "It's good to have you home, hon."

"We make a good team," Sierra shot back, the phrase a callback to all those years when those words had been something of a motto in their household of two. They'd been partners and friends. Just the two of them against the world.

Until Sierra had gotten a scholarship and left for a different world. Not all that far away—she was still in California—but the way her mother reacted, she might as well have fled the country.

And then, of course, Sierra *had* left the country, and things between them had never quite been the same.

But for now, at least, they were on the same team again. It wasn't easy dealing with her grandmother's passing, but she'd been sick for a long time, and in a way, it was a relief that she was out of her misery.

Sierra could hear her mother getting to work organizing Grandma's things on the first floor as she climbed the two sets of stairs that led to the cramped and cluttered attic. For a second, she stopped to assess the situation.

There were boxes stacked upon boxes, and it was hard even knowing where to begin. When she'd moved into this place after Grandpa died, she'd been a bit of a wreck, and it had taken her months to properly unpack…which clearly she hadn't. This attic was storing more than its fair share, and Sierra guessed her grandmother had forgotten about most of it.

She dropped the empty box and blew a lock of hair out of her face. She'd been born with the same brown hair as her mother, but she hadn't seen her natural color in an age. Right now it was dyed bright red, which had seemed like a fun, vibrant color when a fellow nurse had talked her into it back in Venezuela but had felt absurdly inappropriate at her grandmother's funeral.

The small chapel had been filled with Grandma's church friends—there wasn't much family left aside from Sierra and her mother—and Sierra had sat in the first pew, feeling like a red fire hydrant in a sea of black.

But at least she'd made it home for the funeral, right? That was something.

"Where to start?" she muttered to herself as she eyed the stacked boxes beside her. With a sigh, she pulled out her phone, called up her running playlist, which was a mashup of old glam rock hits and songs from her favorite

Zombie Town album, which was tragically underrated, in Sierra's opinion. With the music blasting from her admittedly tinny little speaker, she hauled a box off the top of a stack and dove in.

Her mother found her covered in dust and singing under her breath when she climbed the attic stairs an hour later.

"Just checking in," she said when Sierra looked over her shoulder.

"Good." Sierra nodded. "It feels like I'm not making a dent, but I've got time, right?"

It was a rhetorical question, but her mother pursed her lips. Sierra tensed, knowing what was coming.

"I wish you had more time at home."

"Ma," she groaned. "I'm home for *six weeks*."

And it was by far the longest amount of time she'd spent at home since she'd graduated from college more than a decade before. But was that enough to satisfy her mother?

Nope.

"I know, but do you have to go back to that place? Why don't you find a nice job somewhere around here? Patty at the clinic said they were hiring nurses and—"

"Ma." She tried to keep her voice even, her tone gentle. *She's grieving*, she reminded herself for the tenth time that day. "I love my job. I'm proud of what I do."

"I know, but you'd still be nursing if you came back here, and—"

"Let's not do this right now, okay?"

Her mother clamped her lips shut, and Sierra could feel her disappointment. But honestly, if her mother didn't understand by now that it wasn't just nursing that made

5

Sierra happy but bringing her gifts to people in need, then she didn't know what else to say.

"I'm back for six weeks, Ma. Can we just...enjoy our time together?"

Her mother's smile was more of a grimace as she nodded, turning back toward the steps. "I'll heat up one of the casseroles the neighbor dropped off. Come down soon."

Sierra turned back to the box she'd been sorting through but barely saw what she was looking for as her mind raced. This was how it always went when she came home to visit. No matter how long she stayed, it wouldn't be long enough. No matter what she did or how often she called, it wouldn't be enough.

But the worst part was, being home made her feel like she was a teenager again. Gone was the grown woman, the competent, world-traveling, well-respected nurse, and in her place was a teenage girl ready to have a temper tantrum.

She blew out a long breath as she moved the box aside to dig into the next. "Papers. Wonderful."

Stacks and stacks of papers and documents and...cards?

She knew her grandmother was sentimental, but had she seriously kept every birthday card? That seemed a little extreme.

It...

Wait a second...

Her brows drew down as she lifted the top card in a stack that was bundled together. The pink envelope wasn't addressed to her grandmother. It was addressed to her.

"Sierra McNeal" was written in a scrawl she didn't recognize, but the address was familiar. It wasn't addressed to this house, where her grandparents lived, but the house she'd grown up in a couple towns over.

"What the...?" She lifted the rest of the bundle and quickly sorted through them, her breath hitching as she realized they were all made out to her. They'd been opened, but Sierra couldn't recall ever getting these cards.

She couldn't remember anyone but her mother and grandparents even remembering her birthday.

With a shaky hand, she slid the card out of the top envelope, and the moment she started to read, her belly pitched, and her heart pounded.

She reached for the next card and then the next. The messages were always similar.

I'm sorry I can't be there to celebrate with you...
   I hope you know I'm thinking of you...
   You're on my mind today as you become a teenager...

Her breathing was coming in shallow gulps by the time she got to the last card. It was postmarked a few days before her twenty-fifth birthday, nearly ten years before.

Another message saying the same thing, and with the same signature at the bottom...

Frank O'Sullivan.

Who the heck is Frank O'Sullivan?

She sat there staring at the cards in her lap for what felt like an eternity, a small suspicion swirling inside her. One she wasn't quite brave enough to unpack yet.

"Sierra! Lunch is ready, hon!" her mother called up the stairs.

Sierra got to her feet, but her legs felt shaky, her stomach queasy.

Shock, she knew. This was a mild case of shock. It would pass.

She headed toward the steps and made her way to the kitchen. For a long moment, she watched her mother bustle about, so familiar and homey, even with the cupboards thrown open and half the contents piled up in boxes.

"Mom."

Her mother turned, her eyes wide, no doubt at Sierra's serious tone. "What's up, sweetie?"

Sierra held up the stack of cards. "Who is Frank O'Sullivan?"

Her mother jerked to a stop, the serving spoon suspended in midair. Her lips quivered, her chin bunching for a moment as she obviously tried to control whatever emotions were coursing through her.

"Honey, I…" She shook her head. "He…he's no one."

"He's obviously someone." Sierra shook the cards in her hand, the shock she'd worked her way through now morphing into a sharp anger. She didn't even understand why until that suspicion she'd been trying to ignore started to rise up and fill her brain.

Like a pulsing heartbeat, the words rang between her ears. *You know who he is. You know!*

Crossing her arms, she couldn't stop her voice from trembling. "Who is he, Ma?"

She needed to hear the woman who raised her say it. She needed the truth after all these years. All the times she'd asked about "Daddy" and her mother had said she didn't need one.

"You've got Grandpa, Gran, and me. You don't need anyone else, my sweet."

She'd bought it as a child...or at least swallowed it. Even in her teenage years, when the questions burned brighter and hotter, her mom had always managed to brush her off, change the subject, distract her with something else.

But not this time.

She squeezed the cards in her hand before slapping them on the table. "Tell me the truth! Who is he?"

Her mother's arms dropped, her chin dipping toward the floor when she softly mumbled, "He's...the sperm."

Sierra scoffed. "You mean my father."

Her mom's nostrils flared as she made two fists and turned to face out the window.

"You told me he'd gone somewhere we could never find him. I thought you were trying to tell me he was dead, but you didn't have the heart to say it so bluntly." The words came out low and lethal as her whole history seemed to shatter and reshape itself right before her eyes.

"I had to tell you something. You wouldn't stop asking!" her mother snapped, then spun back, her face a mask of anguish. "You were so persistent, and I just blurted it out to make you stop!" Her eyes sharpened, blazing with a hot glow that made Sierra flinch. "He didn't want anything to do with us. He might as well have been dead. I was trying to protect you from getting hurt!"

"He wanted nothing to do with me?" Sierra lifted the stack of cards accusingly. "Did you know about these?"

Her mother's silence was her answer.

Sierra took a few halting steps back toward the kitchen door. "How could you?"

"Sierra..."

Sierra shook her head. For a moment, she didn't trust herself to speak. Betrayal made her stomach turn violently, and she clapped a hand over her mouth.

"He didn't want us!" Her mother's voice pitched.

Sierra's hand dropped. "No, he didn't want *you*."

It was a horrible thing to say, and guilt made her insides sink even as she trembled with anger.

Her mom's expression was stricken. "Honey, I did what was best for the both of us."

Sierra felt tears welling, her throat choking. Dang it! She hated crying.

She *never* cried.

Swallowing convulsively, she held up the envelopes again, most pink or purple like they were meant for a kid, and all worn and battered at the edges. "Were you ever going to tell me about these? Were you ever going to tell me that my father was alive and wanted to meet me?"

Her mother's mouth worked, but no words came out.

No.

That was the answer. She might try to deny it, but Sierra could see it plain as day. She spun around, heading toward the front door.

"Where are you going?"

"Out," Sierra snapped.

She grabbed her battered leather jacket from the back of her grandmother's armchair and picked up the satchel she'd strewn beside it. It wasn't until she was standing next to her motorcycle, her helmet in hand, that she stopped to think about her mother's question.

Where was she going?

Her pulse pounded furiously as she sorted through the envelopes again, dumping all but the last one in her satchel. It was postmarked Aspire, Montana.

Was he still there?

She had no idea.

Sierra threw one leg over the bike and slung her satchel on her back.

She didn't know if he was still there...but she was going to find out.

CHAPTER 2

The kitchen at the main house of the O'Sullivan ranch was filled with laughter when Cody slipped in through the back door.

"Morning, Cody!" Daisy beamed at him from where she sat on a countertop, a cup of steaming tea in hand as she watched her half sister Emma load the dishwasher.

Their sister Lizzy was bustling around in her high heels, cleaning up after Cody's niece and nephew, who still sat at the kitchen table and wore matching grins when he came over to ruffle their hair.

"Morning, Uncle Cody," Chloe sang in a sweet, high-pitched voice that never failed to make his heart soar.

"How was Sunday school?" He slid into the seat beside Corbin.

"Fun!" Chloe shouted.

"We did arts and crafts." Corbin's upper lip curled. He didn't have to say any more. Arts and crafts were Chloe's idea of fun. Corbin? Not so much. Like his father—Cody's older brother, Kit—Corbin hated to be kept inside on sunny summer days like this one.

Lizzy paused in her cleaning up to swipe a napkin over Chloe's syrup-covered cheeks. "Note to self," she said wryly. "Change them out of their Sunday best before the pancakes are served."

"They're going in the wash anyway." Cody chuckled when Lizzy gave him a good-natured eye roll. His new sister-in-law was still getting used to being a mom to twins, but she clearly adored this new role. And the twins adored *her*—Kit, too—which was really all that mattered.

"Kit and I are taking the kids to a rodeo with your mom and dad this afternoon," Lizzy called over her shoulder as she joined Emma by the sink. "Wanna come?"

"Nah, thanks." At Chloe's look of disappointment, he added, "I've got a surprise to plan for when I babysit this week." He rubbed his hands together, narrowing his eyes like he was concocting some evil plan. The twins giggled like he knew they would.

"Are we still on for Thursday?" Lizzy asked. "If you have other plans…"

"Of course we're on," he said quickly. He knew how much Lizzy and Kit enjoyed having a date night once a week, and truth be told, he enjoyed his night alone with the kids. But after helping to corral these two wild things at his friend JJ's wedding to Dahlia O'Sullivan the day before, he wouldn't mind taking today off from kid duty. And with his parents there, plus Kit and Lizzy, they wouldn't need him anyway.

"If you're not going with Lizzy, you should come hang out with me and Levi," Daisy chirped. "We're taking the kids over to Rose and Dex's house to give them a hand with the baby." Her smile widened at the mention of her sheriff boyfriend and his family. "Those kids are so psyched to have a new cousin, they actually fight over who gets to change the baby's diaper."

Everyone laughed, and Emma straightened from where she'd been putting the pots and pans away. "Oh! That reminds me. Would you mind taking Rose the lasagna I made for them? I don't want them to have to think about cooking while little Kiara still has them up around the clock."

"Sure thing," Daisy said, swinging herself off the counter to fetch the lasagna. Apparently, she already forgot that she'd invited Cody, and he was happy to let the conversation carry on without him.

Emma turned toward Cody. "Have you heard from JJ today?"

He shook his head. "Nah, but he and Dahlia are probably still on that first flight."

"It takes a long time to get to Africa," Kit said as he strolled in through the front hall. He gave Cody a nod of acknowledgment just as Chloe and Corbin burst out of their seats to tackle their dad with a hug. "Well, hello to you too," he teased as he scooped one child up in each arm and carried them over to Lizzy. "Look out, darlin'," Kit drawled as he stalked toward his wife. "A three-headed monster is coming to get you."

"Oh no!" Lizzy held her hands up and widened her eyes, pretending to be scared as she ran away from Kit and the giggling twins.

Cody and Emma shared a grin as she slid into the seat beside him.

"I'm sure JJ and Dahlia are just fine," he said, his voice barely audible over the shrieks of laughter as Daisy got in on the fun, pretending to battle Kit's "monster" to save Lizzy.

"Yeah, I know you're right." She gave him a rueful smile. "I'm just a nervous traveler...even when I'm not the one traveling." She went to reach for one of the empty plates still lying on the table, but Cody beat her to it.

"Sit," he said. "Relax for a bit. You look tired."

She sank back into her seat with a grateful smile. "Thanks, Cody. I'll admit, helping to plan a wedding kinda took it out of me."

"You know you didn't have to do that, right?" he teased as he gathered up the last of the dirty dishes.

It was a rhetorical question. Of course Emma didn't *have* to help plan her half sister's wedding, but that was just who she was. The first O'Sullivan sister to arrive at this ranch and flip their ordinary world upside down, kindergarten teacher Emma was definitely a natural-born caretaker. She'd taken it upon herself to track down all the sisters she hadn't even known existed, per her deceased father's wishes. And she'd done a good job. All but the elusive eldest, Sierra, and the youngest, April, had descended on Aspire and taken the small town by storm.

"I hope you and Nash have a relaxing day planned," he said. "You deserve it."

Emma's husband, Nash, was the ranch's foreman and one of Cody's good friends. And Cody found himself smothering a grin that the mere mention of her husband still had the ability to make Emma blush.

"Yeah, we're planning to relax this afternoon," she said. "And then we're having a family dinner with Nash's parents and sister." Her eyes widened expectantly, and he knew what was coming before she even added, "If you want to come—"

"I'm good," he said, softening the words with a smile.

"I'm beat too. Think I'm just gonna take a drive. Maybe get some chores done."

Emma nodded easily. "That sounds like a great day."

He wasn't sure if she was just being nice or if she actually understood how much Cody needed to take these little solo adventures on his days off. He didn't go far—there weren't all that many towns he could drive to in a day and still be back by nightfall—but hitting the road with just some music and his thoughts always helped him come back to his day-to-day life feeling refreshed.

Cody headed over to the sink just as Kit and Lizzy were gathering up the kids to leave.

"Sure you don't want to come, bro?" Kit called out as he tried his best to herd the twins toward the door.

"I'm good," he said.

Minutes later, the kitchen was silent as the O'Sullivan sisters all went off to be with their new families.

He finished loading the dishwasher and chuckled as he soaked in the calm that followed in the wake of the family's chaos. "And then there was one." He let out a contented sigh and headed for the door as well.

After a long, winding drive, during which he did, in fact, stop to take care of some chores, he found himself in Wellspring, a small town close to Aspire. He pulled over to grab a bite to eat, unwilling to head back home just yet, because there was no doubt he'd run into several people he knew, and he wasn't sure he was up for that.

He had no complaints about growing up in a small town in the middle of nowhere, but there were days he wouldn't mind just a little anonymity. But everyone knowing everyone was part of life in Aspire. "It's a blessing and a curse," his mother always said.

He hopped out of his car and headed into the old saloon.

Heck, he'd probably run into at least a few people he knew in Wellspring since he'd been born and raised in the next town over, but at least he stood some chance of going unnoticed. A burger and a beer, and then he'd head back to the ranch.

But all thoughts of burgers fled his mind the moment he flung the saloon door open, and his gaze found her.

It was impossible not to notice the flaming red hair in the middle of a long row of cowboy hats and baseball caps. He blinked as his eyes adjusted to the dim lighting inside, and then they narrowed as he tried to drink in every last feature.

Good grief. He ran a hand over his hair as he took a deep breath to steady himself. It wasn't like he'd never seen a pretty woman before. Aspire had plenty. But there was pretty, and then there was…

Well, then there was *her.*

"Hey, Cody." A woman's twang had him glancing over to see the cocktail waitress. What was her name…?

"Sheila, hey." He sauntered in farther, following Sheila as she headed toward a table in the corner.

"How's your brother?" she asked.

"Good. Real good."

"Is it true JJ's in Africa?" Sheila's voice went high at the end in disbelief.

He chuckled as he knew he should, but he couldn't tear his gaze away from the redhead. She was leaning against the bar, not sitting even though there was a stool available. She was resting on her elbows, her body stretched out, all lean lines and gorgeous curves.

Her black jeans were formfitting, and his breath caught

when he noticed a strip of skin along her lower back where her worn leather jacket rode up. A delicate, finely drawn tattoo peeked out, but not enough for him to make out what it was.

His mouth was dry, his heart racing. And for no reason he could ever explain...he was desperate to know what that tattoo was of.

Whatever it was, it was almost...dainty, at odds with the leather, denim, and dyed hair. And yet, at the same time, it fit her perfectly. Her clothes and hair said she was a tough, "don't mess with me" woman, but her features in profile were breathtakingly delicate and just as elegant as that tattoo.

He wet his lips, only just catching the end of Sheila's long-winded monologue about her sister's latest screwup of a boyfriend. He murmured what he hoped was the correct response and then placed his order.

The moment she was gone and he was alone, he knew he had to talk to the redhead. He only hesitated a moment, even though this wasn't his usual style. His brother was the outgoing flirt in their family. Kit was shameless in his ability to stride up to the hottest woman at the bar and strike up a conversation. Not that he did that anymore.

But Cody had every right to.

He just...didn't.

It wasn't that girls didn't like Cody.

They did. He had no problem there.

But every woman in Aspire knew Cody, and, for whatever reason, they seemed to like making the first move with him. Unlike JJ, who they got all flustered around, or Kit, who beat 'em to the punch, or even Nash's cousin Boone, who was treated with care because "once a player, always a player."

Nope, when it came to Cody, women saw him as safe. Kind and approachable. And he was. Which was why he never had to do much to get a little flirty conversation going.

But he couldn't imagine that stunning redhead spotting him across the saloon and sauntering over. No, if he wanted to meet this woman, it was all on him.

So, what's the best way of doing that?

He ran through a few different lines, cringing at the cheesy ones and licking his lips as nerves started to rattle him.

Just go over there and be yourself, you big dope!

He'd regret it forever if he didn't at least try to catch the attention of the most gorgeous woman he'd ever seen. The seat beside her was empty, so Cody slid up to her, nodding to the bartender, who he recognized. "Excuse me, ma'am…"

She turned to face him, and he stopped, temporarily stricken senseless.

Gorgeous. Her eyes were a striking shade of blue, her cheekbones sharp and high, her brows delicately arched, and her lips so full and lush it was impossible not to stare at them.

When they quirked up at the corners, his gaze darted up to meet hers. Amusement made her eyes twinkle. "Can I help you?"

Her voice was low and a little raspy.

He swallowed hard.

It was sexy as all get-out. But the teasing in her tone, the playful tilt of her lips…

It made him smile in turn and eased his nerves. "Yes, ma'am," he said, raking a hand through his too-shaggy brown hair. "You see, I'd love to play a round of pool, but I'm here all on my lonesome."

He drew out the words, giving her a "What are you gonna do?" expression.

Her answering smile made his heart flip. "That's a shame."

"It is, isn't it?" he shot back. "I was hoping maybe some kind soul would take pity on me and join me for a round. What do you say?"

She was outright laughing now, and the sound was better than any of the music he'd been cruising to all day. Her grin tilted up slightly on one side, giving her a coy look as she pushed away from the bar. "Never say I don't do my part for those less fortunate."

"No, ma'am," he said, starting to chuckle at this odd but easy little banter they'd fallen into. Almost like they were already friends who shared inside jokes.

She led the way to the pool table in the back, her hips a mesmerizing sight as he followed. Stopping short at the table's edge, she bit her lip as she peeked up at him. "We have one little problem, though."

He rested a hip against the table to study her, and when she wrinkled her nose in a self-deprecating grimace, it took everything in him not to pull her into his arms and hold her tight.

"The problem is I haven't played much." She cast a wary look at the pool table. "Not sure I'll be much of an opponent."

"Not a problem. I'll teach you." His mind instantly filled with an image of how he was going to do that, and his heart raced off at a gallop.

"Mighty neighborly of you, stranger," she said, going back to their earlier routine with a little wink.

The "stranger" bit gave him pause. Heck, he really was out of practice if he hadn't even thought to give her his name...or ask for hers.

"I'm Cody, by the way." He stuck out a hand for her to shake.

She eyed him up for a moment, her lips curling into a lopsided grin as she slid her much smaller hand into his and held on.

His lips twitched into a smile. Good grief, none of his flirtations in Aspire had prepared him for a woman like this.

He leaned in slightly, dipping his head with a crooked grin as her silence went too long. "And your name is...?"

She pursed her lips. "Hmmm..."

"You don't know?" he teased.

She arched a brow. "I don't know if I'm ready to tell you."

"Okay then." He slid his thumb over the soft skin of her hand. "What'll it take to get you to trust me with your name?"

Her lips quivered, the only hint that she was trying not to laugh. "Let's play and find out."

He ducked his head to hide a grin he knew must be foolish. He could feel his wits evaporating like beads of sweat on a cold winter's day the longer they stood here holding hands like this. So close, all it would take to taste those lips was a quick dip of his head. A tug of her hand and she'd be in his arms.

But she gently slid her hand from his, and he let her go.

She frowned when he passed her a pool cue, her soft, full lower lip sticking out in a slight pout. "What am I supposed to do with this?"

Heat coursed through him as he came up behind her,

gently adjusting her grip on the stick and helping her line up her first shot.

She smelled like lilacs and something with a little spice. Cinnamon, maybe? Whatever it was, the scent wrapped around him as he bent over her, not so close as to take advantage but close enough that their thighs brushed, and the heat of her body made him feel like his skin might start burning.

"Like this?" she asked, turning her head to catch his gaze.

Her eyes danced with mischief, and he couldn't bring himself to look away, not even to make sure she was properly lined up for her shot.

"Perfect," he whispered. "Just...perfect."

CHAPTER 3

Perfect was right.

Sierra leaned against the pool table when he pocketed the eight ball. "You win," she said with a sigh. "Again."

"You're getting better, though." Cody grinned.

Sweet, sweet Cody.

"I am, aren't I?" She flipped her hair, which made him laugh. It didn't take much to make the man smile—and oh, that smile.

She soaked in the view, and just like every other time he'd laughed, the low, rumbly chuckle made butterflies swarm her belly.

"You want to play again?" he asked. The eagerness in his eyes was nearly her undoing. She couldn't remember a time any man had been so eager just to play a round of pool with her.

Though she supposed he was enjoying these lessons as much as she was.

"Maybe after we've eaten?" She nodded toward his

table, where the waitress was setting down his burger and the steak she'd ordered at the bar.

"After dinner," he agreed.

He gestured for her to go ahead of him, and then he did that move that she'd only seen in movies and never quite understood. He placed one hand at the small of her back as they weaved through the thickening crowd that blocked their way to the table.

She might not have understood it before, but she did now. It was a bizarrely chivalrous gesture and totally unnecessary, of course, but warmth spread from her lower back to her belly and then out to her limbs until she all but melted into the seat across from him.

"Beverly," he said abruptly when he sat down. "Your name's Beverly."

She burst out in a laugh she barely recognized. *Was that...?*

Oh man, am I giggling now?

"Not Beverly," she choked out, reaching for her knife and fork. "Try again."

His lopsided smile made her belly flutter again as it spread across his face, all slow and languid, just like his way of talking. Everything about him was...easy. From his overgrown stubble to the faded old T-shirt that did nothing to hide his broad shoulders and bulging biceps, the guy oozed confidence the way most men she knew could only try.

It wasn't the in-your-face kind of confidence but the real kind. The kind that said he was so comfortable in his own skin, he didn't have to bother flexing and impressing.

The kind that made a woman feel like she could be herself too.

There was no trying with a guy like Cody. He just was

26

who he was, and Sierra could be who she was, and right now…

"Tabetha?" he asked between bites of his burger.

She pressed her lips together and cut into her steak. "Nice try."

Right now she was no one. She was anonymous.

And it felt amazing. After days of being on the road alone, stewing in her own thoughts about her father, her mother, what she'd find when she got to Aspire, and what she'd say when she returned her mom's calls…

It was a relief not to talk about family or where she was from but just live in the moment for a while.

"C'mon, one hint," he said, his tone teasing.

She tilted her head to the side. "What do you need my name for?"

He shrugged. "How am I supposed to look you up online if I don't even have a first name to work with?"

She rolled her eyes. "You just want my name so you can Google stalk me?"

"Might be the only way I can learn anything about you, mystery lady." His dark eyes sparkled, and not for the first time, Sierra found herself forgetting everything—the rest of the patrons, the reason she'd come to Montana. All of it seemed to disappear when he looked at her like this—like she was endlessly fascinating, and the only person on the planet.

She swallowed hard, belatedly registering his words as she reached for his beer to steal a sip, a laugh bubbling up at the thought of what he'd find online even if he did search her name. "Good luck with that," she murmured.

It wasn't like Sierra was morally opposed to social media or anything. She wasn't. She just never really got into it, that was all. The idea of having friendships that weren't in person or at the very least over the phone was just plain depressing.

What kind of friendship was that?

And her mother had always been big on protecting their privacy when she was a kid. Always making sure their number wasn't listed and her name wasn't mentioned online and—

Sierra froze, her fork hovering in midair as another piece of the puzzle fell into place.

She felt the blood drain from her face and caught Cody's eyes focusing on her with a new intensity. "Mona Lisa? You all right?" He'd been teasingly calling her that for the last hour, insisting that he had to have something to call her, and Mona Lisa seemed a good fit.

The name now broke through the sudden flood of emotions, and she let out a huff of amusement. "I'm fine," she murmured.

Just fine. It'd been like this for days now. Pieces of overheard conversations from her childhood coming back to her with a whole new meaning. The looks her grandmother would give her mother when another lie about her father was being told.

It all added up now, filling in pieces of her life she hadn't known were missing. But now her mother's quest to keep Sierra's name and contact information private made sense. It wasn't about avoiding scammers but evading her father's attempts to get a hold of her.

He'd known how to find her grandparents, but her mother must have insisted they didn't tell him how to get in touch with her directly.

A large, warm hand slid over hers, and Sierra's head snapped up to find brown eyes gazing back at her, so warm and gentle she thought she might melt if he looked at her like that one moment longer.

His thumb stroked the back of her hand. He'd done that earlier, too, and just like then, the innocent gesture sent a bolt of electricity to her core, jolting her back to the present. "You sure you're all right, darlin'?" he asked. "If you're in trouble or need to talk, you know—"

"I know," she said quickly. Even though she didn't. What did he want, for her to spill all her secrets?

Please. She barely knew this man.

But he was here, and she'd been having the time of her life, up until thoughts of her family threatened to ruin it all.

She set her fork down with a clink. His burger was already gone. Big, broad, muscular guy that he was, it shouldn't have been a shock that he could down a burger in under a minute.

"You ready for that next game?" she asked, already coming to her feet and drawing him up with her.

He hesitated for a second, and she caught the genuine concern there.

Her heart did a crazy little twist. Sweet guy. He was gonna make some small-town cowgirl one happy lady someday.

He eventually relented with a shake of his head. "All right, Penelope. Lead the way."

She giggled at his guess, and they reached the table just as another twosome was finishing up.

"Okay, Cowboy." She started chalking her pool cue. "How about we put some money on this one?"

His arched brows were full of skepticism. "You serious?"

She couldn't blame him. With a shrug, she said, "I feel like I'm getting better."

He scratched the back of his head, and she pressed her lips together to hold back a grin. He really was adorable when he was trying to spare her feelings. "Well, yeah, your second game was a little better, but I don't want to go robbing you blind."

She gave him an exaggerated frown. "Please, Cowboy. Your chivalry is insulting. Just put your money on the table and let me try to win it off you."

"All right then." He shook his head, slapping down a ten.

She snickered as the reckless part of her that had come alive the moment he'd leaned against the bar beside her flared to life, and she found herself leaning into him with a flirty grin. "Now where's your sense of adventure?" Slapping down two fifties, she wiggled her eyebrows.

He gaped at her. "You sure you want to be throwing that much away?"

"Aw, let a girl try. Come on." She batted her eyelashes and was rewarded with one of his low, rumbly laughs.

"Okay then." He sighed, and she just knew he was going to do something chivalrous again. This guy didn't know how *not* to be a proper gentleman.

Someone's mama raised him right.

Sure enough, he broke and then downed five balls straight.

She bit her lip and cocked a hip as she studied the rapidly depleting layout on the table. And then, just as expected...the man threw the game. Well, he threw the next shot, aiming so wide it was a wonder the cue ball stayed on the table.

"My turn," she sang cheerfully as she snagged the cue

stick from his hand. "Let's see..." She wiggled her hips, enjoying herself far too much as she glanced over her shoulder. "Like this?"

The cue stick connected with a loud clack, and the balls scattered, three of her striped ones going in one after the other.

Cody stood there gaping, so dang cute she couldn't stifle another giggle as she glanced up at him between shots. "You're a good teacher, Cowboy."

His mouth clamped shut, but while some men might've gotten annoyed, this one...

Oh boy.

This one gave her a lazy, lopsided grin that made her tremble from her head to her toes.

She finished the game in record time, sinking the 8-ball with a sweet sigh before leaning back to smirk at him.

"You...," he said when she slowly walked around the table, snatching her winnings with a grin.

"Me?" she prompted.

He reached out and wrapped his hands around her waist, pulling her in close and leaning down until his nose grazed hers. "Charlene Marie, you hustled me."

Her laugh was an embarrassingly girly giggle as she clutched his hard biceps, her heart tripping over itself as she reveled in his warmth. "I did. But if it makes you feel any better, the next round is on me."

His head fell back with a rough bark of laughter. "You're on. But make it a pop for me. I've still gotta drive home."

The words threatened to dampen her giddy mood, but she cast a quick look toward the grungy window, where the sun was starting to set. "Yeah, I've got to get on the road soon too."

A silence fell between them as reality loomed overhead. "But I've got time for a pop. And maybe...some fries?"

His smile hitched up on one side, and he settled a hand on her lower back, making her veins flood with warmth. He leaned down so she could hear him over the music and the crowd. "*Definitely* fries."

CHAPTER 4

Cody didn't want the evening to end.

But he tried to keep that thought at bay as his fingers brushed hers when he reached for another handful of fries.

She stilled, her eyes darting up to meet his.

Satisfaction rippled through him when he saw the way her eyes flared wide for a second and she made no move to pull away.

She felt it too.

He was certain of it. She felt this strange electricity that zapped between them every time their bodies came into contact. Even with something as innocent as brushing fingers over the basket of fries.

She grabbed a few and took a bite, settling back in her seat with one knee up and that little mischievous tilt to her lips.

Mona Lisa had been his best guess yet, because it was so very fitting. This woman was an enigma. At once sweet and soft, while also tough as nails and with a wicked sense of humor.

Good grief, when he'd realized she'd hustled him, his first thought wasn't *Oh crap, I lost my money*. It'd been *I think I'm in love*.

He gave his head a little shake with a rueful huff of laughter. "Okay, your turn." He dunked a french fry in ketchup and smiled at her. "Favorite ice cream topping."

She pursed her lips, her gaze going distant like she was really giving this a lot of thought.

He chuckled, soaking in everything he could. He wanted—*needed*—to remember every detail later when he was back at the bunkhouse without JJ and only some nomadic cowboys he barely knew for company.

He took note of the way she nibbled on her lower lip when she was thinking. The way she moved in her chair, graceful and sleek as a ballerina. She'd taken off her leather jacket during their last game, and he could make out another tattoo peeking out over the edge of her T-shirt. Again, it was thin, simple lines, but he couldn't see enough to know what it was.

And he knew better than to ask. For hours now they'd been laughing and talking, but they managed to talk about everything…and nothing.

"Butterscotch," she said abruptly, breaking into his thoughts.

He feigned confusion. "Wait, is that your name or…?"

Her laugh made his gut clench with desire.

She leaned forward, her elbows on the table. "So tell me more about this ranch hand job of yours. What do you actually do all day?"

There was nothing patronizing in her tone, which he appreciated. He'd dated a girl once who kept asking him about his career aspirations.

Aspirations. She'd actually used that word. Like it

wasn't enough that he loved being out on the range, and that he enjoyed working alongside his brother and best friends.

Like he wasn't worth anything if his life wasn't all about making more money or climbing some invisible ladder.

But not his mystery woman. Nope, she listened intently, a hint of a wistful smile on her lips as he gave her the lowdown of what a typical day looked like for him.

"Must be beautiful on this ranch of yours." Her tone had a wistful lilt, another dimension to her varied tones and nuances. He filed it away to relive later.

"What about you?" he asked. "What do you do for a living?" When she didn't immediately answer, he added, "Aside from hustle innocent ranch hands, of course."

"Of course." Her eyes glinted with amusement, but she might as well have plastered caution tape across her features. "I don't want to talk about the real world, Cody. It'll be there waiting for us soon enough."

He nodded, keeping his expression even despite his disappointment. "Fair enough…Barbara."

She grinned and snagged a few more fries.

"Want me to ask Sheila for more ranch dressing to dip those in, Clarabell?"

She giggled. "Yes, please."

He now knew she liked ranch dressing on her fries. He added this mundane fact to the running list he had going on. He knew she didn't watch much TV because she couldn't sit still long enough to get invested in any shows, and that her favorite color was orange, and she preferred dogs to cats, and she didn't think anyone should ever eat kale under any circumstance.

He found himself smiling a goofy grin at the memory

of her over-the-top disdain for the vegetable. But honestly, he didn't know anything real about her.

So why did he have this feeling like he knew her so well? And that she knew him better than just about anyone?

It was ridiculous, obviously. She was a stranger, and from what little she'd told him about where she was coming from and where she was going, it was obvious that she wasn't sticking around these parts for long.

It was one night, that was all.

It definitely wasn't love. Probably wasn't even a real crush. How could it be real when this was based on nothing more than a little fun flirtation?

Nope. Cody wasn't looking forward to this evening ending, but he knew it had to. There was no future here.

He might have seen his brother and friends fall hard and fast for their wives, but he wasn't such a romantic that he truly believed in love at first sight.

Lust at first sight, sure.

He reached for a fry and came up empty.

"Huh." His mystery woman frowned. "Looks like I won't need that ranch after all. We're out."

A silence fell, the first awkward quiet of the night.

Her lips curved up in that impish little grin, but it was tempered by the regret in her eyes. "Well, I guess that's it, then."

"Guess so," he agreed.

Neither of them made a move to stand.

"That all, hon?" Sheila was the one to break the stilted moment as she hovered over their table with a check in hand.

Cody grabbed it before Mona Lisa could. She scowled at him with feigned irritation, and he donned his best cocky swagger. "You might win at pool, sweetheart, but I'll be the one to pay for dinner every time."

"Every time, huh?" Her voice was filled with laughter, and he knew what she meant.

"Yeah, all right. This one time," he shot back, handing a hovering Sheila the bill along with a wad of cash to cover the tab and tip. He held out a hand, helping his date to her feet. "But if you ever come through Southwest Montana again...," he started.

She gave a little snort as she led the way to the exit. "Chances are I won't be coming back."

He nodded, shoving his hands in his pockets. "Right. I figured."

And that was not aching disappointment nagging at his gut. There was something wrong with the oil they'd used for the fries, that was all.

"So, how long *are* you staying, then?" he asked.

"I..." Her expression faltered a bit, the impish little hint of a smile replaced by a flicker of worry or something like it. "I don't know. Probably not long at all."

She tried for a smile, but it looked strained. "Might be back on the road as of tomorrow. It all depends."

Depends on what? He bit back the words. This had been one of the best nights of his life. The last thing he wanted was to ruin it now by asking her questions she wouldn't answer.

"This is me." She stopped right next to a motorcycle, and he blinked in surprise before letting out a bark of laughter.

"Of course you ride a motorcycle," he said with a shake of his head. "I should have known...Rhonda."

She smiled up at him, her eyes sparkling with humor in the light of the streetlamp. "Not Rhonda." She reached under the seat for a helmet and set it on the bike. "But nice try."

"C'mon, Hustler," he said. "Just give me a name. That's all I ask."

She pursed her lips and planted her hands on her hips, thinking it over before giving a firm shake of her head. "Sorry, Cowboy."

She surprised him by going up on her tiptoes and wrapping her arms around his neck. His breath caught and held as he instinctively reached out to hold her.

Her eyes held a shimmer of sorrow, like maybe…

Maybe she was feeling this same disappointment too. This gut-wrenching resistance to saying goodbye.

"If not a name," he tried, "what about a number?"

Her lips hitched up, but he saw the answer before she spoke. "The chances of us ever meeting again are slim to none, so let's not make this something it's not, 'kay? I just want to remember you as the cowboy who made me laugh." She moved in closer, peeking up at him as she leaned her weight against his. "And I kinda like that you'll remember me as that mystery woman…who stole all your money."

He let out a short laugh, but it ended a second later when she pressed her lips to his.

His heart stopped.

Heck, the entire earth seemed to stop spinning as his whole world came down to this moment. This woman.

This kiss.

Her lips were even softer to the touch than he'd expected, and he groaned as he tilted his head for a more thorough taste. She parted for him, soft and welcoming, warm and tasting of some spice he couldn't name and would never be able to get enough of.

She kissed him back with a hunger that fueled his and made him forget where they were and what they were doing.

Saying goodbye.

It didn't come back to him until she pulled away with a breathy "Wow" that made his heart swell, and then she took another step back until the brisk night air replaced the warmth he'd held in his arms.

"Thanks for the memory, Cowboy." Her voice was husky and soft, and maybe just a little sad, before she hopped on her motorcycle and drove away.

CHAPTER 5

Sierra took her time meandering down Main Street Aspire. It had been late when she'd finally left her handsome cowboy and checked in at the Aspire Inn, and she hadn't seen much of the town before falling into bed, her heart still racing as she replayed that kiss over and over.

It had been one heck of a kiss.

It'd been too hot for her leather jacket this morning but not quite warm enough for a T-shirt, so now she pushed her hands into the pockets of a lightweight sweatshirt as she forced her mind away from that kiss.

She couldn't avoid this any longer. Today was the day she tried to track down her father. Letting out a sigh that did nothing to ease the knot of apprehension in her belly, she eyed the lineup of stores and restaurants.

Where was she supposed to start? And how? Did she just look up his address in the white pages and then show up on his doorstep?

Did she call ahead of time?

She stopped short in the middle of the sidewalk with

another sigh, this one filled with exasperation. What exactly was the etiquette in confronting one's long-lost father?

But then again, maybe she was stressing out over nothing. Ten years was a long time. He could have moved since then. She could be barking up the wrong tree entirely, for all she knew.

A woman with a stroller murmured an "excuse me" as she passed, and Sierra started to walk again.

One thing was certain: she couldn't spend the whole day standing still and stewing.

For a Monday morning, it was surprisingly busy. Not to mention adorable. She walked the few blocks that made up the most bustling section of Main Street before turning around to retrace her steps on the opposite side of the street.

Yup. Adorable.

Too bad adorable wasn't really her thing. Oh, it was nice to visit a Norman Rockwell town like this, but she'd spent too many years surrounded by too much poverty to ever really forget that a well-maintained, upper middle-class town like this one wasn't the norm.

Surrounded by high snow-covered peaks on every side, even now in early July, she had a rather disconcerting sensation of having stepped straight into a scene from a postcard. And the friendly greetings from strangers she passed only reinforced this feeling.

This must be what people talked about when they spoke of small-town friendliness. And she supposed it was nice…

And a little freaky.

But mostly nice, she decided as an older gentleman

sitting out front of the coffee shop called out a greeting for the second time that morning.

Before she could think better of it, she found herself heading toward the man and his friends.

Cal's Coffee Shop, the sign read over the front door. She could definitely do with a coffee this morning, and if people here were really as friendly as they seemed, maybe she could do a little digging and figure out where to start.

"Hey there," she called out as she drew near.

And just like that, one of the gray-haired men sitting at the small table pulled out a chair for her to join.

Well, that was easy.

"You're not from around here," one of the men said matter-of-factly.

"How'd you know?" she teased.

"Oh, something tells me I'd recall seeing a pretty woman like you." The first man chuckled.

"And I'd never forget that hair," his friend added.

She smiled at their good-natured teasing.

A third one leaned in, his eyes twinkling with amusement. "And then there's the way you've been walking around looking lost for the past twenty minutes."

She laughed. "Okay, you caught me. I just got here last night."

"Were you looking for someplace in particular?" the first man asked. "We can point you in the right direction."

Sierra wet her lips, her belly twisting with nerves and maybe a hint of excitement. Was she really going to meet her father? She took a deep breath. "Not someplace," she said slowly. "Some*one*."

The second man slapped his knee with a guffaw. "Then you're definitely in the right place. There's no one in this town we don't know."

She smiled. "I had a feeling."

"So who're you looking for?" the first man asked.

She swallowed hard. "A guy named Frank. Frank O'Sullivan."

The moment she said his name, she knew. Their expressions said it all.

Her belly sank and her heart ached, even before the second man gently said, "I'm sorry to tell you, honey, but Frank O'Sullivan passed away."

For a moment, she couldn't speak. She could hardly breathe.

Too many emotions rippled through her, and much too fast. She couldn't see up from down as she ricocheted between anger and hurt and a pain she couldn't justify.

She didn't even know Frank O'Sullivan! Never met the man.

Why did her heart suddenly feel too big in her chest, beating fiercely like it was trying to escape?

The man was a stranger. You couldn't miss a stranger.

You couldn't grieve for a stranger.

The group at the table were watching her closely, and Sierra cleared her throat as she clasped her hands together tightly. "I'm sorry to hear that."

She kept her voice and her expression bland, like they were, in fact, talking about a total stranger.

Because he is.

He was.

Her throat felt too tight, and she started to move, to get up from her seat and make her excuses.

There was nothing for her here. This whole trip had been a waste of time.

"If you've got business for the family, you can always

go up to the ranch and see his daughters," the first man said.

Sierra froze in her seat. "His...his daughters?"

Her heart was thundering now, and her body felt numb in a way that was both alarming and a relief.

Numbness was better than pain at the moment, and it helped hold her together long enough to listen to the men's chatter.

"Oh yeah, old Frank left behind seven daughters, if you can believe that." The second man grinned like this news was amusing. Like it wasn't shocking. Appalling. Just a little earth-shattering.

"Seven," she repeated woodenly.

Seven daughters.

Seven...sisters?

No, that couldn't be right.

"That's right," the first man said with a wide smile. "Lovely girls, each and every one of them."

He kept talking, throwing names around that barely stuck. Her mind was whirring too fast, but she heard Rose, Daisy, and another flower name.

One of the other men chimed in, "Yes, ma'am, the O'Sullivan sisters have really lit up this town. We wouldn't want to be without them now."

"They all live here." Her voice dropped to a husky whisper. It wasn't really a question, just a confirmation. Her father had a whole slew of daughters, and they all lived together in this Norman Rockwell town.

"Oh you bet." The third man nodded. "One of 'em moved out to live with our town's favorite doctor, you know, but the rest are up at the family ranch."

The family ranch.

The words felt like a blow. The family ranch. A group of sisters.

All of Frank's daughters…except her.

She swallowed hard, but this time it didn't work. A burning sensation stung the back of her eyes, and her throat grew too tight to speak.

All living together like one big happy family. Did they even know about her?

Did they care?

"When did—" She cleared her throat. "When did he pass away?"

"Oh, let's see." The third man rubbed his chin. "It's been more than a year now, I'd say."

"At least. It happened all quite suddenly."

"Car accident."

"He wasn't himself. When Loretta got real sick that way…it really changed him." The man closest to her shook his head with a sad smile, but she was barely registering the conversation.

She was too busy still trying to wrap her head around the number seven. "I see."

And she did see. Frank had been alive for years after that last card he sent her.

Obviously birthday number twenty-five was the cutoff. After that, he'd just stopped trying. Ten years of not trying. And these…these sisters by blood, they were some happy family on some idyllic ranch, no doubt.

Her breathing was growing shallow, and she could barely see past the burning in her eyes. She had to get out of here.

There were more questions racing through her mind than she knew how to handle, and her mother was the only person to answer them.

The first man seemed to realize she wasn't okay, because he leaned forward with a frown. "We never did ask…what's your connection to Frank O'Sullivan?"

She let out a choked sound that was somewhere between a laugh and a sob. "My connection?" She stepped back, swiping at her eyes. "I don't have one."

CHAPTER 6

The seasonal crew was out when Cody swung by the bunkhouse that afternoon to grab some lunch. He didn't even stop to take off his muddy boots or his hat before heading straight to the pantry.

He was starving, but it was his own fault. He normally would have eaten hours ago, but he was slow as molasses getting through his morning chores.

So yeah, it was his fault his stomach was growling. Although, really…it was mostly *her* fault.

Mona Lisa. He found his lips twitching into a smile as he rifled through the cabinet, which was horrifyingly bare.

Dang it.

JJ hadn't even been gone a full week, and already this place was falling apart without him.

He grabbed the last two pieces of bread he could find and shut the pantry with a loud click that seemed to echo in the empty space.

Normally he didn't mind alone time. Actually, living in a bunkhouse, he typically sought out time alone, but right now…

Right now, his racing thoughts were driving him nuts. When he wasn't replaying every conversation from the night before, or reliving that epic kiss in agonizing detail, his mind was whirring with doubts and questions.

Should he have let her go like that? Had he had any other choice?

What if he still wanted to find her, to talk to her? Would it be too much of a stalker move to try and track her down?

After all, it wasn't like there were a lot of towns near Wellspring where she could have been staying the night. There were only so many hotels available…

It wouldn't be the craziest idea ever to call 'em up and…

And say what? They wouldn't just hand over information about a guest, especially if he didn't have a name to inquire about.

With an irritable huff, he finished slathering his bread for one of the most pathetic lunches of all time.

Heck, he really missed JJ. And not just because JJ always did the grocery shopping when he was in town. He could really use his friend's company right about now. He'd know what to say to Cody about the whole mystery woman situation. Because the thing with JJ was he didn't say much, but when he did talk, people listened.

Cody listened.

Unlike Kit and Nash, JJ never gave his opinions, he just told you what you already knew. But he put it in a way that made the answer to whatever you were struggling with seem obvious.

He didn't hand you the answer, but he helped you find it on your own.

JJ was cool like that.

And he deserved to be off with his new wife exploring the world, Cody reminded himself. Just like Kit deserved his happiness with Lizzy, and Nash ought to be all lovey-dovey with his kind wife.

He was happy for all of them. He really was. But right about now, he could use a friend who wasn't so caught up in his own romantic bliss.

The door swung open behind him with a whoosh, and Cody turned to see Boone striding in like a whirlwind of youthful energy and testosterone.

"Hey, man," Boone said in that booming voice of his as he slapped Cody on the back in passing.

"Boone." Cody leaned against the kitchen counter, watching as Nash's young cousin heaved a duffel bag over one shoulder and then strode in like he owned the place.

"What're you doing here, man?" Cody couldn't help but smile as he watched the early twentysomething former high school football star check out the place.

"Moving in, bro." He turned to flash Cody a crooked grin that made his eyes crease at the corners and lines form around his mouth.

Boone was a handsome young devil, and he well knew it. Thanks to his stint as the star quarterback at the local high school, he was something of a celebrity in these parts...

Especially with the ladies.

He was only twenty-two, but he had women young and old fawning all over him whenever he went out with Cody, Kit, and the guys.

Boone dropped his duffel bag by JJ's door. "Nash was telling my uncle about how y'all are shorthanded without JJ, so Uncle Patrick told me to come here for the rest of the summer and give you guys a hand."

"Awesome." Cody stuck out a hand to shake Boone's. "Welcome aboard. We appreciate the help."

"No worries, man. That's what family's for, right?" His grin was infectious, as was his good mood.

Boone had the sort of personality that made you feel like there was nothing he couldn't handle, and nothing in the world could bring him down. There were times his self-assuredness crossed the line into cocky arrogance, but right now, his easy chatter as he helped himself to the meager contents of the cabinets was a blessed respite after all the angsting and stewing Cody had been doing ever since he'd watched his mystery woman drive off.

"We better get out there," Boone said around a mouthful of food. "I don't want Nash thinking I'm gonna slack off just because I'm his cousin."

Cody laughed. "You're right."

"You look beat, man. Maybe you should call it for the day." The concern in Boone's expression was a little surprising.

"I'm all right."

"You sure?" Boone arched his brows. "I can cover for you."

Cody grinned. And that right there was why he and Kit and the others always enjoyed having Boone around, even if he was nearly ten years younger. Beneath all that booming confidence and swagger lay a heart of gold. As Nash said on more than one occasion, "My cousin would give the shirt off his back to anyone who needed it."

"I didn't get much sleep last night," Cody admitted. "I went out…"

Boone's lopsided smile grew wicked. "Late night with a lady, huh?"

The way he waggled his eyebrows had Cody rolling his eyes. "Not like that."

Not really, anyway. It had ended way too quickly, and with just one kiss, which felt like far too little after what they'd shared.

"Aw, man," Boone said with a drawl. "That bad of a date, huh? Don't let it bring you down, bro."

Cody started to protest but thought better of it. Boone was a good guy, but something told him he wouldn't get JJ's wise words of advice if he tried to explain what had happened the night before.

"It's not that," he said. "I was just up too late…"

Thinking. Stewing. Wishing like heck I hadn't let her slip away without some way of getting a hold of her.

"I need some caffeine, that's all," he finished.

"Right on. Take your time. I'll check in with Nash and see what needs doing."

Cody watched him head back out with that same intense energy he'd come in with. The guy was a force of nature, all right.

And now…his new roommate.

Cody laughed to himself as he went to fix a cup of coffee. From quiet, wise JJ to loud, cocky Boone. This was going to take some getting used to.

He'd already started brewing the coffee when he realized they'd run out of sugar. He frowned, studying the black, tar-like coffee JJ supplied them with.

He swore it was a good brand, but quality or not, all coffee tasted like tar to Cody without some milk and sugar.

He grabbed his hat and headed toward the door. The nice thing about being so close to the main house was that they had an open-door policy—especially the kitchen.

Emma was always making them food and sending them home with desserts.

He'd bet his paycheck that they had a stockpile of sugar in their pantry and wouldn't mind sharing. He set off for the main house, determined that from here on out, his day would be focused on work and work alone.

No more thoughts about a certain magnetic mystery woman.

Even if her smile still haunted him with every step he took.

CHAPTER 7

Sierra had thought the small room at the Aspire Inn was cute when she'd checked in. Right now, it felt like a closet—stuffy and suffocating.

She tugged at the collar of her T-shirt as she paced from one end of the room to the other before turning on her heel and retracing her steps.

Yep, the room was definitely too small.

Maybe she should go for a ride. Or go back to that saloon she'd been to the night before.

Not that the hot cowboy would still be there. But man, the thought of seeing him right now was just about the only comfort she could find.

He'd know how to make her smile. He'd probably even make her laugh about this whole situation. Because, honestly, it was laughable, right? Going her whole life not knowing who her father was, only to find out he was dead. After fathering seven other children, of course!

She sat on the edge of the bed with a huff, her sight temporarily clouded by tears.

Yeah, real funny.

She swiped at her eyes. Gah! She was a mess. What was she doing crying over a man who'd wanted nothing to do with her?

Except...he had sent those cards. And her mother had purposefully hidden them from her.

But then again...those cards came once a year. Twice, tops. And rather than move hell and earth to find her, he'd gone off to start a new family and sire a whole freakin' gaggle of little girls to replace the one he'd lost.

She'd been an afterthought to him, at best.

And those girls...the sisters. Did they even know she existed? Or had her father just been Dad of the Year to these seven daughters and forgotten all about his first kid?

She frowned at the wall. *I was* the first, right? An ugly thought took hold. Maybe her mom had lied about everything. Maybe she'd been some affair, and that was why he had a whole other family that never acknowledged her.

Swallowing hard, she dug out her phone. She could spend an eternity wondering about the past, or she could get some answers.

Her mother answered on the first ring, and she sounded aggrieved. "Sierra, thank goodness you called me back. Do you know how worried I've been?"

Sierra ignored that. "Why didn't you tell me about Frank's other family?"

"His...his what?" Her mother's tone grew sharp. "Sierra, have you seen your father? I don't know what he told you, but—"

"I haven't seen him, Ma," she snapped. And then, softening her voice, she added, "He passed away."

There was a beat of thick, heavy silence before her mother spoke.

"What? When?" she rasped. She didn't sound heartbroken, exactly. Definitely a little shocked, but there was no tremble of sadness in her voice.

This man must have been important to her at one point, so Sierra pushed aside her own battered emotions to tell her mother what she'd heard from the town gossips at the coffee shop.

"Seven daughters?" She sounded just as shocked as Sierra felt.

"I take it you didn't know."

"No, of course not. I told you, that man wanted nothing to do with us." Before Sierra could argue and point out the cards, her mother added, "Not until it was too little, too late."

A silence fell as Sierra's anger with her mother wavered.

"I know you're mad that I kept secrets, sweetheart. But I've always wanted what's best for you. And Frank O'Sullivan would only have hurt you in the end."

Sierra didn't respond. She couldn't. Her insides were a mess of careening emotions that she couldn't begin to name. Ever since she'd found those cards, her world felt topsy-turvy. Hopeful one moment, sad the next.

She scrubbed a hand over her face as she drew in a deep breath. And now finding out she'd never meet the man who'd sired her...and that there were seven women out there who shared her blood...

"I don't know what to think anymore, Ma," she admittedly wearily. "I'm so...so..."

Confused. Heartbroken. Betrayed.

She never finished the sentence, so her mother finished it for her. "Angry." Her voice took on a sharp, metallic edge. "That's what you should be."

Sierra straightened. "I didn't even know the man. And

he's gone. It seems a little wrong to be angry with him now when he can't even defend himself."

"No, but that family of his shares some of the blame!"

Sierra squirmed with unease. She knew this tone. Her mom was getting herself worked up on Sierra's behalf.

"I bet there was a will," her mom clipped.

Sierra frowned. "Ma, it's not money I'm worried about—"

"Of course not." Her mother huffed. "But that's not the point. The point is you never received anything from that man. Neither of us did. My guess is everything went to his new family, without a single thought for you."

Bitterness formed a toxic pit low in her belly, and much as Sierra didn't like to encourage her mom when she got like this, the self-righteous anger brewing was a relief compared to the other muddled, complicated feelings she'd been stewing in this week.

"I know you think those cards mean something, sweetheart, but they were nothing. Just a sign that occasionally the man felt a pang of guilt for walking away from us."

Sierra gripped the edge of the bed. Was that all they were? Acts of guilt?

"Meanwhile, he was off building a life, creating a family." Her mother let out a bitter laugh. "If he'd actually wanted to help us, he could have found a way. He could have tracked you down if he'd really wanted to."

Sierra nodded, her grief and heartache slowly but surely being pushed aside to make way for anger.

Her knuckles turned white from gripping the bed so hard, and her jaw clenched tight.

"If he'd actually cared about your welfare, he would have been diligent with child support! He—" Her mother sniffed and went suddenly quiet, like she was too enraged to form any more words.

Sierra nodded, her mind going back to all those years when she and her mom had worked so many jobs just to make ends meet.

"If he'd cared at all about you..." Her mother huffed, building up steam again. "He...well, he sure as heck would have put you in his will!"

Sierra had the sudden urge to shout, "Amen!" But she couldn't bring herself to make a joke about this.

Her whole body was trembling with rage.

With hurt.

With rejection.

Her mom was right. It'd been the hopes of a little girl that had led her here. Some wishful thinking that maybe her father had been out there looking for her. That he'd actually cared.

But no. He'd abandoned her, plain and simple.

He'd given her nothing. Not his name. Not security. Definitely not love.

He hadn't seen fit to give her a dang thing when he'd been alive, and it seemed his family was content to continue leaving her out of the mix.

She shot to her feet.

"You deserve that property and whatever else Frank left behind just as much as his other daughters do," her mother continued, clearly on a roll now.

Sierra could practically see her pacing in her apartment. Normally Sierra would try to calm her down, but right now...

This anger felt *good*. It felt right.

Her free hand clenched and unclenched at her side.

"You deserve whatever they get," her mom spat.

"More! Heck, they had a daddy, didn't they? They had Frank's support all their lives, while you got nothing from the man."

"Dang straight," Sierra muttered.

"Don't you dare let any of Frank's family make you think you don't deserve what's yours. You've suffered long enough, and it's about time your father gave you something."

"You're right, Ma." Sierra snatched her keys, the metal digging into her palm as she stormed out of the room. Slamming the door shut, she barked into the phone, "I'm gonna go find that ranch and take what's mine."

CHAPTER 8

Cody always enjoyed chatting with Daisy, and this afternoon the diversion was more welcome than ever.

He ran into her when he was grabbing the sugar and she was hanging out in the kitchen, and for a little while, they'd been having a nice conversation about the wedding and JJ's replacement on the ranch. But now he caught a familiar glimmer in Daisy's eye when talk turned to the romance epidemic taking place at the ranch.

"All these men falling in love left, right, and center." She sipped her tea, her eyes sparkling. "Must be making you a little crazy."

Cody snickered. "I've had my moments."

Her gaze sharpened. "Do you think you want to fall in love one day?"

Uh-oh. He backed up a step. The last thing he needed was a matchmaker in his life, but he could feel heat crawling up in his neck, because her innocent question had brought the image of his mystery woman to the front of his mind all over again.

Daisy was watching him with unabashed interest. He shuffled toward the door. Any second now, the questions would start.

Have you met someone?

There are some lovely girls in this town, right?

Tell me all your secrets, Cody!

Nightmare.

He cleared his throat, scratching the back of his head and inching closer to the door.

"Cody, come on. You can tell lil ol' me." Daisy batted her eyelashes, her melodic laughter dancing through the air toward him.

He felt his skin start to prickle and was pretty sure he'd rather die than be blushing in front of this woman. He'd never hear the end of it!

The roar of an engine from the front driveway made his head snap toward the window. Relief filled him as Daisy's brows drew down in confusion. "Who could that be?"

He shrugged. "No idea."

But whoever it was, he owed them a thank-you for saving him from any questions about his love life.

Or lack thereof.

Daisy set down her tea and headed toward the front door. He followed, curiosity getting the best of him. The ranch was far enough outside of town that guests didn't just drop by, and everyone who lived and worked here was accounted for.

Daisy paused at the top of the porch steps, and Cody stuttered to a stop right behind her, his lips parting and his stomach clenching like he'd just been sucker punched.

It couldn't be.

But it was.

When the slender woman atop the motorcycle tugged off her helmet, there was no mistaking that vivid red hair.

The air rushed from his lungs, joy flooding through him fast and fiery. She'd found him.

He moved forward but paused when he reached Daisy's side. That joy faded into wariness because…Mona Lisa wasn't looking at him. And she sure as heck wasn't smiling.

Setting her helmet down, she slid on a dark pair of shades as she eyed the house and property with a disdainful sneer.

What the…?

Daisy turned to him, looking just as confused as he felt.

"Who is this?" she murmured.

He didn't answer. His gaze was fixed on his mystery woman, his mind racing to reconcile the funny, sassy hustler from the night before with this woman who looked…hard, furious, and…kinda scary.

"Hi," Daisy called out, trotting down the porch steps, no doubt sporting her sunshine grin.

Cody couldn't bring himself to move. Shock and confusion held him in place, along with a sick feeling of disappointment. Not to mention wariness.

Mona Lisa hadn't come here for him, that much was obvious. So what was she doing here?

His redhead paused, yanking off her shades to give Daisy a narrow-eyed glare that startled Cody.

This…was *not* the woman he remembered. She seemed to vibrate with anger.

Or was that hurt?

His heart pounded furiously. He wanted to go to her. To hold her and tell her everything would be okay. But he still had no idea what she was doing here, and something held him in place as he listened to the tense exchange going on in the driveway.

"I'm, uh, Daisy. And you are?"

Mona Lisa ignored her.

"This is the O'Sullivan ranch." Daisy pointed over her shoulder, and you couldn't miss the pride in her voice.

In contrast, the taller woman shot Daisy a disparaging look before muttering, "I know."

Cody's heart did a flip as her gaze traveled across the house, then landed on the porch, and...

There it was.

She'd spotted him.

He tensed as her expression morphed from anger to complete shock.

Daisy whipped around to look over her shoulder, but he held his mystery woman's stare, taking a step forward.

Mona Lisa gave a shake of her head as if coming out of a trance. "What are you doing here?"

He scratched the back of his head. He could ask the same. "This is where I work."

Daisy pointed between them. "You guys know each other?"

They both said nothing, and Daisy let out a huff. "Can someone please tell me what is going on?" She threw her hands up before pointing at the woman. "Who are you?"

Yet again, his redhead ignored her, shaking her head at Cody. "You didn't think to mention that?"

He frowned at her accusatory tone. What was she so bent out of shape about? "I didn't think it was important at the time."

"Oh, it's important." She pointed to the ground. "This is my land."

Cody's lips parted, rocked by the anger in her tone. The tremble of her voice.

His gut wrenched when he spotted the hurt beneath her heated glare. Yeah, he could see it—pain sharpening the edges of her expression, her brows drawing together and up.

What had happened to his mystery woman between last night and this afternoon?

He would have killed for a moment of privacy. A chance to find out what was hurting her.

But Daisy spoke up first.

"Excuse me?" she snapped. "I don't think so. This place belongs to the O'Sullivan sisters."

Mona Lisa stepped forward, her stance aggressive, and she glared down at Daisy. "I'm Sierra, Frank's eldest." Her eyebrows puckered, like for a second she wasn't completely sure on that fact, but then she lifted her chin as if she couldn't let any uncertainty show.

There was a thick silent beat that stole the tension for a microsecond, replaced it with a rapid-fire moment of joy and surprise. They'd found another sister!

"Sierra," Daisy breathed.

Cody was outright gaping now.

Sierra. Her name was Sierra.

His mystery woman was...

Oh good grief.

He'd spent the best night of his life...with one of the missing O'Sullivan sisters.

Daisy recovered quicker than he did, her smile bright and cheerful. "Well, welcome. We've been looking for you. I'm so glad you finally came."

Sierra scoffed, ignoring Daisy's outstretched hand and

wrenching the tension back with her jarring rancor. "Enough with the small-town plastic-coated pleasantries."

Cody flinched. The hardness in Sierra's tone was grating—especially since she was currently being rude to Daisy, who was kind to a fault. But what made Cody's heart buckle was the sorrow that seemed to ooze from Sierra. It tinged every word and permeated the air around them.

Daisy frowned. "I was just trying to be ni—"

"This land belongs to me. It's my right. I'm the oldest. I should get first claim."

"It's not..." Daisy shook her head. "It doesn't work like that. I can show you the will. Frank left the land to all of us. He—"

"Frank gave me nothing!" Sierra snapped. "My whole life, he forgot about me, treated me like I didn't even exist. Now he's dead, and finally it's my chance to take a little something back. He owes me this place."

Cody's heart was pounding. Sierra. He wanted to say her name. To touch her cheek. To pull her into his arms and let her cry.

Because that was what she needed. It was obvious to him, and maybe to Daisy, too, because when she spoke again, her voice was feather soft and filled with sympathy. "Sierra, this land is yours, but it's also mine and Emma's and Lizzy's and Rose's and Dahlia's...and April's." Daisy winced. "If she'll ever choose to acknowledge it. We've been trying to find you both for so long now. We want to—"

"Enough." Sierra frowned, rubbing her forehead. "I don't want a list of names I've never heard before. I just want what's mine." Her voice broke, then started to tremble, and Cody felt like someone had taken a knife and cut him open.

"Frank owes me this," Sierra finished, her voice cracking like she was on the verge of splintering into a thousand pieces.

Even Daisy could see it. And while Cody was rigid and motionless as he took in the scene before him, Daisy reached out to Sierra.

She flinched away from the comforting touch, whirling around to glare at Cody.

Her gaze darted up to his face, and she pointed an accusing finger at him. "You should have told me."

Now, finally, his body moved into action, and he hurried down the steps toward her. "I didn't know who you were."

He could feel Daisy's stunned stare, but he ignored her, transfixed by the sadness that etched Sierra's features as she met his gaze.

There she was.

The woman he'd met was in there. And she was suffering.

But he knew she'd balk if he tried to comfort her right here and now, so he didn't make a move to stop her when she whirled around and straddled her bike.

She gave them both a hard look. "This isn't over," she shouted over the engine's roar. "I'm going to be contacting my lawyer about this. I want what's mine."

And with that, she spun the bike around and took off down the driveway.

Daisy watched the cloud of dust bloom for a moment before spinning to look up at Cody. "You know that woman?"

Yes. No. I hope so.

He had no idea, but he knew what she meant, so he shook his head. "Not really."

Turning for the house, he started up the stairs, but Daisy chased after him. "You better tell me something, Cody Swanson!"

He paused with his hand on the screen door and let out a sigh. "I'm sorry, Daisy, but...I don't want to."

He heard Daisy squawk behind him, irate that he was holding out on her. But there was nothing to be done about that right now, because he had too much to sort out.

He had too much he needed to say to Sierra before he made any attempt to explain to friends how he'd met this woman and had the best night of his life.

CHAPTER 9

S ierra's whole body shook as she drove away from her father's ranch.

She gripped the motorcycle's handles harder, but it only made the trembling worse. With a curse she realized...she couldn't ride like this.

Even if her body wasn't trembling in the aftershock of meeting a sister and seeing her father's home—not to mention Cody!—her mind was too rattled to concentrate. One wild animal on the road and she'd be too distracted to notice.

At the next exit, she pulled off the highway, following a sign for a trailhead. Parking in the near-empty lot, she got off her bike and started walking.

If she didn't, she was a little afraid she'd collapse into a ball of tears.

As it was, she swiped at her cheeks in annoyance as she took long, quick strides up a winding trail, heading...where?

Who cared?

She wasn't racing toward something—she was running away.

"Stupid," she muttered under her breath. "Stupid move, Sierra."

She swallowed hard and pumped her arms, as if she could actually work out all these emotions.

As if fat, salty tears weren't currently pouring out of her.

She swiped at her cheeks again as regret rose up like bile—bitter and unbearable. Why had she charged in there with a red-hot temper? Barreling in like a thunderstorm.

That wasn't what she'd meant to happen the first time she met her family.

She stopped short and squeezed her eyes shut, the sound of her breathing labored in the otherwise peaceful silence of this green hillside.

That woman was her sister.

Her half sister.

Sierra had only had a mother in her life now that her grandparents had passed away, so meeting a relative was a huge deal. And she'd…

Oh heck, she'd blown it.

The blonde chick had been nice. *So* nice. And somehow that had just made Sierra feel worse for showing up like a raging crazy person. The fire of anger that had driven her there had burned out of control for some reason.

But no, she knew the reason. She'd been hurt.

Her mind called up the cowboy. Cody.

It didn't make sense and she knew it, but somehow seeing him standing there, watching him go to the sweet blonde's side like he was protecting her…

She swallowed hard and choked on a sob.

It was stupid. Of all the feelings that had caught her in

the gut and left her winded, feeling betrayed by a stranger she'd only just met was the least reasonable of them all.

She started walking again, this time following the path to the right, which led into a thick grove of trees.

The tall pines provided some shade from the harsh sun, and she slowed her steps, her muscles relaxing as fatigue started to set in.

She should tell her mother what happened, but a glance at her phone showed she had no reception.

She had no doubt that the moment she returned to an area where she could receive texts and calls, her mother would be all over her for answers.

All at once the adrenaline that had fueled her rant at the ranch drained out of her, and she sat heavily on a log at the side of the trail.

For the first time, she truly looked around her and realized just how poor of a plan this was. Hiking alone in a strange place where there were bears…

Wait, are there bears here?

Oh heck.

She shot to her feet. The thought of the giant mammals with their sharp claws heading her way had her marching back to her motorbike.

And along the way, her thoughts started falling into a pattern that was closer to normal. Steady. Logical. Void of treacherous emotions.

She pushed aside images of Cody—that had been too much. The straw that broke the camel's back. But she let herself replay everything the blonde had said.

Daisy, that was her name. And just like those old men at the coffee shop, she'd rattled off others' names as well, as if it was second nature.

Sierra couldn't recall them all, but she thought she heard six. Was it?

Did that make her the seventh daughter?

Well, the first.

Sierra stopped, the air rushing out of her lungs as another key point registered.

Daisy said the land was all of theirs, which...

Did that mean they had known about her?

She'd repeated Sierra's name and had stuck her hand out with a smile, so...yeah. She'd definitely recognized her.

Which meant...

Sierra stopped to rub her temples wearily. Which meant...what?

Daisy knew about her existence. And maybe the others did too. Because their father told them about her?

The idea settled inside her—a cooling balm that soothed the scorching burns.

She still had questions. Actually, now she had even more questions than when she'd first set out this morning.

Her one chance to get answers, and she'd blown it by losing her temper and getting all distracted and upset over some guy who shouldn't mean anything to her.

Who didn't mean anything to her.

She started back to her bike, her earlier storm of emotions more under control but her mind still racing with questions.

So Daisy was nice.

So the blonde had heard of her.

That didn't change anything. She'd still had to learn about her father's death from a bunch of old men outside a coffee shop.

And her father still hadn't given her a dang thing.

CHAPTER 10

Cody typically prided himself on being a levelheaded guy.

He wasn't quick to anger, even when his friends and family got all worked up over something. But right now...

Right now, he was having a heck of a time keeping cool.

"I'm just saying, she looked like trouble." Daisy was pacing the length of the now-crowded kitchen.

Her boyfriend, Levi, leaned against the counter near her, watching her with an expression that was part amusement, part exasperation, and total adoration. "I understand you're worried, sweetheart, but that's not a good enough reason for me to run a background check and invade her privacy."

Cody's death grip on the counter eased somewhat at Levi's voice of reason, but his jaw was still clenched tight as he listened in on the emergency meeting Daisy had called.

All of the sisters were gathered—minus Dahlia, of course. Even Daisy had agreed that Dahlia's honeymoon shouldn't be ruined because of one bad encounter with the newfound O'Sullivan sister.

"Maybe one of us should go talk to her," Rose said as she rocked Kiara from side to side.

Lizzy crossed her arms with a stubborn pout. "Oh, I'll talk to her, all right. I'll tell her where she can shove—"

"Easy, Angel." Kit wrapped his arms around her from behind, soothing her with a quick peck to the cheek.

For a second, Cody felt a flicker of gratitude toward his brother for defending Sierra, who wasn't here to defend herself. But then Kit added, "If it comes to a fight, this biker chick doesn't stand a chance."

"Kit," Cody snapped.

He arched his brows in surprise. "I mean legally. I'm not condoning violence."

Emma was frowning as she turned to Nash. "We do have the legal right to this place. She can't fight that, right?"

Nash grimaced. "I honestly don't know."

"I wish Dex were here. He knows a bit about the law," Rose murmured.

It seemed Dex was too busy at the clinic to get away, but Kit, Nash, and Levi had come running at the first hint that their women were unhappy.

Who's running to Sierra's side?

"Maybe we can buy her out," Daisy suggested.

Lizzy shook her head, rubbing her temples and muttering, "Of all the times for Dahlia to be away."

Kit gave her a light squeeze, then started rubbing her shoulders.

Cody frowned, looking away from the intimate gesture and again wondering who the heck was comforting Sierra through all of this.

"What exactly do we know about this woman?" Levi asked.

After that, Cody couldn't keep track of who was talking because they all started speaking at once. Daisy was the only one who seemed to even notice he was there, and the curious glance she shot his way had him backpedaling toward the door.

It was a miracle she hadn't mentioned the fact that Sierra had recognized him, but he didn't expect her to stay silent forever.

Part of him wanted to stick around, to dive into the fray and tell them they didn't know the first thing about Sierra. If anyone had bothered to pay attention, beneath her anger and bravado had been a world of pain.

But that would only elicit a tidal wave of curious questions he wasn't willing to answer.

So he turned and left, heading toward the front door before anyone could call him back.

He might want to play devil's advocate and tell them to give Sierra a chance, but more than that, he needed to make sure she was okay.

Lizzy, Emma, Daisy, Rose…they had each other. They had their significant others.

Who did Sierra have?

His jaw set as he hopped into his truck.

She has me. Whether she likes it or not.

It wasn't hard to track her down. There weren't many places for her to stay, and he hadn't been parked in front of the Aspire Inn for more than a minute before he heard her bike coming down the quiet side street.

He got out of his car just as she was getting off her bike. She tugged off her helmet, her bright red hair flying free as her gaze locked on him.

Shoving his hands in his pockets, he walked slowly toward her, despite the urge to run. But her expression was wary, at best, so he took his time and stopped a few feet away.

She settled the helmet on her hip, her head cocked to the side. "So. You're one of them, huh?"

He flinched. "Sierra, I had no idea who you were or—"

"No, yeah. I know." She looked away, her nose wrinkling. "My guessing game kinda backfired on me, now didn't it?"

He rocked back on his heels as he studied her. She wouldn't look at him, turning away to set down the helmet rather than meet his gaze. And despite her tough posture and the stubborn set of her chin, she couldn't quite hide the tightness in her features or the tension in her voice.

He let out a sharp exhale and closed the distance between them. Screw space. This woman needed comfort.

She looked over, her eyes widening in alarm, but he didn't stop until he was right in front of her. Then he wrapped his arms around her and pulled her in for a tight hug.

She froze, going rigid in his arms. But then, slowly, like the unraveling of a stubborn knot, he felt her muscles ease as she relaxed into his embrace. Her breath was warm against his neck, and her hands tentatively settled at his waist.

"Are you okay?" he murmured against her temple.

She didn't answer at first, and then she shrugged.

No. That was a no. She was just too proud to admit it. He held her tighter, and she made no move to pull away. If anything, she seemed to burrow into him, and for a second, he could have sworn she was tunneling right into his heart.

But then a car passed, and the sound broke the moment. She tugged backward and then pushed against his chest until he let her go. Crossing her arms, she glared at him.

But heck, if that glare wasn't just plain adorable, all the more so because whatever she'd gotten up to after her visit to the ranch, she had faint smears of dirt on her cheekbones and a thin twig dangling from her hair.

"What are you doing here, Cody?"

"I came to see if you were all right."

Her eyes narrowed. "Did they send you to spy on me or something?"

He let her words settle. She was trying to push him away, and maybe it would work if he didn't know better... if he didn't see the hurt she couldn't quite hide.

The longer his silence stretched, the more she squirmed, her stance crumpling as she let out a heavy sigh. "So, you and that Daisy chick..." She kicked the toe of her boot against the asphalt. "Are you, like...?" Her expression crinkled, like the idea tasted vile in her head.

Cody had to fight a grin, his heart filling with helium.

Was she jealous?

"No." He was pleased to inform her. And wait...was that relief he saw in her eyes when he added, "Daisy and I are just friends. Even if she wasn't dating the sheriff, we'd still just be friends."

"Okay." She continued to stub the toe of her boot into the ground.

He pressed his lips together, squashing his smile. Did she have any idea how childlike and cute she looked when she was uncertain?

He doubted it.

She started to nibble on her lip, her brows drawing down and her gaze sliding away as if she was lost in thought.

He could only imagine all she had on her mind.

"Is that why you came here?" he asked gently. "Did you hear about Frank's passing and...?"

He trailed off when she shook her head and crossed her arms even tighter. "No, I didn't even know he'd passed away until this morning." His expression must have given him away because she added in a gruff tone, "Don't feel sorry for me."

"I wouldn't dream of it."

She huffed. "Did you know him? My, er, my... I mean Frank?"

"A little." Cody shrugged, wishing he could give her a different answer. "Not well, though. I didn't start working at the ranch until after he left Aspire and my friend Nash became the foreman."

Her brows knit together. "So you really do work there."

He tipped his chin.

She rolled her lips inward as she thought this over. "And you're friends with all of them...his daughters?"

"Most of them." He nodded, his voice soft and slow.

His gut tightened at her intense gaze. He had a feeling he was on dangerous ground here. She already had little reason to trust him, and the wariness in her gaze said all it would take was one half-truth, one lie of omission, and she'd walk away and never look back. So he stepped closer and said, "I've become friends with the five O'Sullivan daughters who live here in Aspire. I met the youngest, April, because she used to live here with Frank

78

and her mother, but she's a good ten years younger than me, so I didn't know her very well."

Sierra's brows were tightly knitted now, her gaze searching his like she was trying to read something there. Or maybe she was just absorbing what he was saying.

Not for the first time, he wondered how much she knew about Frank...about her sisters.

"So you're just friends," she said. "And you work for them."

She sounded like she was testing out his story, tasting how much truth there was in each of his words.

He took a deep breath. "Well, it's a little more complicated than that."

She arched a brow.

"My brother, Kit," he explained. "He's married to Lizzy, one of your...one of the sisters."

She blinked. "So that makes you...what? My brother?"

He let out a huff of laughter, and he saw her lips twitch too—a hint of the mischievous girl from the night before. But where that woman had seemed so strong and invincible, this one looked soft and vulnerable...and so very hurt.

"Sierra, you should know...your father—"

"I don't want to talk about him." She shook her head, her gaze hard and unyielding.

But he saw it for what it was, and he moved closer, brushing some of those tangled red locks out of her eyes. "We don't have to talk about anything you don't want to."

Her lips twitched again, but it wasn't with amusement. He had a feeling she was fighting back tears. He lifted a hand, cupped her cheek, and swiped away the dirt that was there.

And this close, he could see it. The red that rimmed her eyes, the tearstains on her cheeks.

His heart twisted painfully in his chest. He would give anything to take these tears away. To bear her hurt so she didn't have to.

But it was a matter of trust.

She had to get to know him. To know her sisters and find out the truth she clearly came here to discover.

"I'm not gonna try and talk you into coming back to the ranch or tell you anything you're not ready to hear about your father and the inheritance..." He paused, his gaze meeting hers.

The wariness was still there...but she was listening.

"The lawyer your father worked with," he said. "He's here in town. I'll text you his contact information."

Her pretty face buckled with a frown.

"Why?" Her voice was softer now.

"It's his job to make sure Frank's wishes were honored. I know you're in that will, Sierra, and you deserve to know what you're entitled to, and what Frank wanted for you."

"He didn't want anything for me," she muttered.

But this time she didn't even try to cover her sadness with anger. He stroked her cheek with his thumb one last time and leaned down until his forehead rested against hers. "Before you leave or go declaring war against your own family, get the facts, okay?"

She didn't answer, but she did lean in toward him, and his heart gave a sharp tug.

"You deserve that," he added.

Then he pulled back and kissed her forehead. He wanted to stay. He wanted to hold her. But something told him she had too much to sort out on her own.

He backed away slowly. "Go get your answers, Sierra. And when you're ready to talk...you know where to find me."

CHAPTER 11

The sound of a clock ticking in Mr. Billman's office was enough to make Sierra want to scream.

The lawyer, with his graying hair and monotone voice, wasn't helping matters with that smile of his. It was a kind smile. A paternal smile.

It was also…an expectant smile.

She cleared her throat, and the sound was instantly muffled by the thick carpet in this small, stuffy room. "And Emma was the first to arrive," she rasped.

"Correct." Mr. Billman nodded.

She was still trying to wrap her head around all the old lawyer had told her since she'd first sat down in this overstuffed, uncomfortable armchair a half hour before. Clarifying that one part of this insane story felt like as good a place as any to start.

"Emma took it upon herself to reach out to the rest of Frank O'Sullivan's daughters, but unfortunately, I didn't have much by way of contact information for you, Miss O'Sullivan."

She frowned. "It's McNeal."

He blinked behind the wire-rimmed glasses he'd donned when he'd drawn out a thick file folder and started reading through the documents there. "Ah," he breathed. "I had you down as O'Sullivan. I suppose that was part of the problem in tracking you down, hmm?"

He said this like it was a minor oopsie and not one of no doubt several reasons she'd been in the dark about her father's death and the inheritance.

She swallowed hard.

Did this mean...?

"Emma called me many times asking if I had any more information on you," he continued, answering her unasked question. "Lizzy, too, once she got involved in the great hunt for the missing daughters." He chuckled at his terminology.

Sierra couldn't bring herself to smile, not even a small, polite one.

Her temple throbbed when she thought of the accusations she'd hurled at Daisy.

Daisy, who...

She glanced down at the notes she'd scrawled while the lawyer had explained everything to her. Daisy, who hadn't known Frank either. Maybe as a small child, but definitely not as an adult. By the sounds of things, all of Frank's daughters had arrived after he died. Except April, who remained a mystery.

And apparently Emma and Lizzy hadn't been aware that their father had sired more children either, which meant...

She frowned at her notes. What? What did that mean?

She had no idea. All she did know was she shouldn't have gone charging into battle without all the facts. She should never have let her mom rile her up. After all these years, she knew better than to make her mother's battles her own.

If she did, she'd wind up as bitter and jaded as the woman who raised her.

"So, now that I'm here, what are the next steps?" she asked, more to get him talking again than anything.

The thick silence in this tiny room felt suffocating. She could hardly wait to get outside, hop on her bike, and go for a ride.

"Well, there's still April who needs to be brought into the loop," he said. "But once she's found, the hope is that all seven of you can come to an agreement."

Her brows furrowed. "Why?"

"What?"

"Why do we all have to agree?"

"Well, it was your father's wish that the decisions regarding the ranch be decided on by unanimous vote."

"That's ridiculous," she snapped, her tone sharper than intended. But really. Her father hadn't had any say at all in her life when he was alive. What made him think he could start giving her orders when he was dead?

"Perhaps," the older man said slowly, clasping his hands together and giving her an infuriatingly patient look. "But that's the stipulation in the will."

"Then I'll walk away," she said. "I don't need the money."

Her heart gave a little pang of disagreement. She could live without the money, and her mother would survive too. But her mind's eye filled with images of the kids she'd left behind in Venezuela.

She might not need the money, but she could definitely use it.

"Miss O'Sull—" He caught himself with a rueful wince.

"Miss McNeal. If you walk away, the land and any money it generates will be tied up in red tape for the foreseeable future."

She huffed. "Then we sell."

"That's a possibility," he said slowly. "But you'd have to get all seven signatures for that to happen."

She narrowed her eyes. "Why do I get the feeling you don't believe that's an option either?"

His smile was small and wry. "Because I've gotten to know the other sisters. And they've made a home here. Perhaps you could—"

"Just because they want to make a life here and be one big happy family doesn't mean I want that."

"No, of course not."

"Isn't there some way around this unanimous clause?" She leaned forward. "There has to be some loophole."

"I'm afraid not."

"But it's...it's ridiculous," she sputtered. "I don't even know these women."

The old man's smile was kind. "Might I suggest you get to know them? It might be the smoothest way to resolve this."

I don't want to get to know them. They're nothing to me!

Her lips parted, but the protest didn't come out as planned.

She was still trying to reconcile her mother's angry accusations about her father's other family with the nice blonde woman who'd given her a welcoming smile when she'd arrived at the ranch.

She toyed with the notebook in her hands. Had they really looked for her?

Pressing her lips together, she gave her head a shake. If they'd really wanted to find her, they could have, right?

Her father definitely could have. He knew where her grandparents lived and how to get in touch with her through them. But he hadn't tried hard enough.

We did move a few times.

Even so, he was a man of means, wasn't he? He could have found her if he'd really wanted to!

And now he was insisting she come to him? Now he wanted to use his money and his inheritance to force her into joining a family she'd never even known about?

I don't think so.

She came to her feet with a sharp exhale. "My father didn't have a say in my decisions when he was alive, Mr. Billman. I'm not going to start playing by his rules now."

He stood from his chair as she stuck her notebook into her satchel and threw it over her shoulder. "Miss McNeal, please—"

She held up a hand to stop him. "No offense, Mr. Billman, but I'd rather hire my own attorney to represent my interests in this matter."

His brows arched slightly, concern wrinkling his salt-and-pepper eyebrows. "You do what you feel is best, Miss McNeal. That is your right, of course."

She felt like there was more he wanted to say, but he kept his mouth shut as she stormed out the door.

All she wanted was a ride in the fresh air, but she'd promised her mother she'd fill her in on what the lawyer said, and she was rapidly learning that cell reception was spotty anywhere but her hotel room, where she had access to the Wi-Fi.

After reluctantly heading back to her suffocating room, she kicked the door shut behind her and dumped her satchel down with a huff. The phone stared at her from where it had spilled out from the top of her bag.

Come on, get on with it.

She wanted to do an about-face and split for another hiking trail, but...

But she didn't want the conversation hanging over her.

Just get it over with, Sierra!

Letting out a growl, she snatched the phone off the bed and was about to call when the hotel phone started ringing.

It gave her a start.

Who would be calling her hotel room?

Cody? Her heart gave an annoying little kick as she reached for it. She'd given him her cell, but maybe—

"Is this Sierra O'Sullivan?" The woman's tone on the other end was brusque.

Definitely not Cody.

She shifted the phone in her hand, wariness coiling in her belly. "Who's this?"

There was a pause and then "I'm Dahlia. One of your sisters."

"One of my half sisters," Sierra corrected automatically.

Again, there was a pause, and then she realized this Dahlia woman was covering her end and mumbling something to someone.

No doubt a room full of the other O'Sullivan sisters.

Bitterness shot up before she could stop it. She was the outsider here, whether these women actually tried to find her or not.

"I heard you came by the ranch." Dahlia's voice was thin, as if it was taking all her willpower to remain calm and polite.

Sierra kept her mouth shut.

"Daisy is my sister," she continued. "My full sister. We grew up together—me, Daisy, and Rose."

"How nice for you," Sierra muttered. "Do you have a reason for calling?"

She winced the moment the words were out of her mouth. What was wrong with her? She was normally levelheaded, dang it, but everything about this situation had her feeling like a hormonal tween ready to lash out without a thought.

Dahlia's tone went from brusque to cold. "Yeah, she said you were making threats, and I thought maybe you and I should talk before you go and do something you'll regret."

"She said you were making threats." Sierra winced again, shame pooling in her belly, but she couldn't bring herself to apologize. Not when this woman was clearly on the offense. Oh, she might be saying she wanted peace, but the tone of her voice indicated otherwise.

This was the mama bear of the family, and she was calling to warn Sierra off.

Sierra straightened. She hadn't backed down when bullies had made her life a living hell in junior high, and she wasn't about to start backing down now just because this woman thought she was tough.

"Are you worried I'm going to do something I'll regret...or something you don't like?"

Dahlia started to respond, but Sierra talked over her.

"Because that know-it-all tone might work with Daisy, but I'm not scared of you, and I don't need your approval."

"Look, you little—" She stopped, and this time Sierra heard her muffled voice saying, "I'm not being rude, JJ. I'm trying to help."

Sierra spoke up while Dahlia was still talking to this JJ person. "Thanks for the call. But if you have anything else to say to me…" She took a deep breath, her gut twisting as her throat grew choked.

This is your sister, a voice was shouting. *You are talking to a sister you don't even know.*

She gave her head a shake. "Next time you want to talk, call my lawyer."

And then she hung up the phone.

CHAPTER 12

C ody hadn't even stepped foot in the kitchen, but he knew what the current conversation was about. He heard Lizzy's and Kit's voices, and they sounded far more serious than usual.

It wasn't a reach to guess that the topic had something to do with Sierra.

She was the only thing anyone on this property wanted to talk about these days—and not in a good way.

Daisy had surprised him by not saying anything to her sisters about Sierra recognizing him, but even without their questions, he felt like he was part of the conversation.

He felt like he was the only person in this town who thought Sierra deserved some empathy. Like she deserved to be heard and understood. But all anyone had heard were the threats she'd made while in pain, and before she'd even known the full story.

The poor thing had only just found out her father had died. She was grieving and reeling, and Cody was the only one who seemed to get that.

He tensed as he headed for the coffeepot. Kit was

resting beside it, his typical easy grin nowhere to be found as he watched his wife with a worried frown. "Babe, you've got to keep calm. I know you're scared, but there's nothing she can do."

"I'm not overreacting." Lizzy flicked her hand in the air. "She told Dahlia to talk to her lawyer. That can only mean—"

"You told Dahlia?" Cody spun with a frown.

"Yeah." Lizzy winced, having the good grace to look shamefaced.

"I thought you all agreed to leave her out of this until she comes home." He gripped his mug, surprised the handle wasn't breaking off. He could only imagine what kind of response Dahlia would have pulled out of Sierra. She probably went in there guns blazing down the phone line, and Sierra would have responded in kind, because she was strong and fiery...and had no doubt ended the call feeling weak and vulnerable. "You shouldn't have done that, Lizzy."

"Cody." Kit warned him off in a tone that said *leave it be*.

But Lizzy answered. "We didn't mean to, but she called when Emma was worried sick, and I guess she heard something in her voice, and she started to panic, and then she called Rose, and Rose panicked, so she told her to call me, and then...well, you know how she can be."

His heart sank because, yes, he knew *exactly* how Dahlia could be. He admired the heck out of the woman who'd taken over the business end of the ranch management, and everyone with eyes could see she was the best thing to happen to JJ. But there was no denying that Dahlia lacked in the tact department.

"Did she...?" He grimaced, scrubbing a hand over the

stubble he should probably shave today if he didn't want to start looking like a mountain man. "What did she say to Sierra? How did she even get in touch with her?"

Lizzy shrugged. "Apparently Dahlia figured out she'd be staying at the inn, so she called and—"

"Geez, Lizzy," Cody groaned. "Dahlia tracked her down and then surprised her with a call." He shook his head, muttering under his breath as he tried to take the burn out of his anger.

"It's not Lizzy's fault." Kit straightened, his expression grim.

Cody rubbed his eyes and clamped his lips together before he said something he'd regret.

But honestly, if the straightforward and, some might say, painfully blunt Dahlia called Sierra out of the blue, it must have been awful.

"Do you honestly think ganging up on Sierra is gonna help matters?" he blurted, his tone more accusatory than he'd intended.

Lizzy gaped at him, and Kit glared.

"Cody, what's up with you?" Kit murmured.

"No, he's right." Lizzy sighed. "I wish Dahlia had talked to us first before she'd called."

And that made Cody's jaw clench all over again. He didn't need Lizzy defending him or Kit getting all protective because he asked a stinking question.

"Still, it's none of your business, Cody," Kit clipped.

Cody's head jerked back a bit, and he couldn't deny that the words stung. "You're right," he muttered. "What was I thinking? I guess I'm just the hired help around here."

He started to walk away.

"That's not what he meant," Lizzy called out.

Cody paused in the doorway, struggling for calm.

"You know you're not just the hired help." Kit rolled his eyes. "What I meant was—"

"It's O'Sullivan sister stuff. I get it." Cody turned with a small smile to let them know he wasn't going to let some flyaway comment rattle him.

The truth was his irritation wasn't aimed at them. It was this situation that had him on edge. Even before Sierra had arrived, he'd had this uneasy feeling, watching all the sisters settle down in this home.

It wasn't that they'd given up on finding Sierra and April, necessarily. But there wasn't the same urgency, and Cody suspected each and every one of 'em would have been happy to just let the matter go untouched if it meant not messing with this happy little world they'd built for themselves.

He backed up a step, only half listening as Lizzy filled him in on what their lawyer had said and what their options were.

"It's none of your business," Kit had said.

He took another step backward, putting a little distance between himself and his brother and sister-in-law.

It didn't help, because Kit's words still stung.

Probably because they had a ring of truth to them. He might be a friend to everyone here, but the O'Sullivan sisters owned the place. And it was them and their new families who had a real home here.

The thought was jarring and uncomfortable. He'd never felt like an outsider before. And he'd always been content to be the doting uncle and the good friend.

But right now...

Right now, he needed to get out of here, because he was in serious danger of saying something he shouldn't.

"I'm sure it'll work out," he muttered when Lizzy paused to breathe. He edged toward the door, but both she and Kit were watching him closely.

"Are you okay, Cody?" Lizzy's expression bunched with that curious but caring look she got sometimes.

He nodded.

"You seem...not yourself," Kit added, resting his hand on Lizzy's back, forming a united front that only amplified Cody's sense of isolation.

How would you know if I'm not myself? He stopped himself just in time, swallowing the words. But honestly, Kit had been so caught up in his new happy family and their new house...

He didn't need Cody's help as much with the kids anymore, which was fine. But now they barely saw each other outside work. He was the reliable babysitter, and that was all he was needed for.

"I, uh...I've got to get back to work," he mumbled.

He rubbed at his chest, hating this feeling, like he was on the outside looking in.

And he imagined Sierra was feeling the same, only a million times worse.

He paused in the doorway and turned back. "I know it's none of my business and all, but you all have each other. Sierra's alone in this town." He turned his attention to Lizzy. "I'd reckon you know as well as anyone what it's like to feel like an outsider in this close-knit place."

Her eyes widened, but before she could respond, Kit shifted in front of her. "I don't know what's up with you, Cody, but don't take it out on Lizzy. She's upset right now, and—"

"And she's got you to comfort her," Cody finished with a pointed look.

He didn't raise his voice, but both Kit and Lizzy looked startled. He supposed everyone was so used to him being quiet and easygoing that they forgot he had a mind of his own, and while he didn't seek out confrontation...

He didn't run from it either.

Keeping his voice even, he drove his point home. "Lizzy's got you, and Emma, and Dahlia, and... Heck, this whole town has her back, and we all know it."

Lizzy frowned, and Cody shrugged. "There's nothing wrong with that," he added. "But try to put yourself in Sierra's place. That's all I'm saying."

Kit's expression darkened into a deep glower. "Now, look here, Cody—"

But Cody turned and headed back to work, not even sparing a glance over his shoulder.

CHAPTER 13

After Dahlia's phone call, Sierra set out for a long ride, heading out of town to explore the winding back roads and the long, twisting two-lane highway that ran along a riverbed.

There was no doubt this place was gorgeous.

But not even the breathtaking landscape could make this itch go away. It was the telltale nagging sensation she got whenever she'd stayed in one place too long.

Maybe it was a side effect of her mom moving them from apartment to apartment so much as a kid, but after she'd gotten her nursing degree, the urge to keep moving only grew stronger. And the more she'd traveled, the more poverty she'd seen, and the more she'd known deep down in her heart that she'd never be able to settle down in some cushiony gig with a white picket fence when there were so many people out there in need of help.

Becoming a traveling nurse with a humanitarian organization had been a no-brainer.

She missed it now, having a purpose. Something bigger than herself that she could throw herself into.

Something that would help her to forget.

But her boss hadn't gotten back to her with an update on the children she'd left behind in the Venezuelan clinic, so she couldn't distract herself with work if she'd tried.

And driving these long, winding roads gave her nothing but time to replay every conversation she'd had since she'd arrived.

Slowly but surely, she could feel the puzzle pieces fitting together, forming some sort of picture of what had happened after Frank passed away.

But the more puzzle pieces she filled in, the more achingly aware she was of the many holes still left to be filled. Including the big empty space in the middle of the puzzle labeled Frank O'Sullivan.

What was he like? Why had he left? Why had he written that ridiculous clause into the will?

Eventually, when the sun started to sink below the mountains and Sierra's grumbling stomach refused to be ignored any longer, she turned back.

But rather than head to Aspire, she pulled off into Wellsprings and found herself parking in front of the saloon she'd gone to her first night in town.

Because their burgers are good, she told herself. Not because she was hoping to run into a certain cowboy.

What would be the odds, anyway?

But the moment she stepped inside the small bar and saw with a glance that a certain hot cowboy wasn't there, her belly dipped with disappointment, making a liar out of her.

Okay, fine. So maybe it would have been kinda nice to see a friendly face.

Even if that friendly face is also friends with the enemy.

Sheila, the cocktail waitress, recognized her. "Hey, hon. You meeting Cody again tonight?"

Sierra opened her mouth to point out that she hadn't met him here the last time. It hadn't been some prearranged date, just...just...

Just the best night of my life.

She stabbed her straw into the water glass Sheila had given her. "Not tonight."

"Too bad," Sheila said, adding with a mischievous wink, "The Swanson boys are always a treat. Polite, good tippers...and easy on the eyes."

Sierra grinned as Sheila walked away with a loud guffaw at her own joke.

"Easy on the eyes" was putting it mildly. She supposed Cody's brother must be just as good-looking...

And he's married to my sister.

She shook her head. No. Nope. She still couldn't think of those women as sisters, even if they were related by blood.

Not for the first time today, Sierra found herself wishing she'd handled everything differently. She had a laundry list of questions she wished she'd asked. Things she should have known before she went charging off to confront her sisters.

Sheila returned a while later with the burger and fries Sierra had ordered, and for some reason, the sight of the fries made her want to cry.

She pushed her food around on her plate as she muttered to herself in annoyance. "Stupid fries. Stupid cowboys." She huffed as she shoved the plate aside. "Stupid families."

As if on cue, her phone vibrated with a text.

She'd been in and out of reception on the road, but it

seemed she had plenty of reception now. Her heart picked up its pace when she saw Cody's name.

She grinned at the way he'd entered his contact info into her phone when she'd given it to him so he could send her the lawyer's info.

Cody the Cowboy.

His text made her laugh out loud.

You better not have fled town. You owe me a rematch, Hustler.

Dipping her head with a silly smile, she started to text back, but then her phone dinged with another text. This one was from her mom.

With a grimace, Sierra set down the phone and pulled her food back in front of her. Her mother had been pestering her with calls and texts asking what the lawyer had to say.

Even though Sierra had yet to respond, that didn't stop her mom from voicing her opinion constantly.

Don't let those women swindle you out of what's yours, Sierra.

And another...

Frank owes you.

. . .

What she means is "he owes us," Sierra thought as she took a bite of her burger. She paused mid-chew as her stomach turned. Or maybe what her mother really meant was...*he owed me.*

She'd tried to get more details about her mom's relationship with Frank the other day on the phone, but her mother had been too focused on her anger toward Frank and his other family to give her any concrete details. Like...when had he left?

Did he know her mom was pregnant when he walked away?

Did he make any other attempts other than those sporadic birthday cards?

She set her burger down. And did it matter if he did? From what the lawyer told her, Frank wasn't much of a father to any of his daughters. Except maybe April, the youngest.

Unease coiled in her gut as she remembered her harsh tone with Daisy and the cold way she'd hung up on Dahlia.

She'd just assumed he'd moved on and given his new family the love she'd been denied. But maybe...

Maybe she wasn't the only one who'd been abandoned.

Not that it matters, she told herself as she snatched up some fries. She hadn't come here to find sisters, and she had no use for a ranch in the middle of nowhere.

No. What she'd come here for was closure.

And closure was what she'd get...just as soon as she found a loophole in that will.

CHAPTER 14

Cody parked his vehicle behind the beat-up old work truck that Nash let the summer help use for their trips into town.

Boone paused with one hand on the door handle. "You sure you don't want to join us?"

Cody shook his head. "Nah. You guys have fun without me."

Boone didn't make a move, watching him with a feigned look of suspicion. "You embarrassed to be seen with us, Cody Swanson?"

Cody laughed at his younger friend's teasing. He'd been a little worried what it'd be like to have Boone as a roommate after quiet and levelheaded JJ, but it'd been a pleasant surprise so far. Sure, he was loud and liked to have a good time. But he knew how to chill out, as well, and could be surprisingly thoughtful as a friend. Like right now.

"Look, I got the feeling there's some tension between you and your brother..."

Cody winced, scratching the back of his head. He

wished he could deny it, but what was the point? "It'll blow over." He shrugged. "It always does."

Boone nodded, and for a second, it looked like he might ask more questions, but after a beat, he just flashed Cody that lopsided grin that made all the girls swoon, according to Daisy. "All right, well, if you change your mind, you know where we'll be."

"Chasing after the ladies?" Cody guessed.

Boone winked. "You know it."

He hopped out of the car as Cody laughed. The more he got to know Boone, the more he was certain that there was a deeper side to him...but he'd nailed the part of the playboy charmer, all right.

Boone waved as he jogged to catch up with the others.

They'd all gotten done with work early, and Nash had given them the rest of the day off. Boone and the other seasonal workers had quickly hatched a plan to head into town for a bite to eat and then some drinks at the bar.

Everyone had been itching to get off the range and spend some time around others. Cody included. But he wasn't in the mood to go to the bar and flirt with the same women who were always there.

They were nice and all, but his head was too full of a certain redhead. She'd never texted him back the day before, which...was fine.

He should probably give her some space. Daisy had finally spilled the beans about how Sierra had recognized him, which was the new tension Boone had picked up on.

Kit had stormed up to him at work the day before and demanded to know what he'd been doing with the black sheep who was dead set on tearing apart their happy home.

Cody had lost his temper all over again. They weren't

kids anymore. He didn't owe his brother any explanation. But the fact that Kit and Lizzy and all the rest of them were so quick to make Sierra out to be some villain in this story really bothered him.

They were so caught up in their own happiness that none of them could see beyond the warm, contented little bubble they'd made for themselves.

Cody climbed out of his truck and started walking. Yeah, he really should give Sierra some breathing room. Let things calm down back at the ranch. Stay out of it.

But all the while he was thinking it, his feet were carrying him toward the Aspire Inn on the far end of Main Street. He couldn't help it. He was worried about her.

And yeah, maybe a little part of him was worried she'd run off.

He couldn't blame her. No one knew exactly what Dahlia had said to her, but the conversation had left Dahlia fuming, so it clearly hadn't been a pleasant exchange.

He hung out in front of the inn for way too long, earning himself some curious looks from the manager when she came outside to get in her car. After a while, he gave up his impromptu stakeout and headed back toward the stores and restaurants that lined Main Street.

He stopped in the flower shop where his mother worked part-time and was greeted with a warm embrace.

"There's my baby." Her voice always sounded like a melody.

"Mom," he groaned.

"Oh, hush," she shot back with a grin that looked just like Kit's. "I don't care how old you are. You'll always be my baby."

He heaved a sigh that made her laugh.

"Now, come on in here and tell me what's been going on between you and your brother."

He tensed, but she rolled her eyes. "Oh, don't worry, he didn't tell me anything. Neither would Lizzy when I tried to pry it out of her. But I know my boys, and I know when something is up."

"Mmm," he muttered, making a show of checking out some flowers to avoid her all-too-perceptive gaze. His attention was caught by some bright red petals.

Unlike his mother, he'd never taken an interest, so he had no idea what kind of flowers they were, but they stuck out amid the pale pink and white petals that surrounded it, and he felt a smile tugging at his lips when he considered buying them for Sierra.

"Fine, fine," his mother was saying with a put-upon air that fooled no one. "I'll just wait until someone deigns to fill me in. After all, I'm just the woman who gave birth to you both, but—"

"Mom." He laughed as he came over to pull her into a hug. "If there were anything serious going on, you'd be the first to know. Kit and I just aren't seeing eye to eye on something at the moment, that's all."

Her lips were pursed when he let her go, but she eventually nodded. "Oh, all right." She jabbed a finger in his direction. "But don't you let this drag on, you hear me? I know you like to keep the peace, but there's being calm, and then there's letting things fester."

He nodded, tucking his hands in his pockets. "Yes, ma'am."

"Good. Now, go on and clear the air with your brother." She winked. "And buy some flowers for whatever young lady it is who has you tied up in knots."

"I...what...no, I..."

His mother's head fell back with a laugh as she turned away from him to tend to a customer. He found himself shaking his head with a rueful grin as she walked away.

Had that been a lucky guess, or was he that easy for his mother to read?

He snagged the red flowers and laid the money on the table before heading back out.

Either way, his mother wasn't wrong. He hadn't been able to get Sierra out of his head from the moment he first set eyes on her.

And now here he was, holding a bouquet of who-knew-what just because it made him think of her.

And for all he knew, she'd already left town!

He laid the bouquet of flowers in the passenger seat of his truck and was about to climb in when he heard a voice calling his name.

He turned to see Dex walking out of Mama's Kitchen, his arms full of to-go bags.

"Hey, you need a hand?" Cody jogged over to Rose's husband.

"I got it." Dex grinned and shook his head. Despite the fact that his hair was mussed and he had circles under his eyes, Cody wasn't sure he'd ever seen the town's doctor looking happier.

Dex nodded toward his car. "I'm just picking up some food for Rose. Daisy offered to watch Kiara for a little while, so I'm taking my wife out for an impromptu picnic."

"Sounds nice." Cody grinned.

"Yeah, well, Rose has been amazing with Kiara. I do my best to help, but the clinic keeps me busy during the day, and…" Dex shrugged, his smile never fading. "Kiara keeps us busy all night."

Cody clapped a hand on his friend's shoulder. "It doesn't look like it's fazing you any."

Dex shrugged. "What can I say? I've never been happier."

"Good for you, man. No one deserves that happiness like you and Rose."

Dex's grin turned sheepish as he ducked his head. "We definitely had our fill of drama in the beginning, but she and Kiara are worth fighting for."

"Well, I won't keep you, man." Cody stepped aside. "You'd better take advantage of your alone time while you can get it."

Dex laughed and started to respond, but they were both startled by the sound of tools dropping and a woman's sigh. They turned to see Bella Cummings, one of the teachers at the high school, frowning in irritation as she bent down to pick up a wreath she'd dropped.

Dex took a step toward her, but Cody stopped him. "You go take care of Rose, Doc," he said with a friendly nudge. "I'll help Bella."

"Thanks, Cody."

"Tell Rose I say hi!" he called out to Dex as he hurried over to Bella. "Can I give you a hand?"

She glanced up in surprise and then smiled. "Why, Cody Swanson. My knight in shining armor."

He chuckled at her flirtatious teasing. Bella had been in the grade below him at Aspire High, and they'd dated briefly years back, before they'd both realized there was nothing between them but friendship.

Not that it stopped either of them from flirting when they ran into each other out on the town.

"What are you up to?" he asked. Although his question

was answered when he picked up the decorations and sign she'd dropped.

She arched her brows. "My class from this year volunteered to help with decorations for this weekend's Music on Main Street festival. Or"—she made a funny face—"I should say I volunteered them to help."

He held up a large stapler and some fake vines. "And yet, here you are."

He looked around pointedly, and Bella laughed. "I know, I know. I have a handful of students coming to meet me. I just got here early to set up."

"In the meantime, what do you say I give you a hand?"

"You don't mind?" Her eyes were so wide and hopeful, he couldn't help but grin.

"Of course not." He leaned down and lowered his voice. "And if your volunteers don't show, point the way, and I'll go kick some teen butts into gear."

Her head fell back when she laughed this time, and she rested a hand on his arm as she smiled sweetly. "My hero."

CHAPTER 15

Sierra was staring.

She swallowed hard, willing her gaze to move away and her hands to unlock from her bike's handles. But she was transfixed by the sight of Cody with another woman.

And not in a good way.

The woman was laughing, her hand on his arm. And Cody...

Oh heck, Cody's smile made her belly do a backflip even when it wasn't aimed in her direction.

Finally, she looked away, snatching her helmet off too quickly and wincing as she pulled a lock of her hair.

The woman laughed again, and Sierra tensed all over. The way she was leaning into Cody...it was flirtatious, there was no doubt about it.

And Cody wasn't exactly holding up a stop sign, now was he?

"And why should he?" she muttered to herself as she climbed off the motorcycle. It wasn't like he was spoken for.

They'd shared one kiss, for heaven's sake. She had no claim to him.

Much as she tried to convince herself of that, her stomach tightened into a knot, and something green and toxic flooded her veins as she walked toward the happy couple.

He hadn't spotted her yet.

She could turn around and go hide out in her motel room.

Her chin came up. She *could*, but she wouldn't. She'd spent the morning driving the country roads and should have stopped for food along the way, but she didn't. And now she was starving.

If she'd known she'd be sticking around this long, she would have rented a place with a kitchen, but as it was, she was stuck eating out every meal. Which meant leaving the inn to hunt for food.

Which meant risking run-ins with her newfound family...and Cody.

She forced her gaze straight ahead, focusing on the sign for Mama's Kitchen like her life depended on it. She'd almost made it when she heard Cody's voice. "Sierra!"

She stumbled to a stop as one part of her ordered her feet to come to a halt and another begged her to keep going.

Awesome. Now she looked like a clumsy weirdo because she still hadn't turned to face him.

"Hey, Sierra." She stared at the concrete, listening to his feet running to catch up with her. "I was looking for you."

She turned and pasted on a smile. "Hi." Her gaze flickered over to the brunette who was watching her with unabashed curiosity, approaching with a small-town smile that Sierra would have normally warmed to in a heartbeat.

"I'm Bella." The woman gave her a little wave.

"Sierra."

"Oh, so you're Sierra," Bella breathed.

Cody shot her a quick look, and Bella blushed. "Sorry." She winced, taking a handful of plastic flowers from Cody's arms. "Sorry, I didn't mean it like that, just..." She cleared her throat and wet her lips. "It's a small town."

Sierra nodded. "That it is."

Her insides were burning with humiliation as she took a step backward toward the diner. She could only imagine what people in this town were saying about her. Even if she hadn't run into those old men on her first day here, she wouldn't have been able to avoid hearing all about the darling, sweet, kind, generous O'Sullivan sisters.

Everywhere she turned, people were gushing about them or asking if she knew them in a not-so-subtle attempt to pry.

"Glad you're still here," Cody murmured.

Her gaze darted back to him, and...dang it, her heart did that thing again. It gave a nudge to her ribs like a puppy looking for attention.

"Yeah, well...I'm not staying long."

His expression fell, his small smile faltering.

Sierra looked away.

"I hope you'll stick around long enough for the festival," Bella chirped. She gestured to a sign that was leaning against the lamp post beside her. "The nice weather doesn't last long here, so our summers are jam-packed with festivals and carnivals and concerts and..." Bella trailed off with a smile. "It's always a good time."

"I'm sure," Sierra said. "But as soon as I finish my business here, I've got places to be."

Bella nodded. "Oh, right. Sure."

But Cody just stared at her, and Sierra shifted uneasily.

Did he know she was lying? Work had given her six weeks off, so they weren't expecting her. And she'd already hired a company to help her mom pack up her grandmother's belongings. She had nowhere she needed to be. Not for a while, anyway.

But she couldn't stay here.

She took another step backward.

"Wait." Cody reached for her.

"I've got to go." Her heart was pounding way too hard. She jerked a thumb over her shoulder. "I just came to grab some food to go, so…" She spun on her heel, leaving Cody behind.

The moment she walked into Mama's Kitchen, she realized her mistake. The place was busy, and there was a line to place a to-go order. But that meant she was trapped in the small lobby with a bunch of curious bystanders. She didn't recognize a single person…

But they clearly recognized her.

She heard "O'Sullivan" and "Sierra." A few of her sisters' names were whispered too. She tried not to notice, and she kept her eyes on her phone, as if she was truly intent on reading what she saw there.

But in all honesty, the words of her mom's latest text blurred together, and she felt the weight of the stares growing with each passing second until finally, like a coward…she ran.

And she nearly ran Cody over as she fled. "Hey, I was just coming in to see if you wanted—"

She brushed past him and forced a polite smile. "Changed my mind. The wait's too long, and I think I've got some snacks back at my room, so…"

She didn't finish her sentence, and she didn't acknowledge pretty, sweet, wholesome-looking Bella, who was watching her with surprise as she hurried back to her motorcycle.

She revved the engine and cut out of her parking spot too quickly, nearly colliding with a passing patrol car.

Wonderful. A fender bender was exactly what she needed. She tucked her head down and forced herself to focus on the road and her driving. The inn wasn't far, and there she'd have privacy to figure out her next steps.

Because one thing was clear. She shouldn't be here. She didn't need to be, not if she found a lawyer who could fight this battle on her behalf.

The only thing sticking around would accomplish was to muddle her head and question her resolve.

She had a flash of Cody's smile, heard his low, even voice in the back of her mind.

Okay, fine, maybe he was easy on the eyes, like Sheila said. And maybe she'd formed a bit of a crush on the guy...embarrassing as that was to acknowledge.

But sticking around would only make matters worse, because she'd made her plans for the future a long time ago. Her plans involved travel and career and helping people.

They definitely didn't include small towns in the middle of nowhere.

And handsome cowboys with killer smiles?

Yeah, that was so not part of the plan.

CHAPTER 16

C ody wasn't sure how long he stood out front of Mama's Kitchen, staring after Sierra.

Bella cut into his thoughts when she came to stand at his side and followed his gaze. "So, that's the new O'Sullivan sister, huh?"

"Yep." His brows drew down as he stared at the now-empty parking space. "That was weird, right?"

"Totally weird," she agreed without hesitation.

He nodded, scrubbing the back of his neck. "Yeah, I thought so."

Bella nudged his arm. "So...was that some tension I was feeling between the two of you, or has my radar been skewed by all the teenage hormones I'm surrounded by all day?"

He let out a huff of laughter. "You caught that, huh?"

He turned to see her giving him a wry smile. "It was hard to miss when she looked at me like she wanted to tear my hair out."

"She did not—" He stopped when he saw her smile widen.

"Trust me, I know a jealous woman when I see one."

His lips twitched, and his gaze drifted back to the place where she'd been...before she'd fled like someone was chasing her out of town. He glanced back toward the diner with a frown. "I wonder what happened back there."

"I don't know," Bella said slowly. "But I can guess." At his look, she shrugged. "I know you don't get into town often, but you know how this place can be. Especially when there's a newcomer around."

He winced. "And one stirring up trouble, at that."

"Exactly." Her expression grew sympathetic. "Poor thing could probably use a friend."

He nodded until he caught her eyeing him pointedly.

"Yeah, okay, okay." Honestly, he was dying for an excuse to chase after Sierra. He'd been over the moon when he'd first caught sight of her, confused by her awkward reaction when she'd joined him and Bella, and then...

Well, then she'd run away from him, and his already battered ego had taken another beating.

Which was why he still hesitated now. "She didn't exactly seem ecstatic to see me," he pointed out. "Not to mention, she just said she's not sticking around for long."

Bella just watched him, her expression one of exasperated amusement. "Cody."

"Yes?"

"Do you want to go run after that woman?"

He pressed his lips together as he nodded quickly. "I really do."

She laughed and gave him a playful push. "Then what are you standing around talking to me for?"

"But your decorations..."

"Will be here when my students show up. Don't worry about me."

When he still hesitated, she sighed. "Cody, I've known you your whole life, and I've never once seen you rattled by a woman, let alone staring after one like some lovesick puppy."

"Hey!"

She planted her hands on her hips, her eyebrows rising with a challenging stare. "Am I wrong?"

He dipped his chin with a laugh, and then he turned toward Mama's Kitchen.

"Wait, where are you going?" she called after him.

He turned back to Bella, walking backward toward Mama's Kitchen. "Trust me. She'll be far more welcoming if I come bearing fries."

A little while later, loaded up with bags that smelled like heaven and two ice-cold sodas, Cody found himself face-to-face with the manager who'd been giving him the evil eye earlier.

"I can't give you her room number."

"Right, but if you just call her or—"

The woman behind the desk was shaking her head before Cody could even finish.

Frustration swirled through him, and he gritted his teeth. He wasn't one to lose his temper with someone who was just trying to do her job, but…

A hallway door swung open to his right, and Sierra stopped in her tracks at the sight of him. "Cody?"

He grinned at the exasperated manager. "Never mind."

Striding toward Sierra, he blocked her path. "Going somewhere?"

"N-No, I just…" Her gaze dropped to the bags in his hands. "Is that…?"

He held them up, the signature smells of Mama's Kitchen making his mouth water. He could only imagine the effect it was having on Sierra. Her nostrils quivered as she sniffed the air, then started fighting a smile. He'd never felt more triumphant. "I thought you might want some lunch."

"I..." Her gaze darted from the bags to his face and back again.

He could all but see the inner war going on. Taking a step closer, he dropped his voice so the manager couldn't hear. "It's just lunch, Sierra."

She wet her lips and took a deep breath. "Yeah. Okay. Thanks."

With a waving motion, she had him follow her back the way she'd come until they were standing in front of her hotel room door. "You didn't have to do that," she murmured, struggling with her keycard.

"You're welcome." He leaned against the wall and gave her an easy grin, seconds away from offering to help her.

But then the light flashed green, and she pushed the handle down, shooting him a sidelong smile as she nudged the door open and ushered him in. "Thank you."

The room was tiny, and a queen-sized bed took up most of the space. That tension Bella had mentioned grew a hundred times over when the door swung shut behind them.

She bit her lip and crossed her arms. "That's an awful big bag of food you got there, Cody. Are we expecting a party?"

He chuckled, opening one of the big bags and pulling out the bouquet he'd bought earlier.

Sierra's gasp made his heart leap. "Wow, these are..."

She trailed off, so he said, "They reminded me of you."

"Thank you." She took the bouquet and stared at the flowers for so long, he started to get uncomfortable. "Now this other bag is filled with food. But no parties have been planned, so far as I know." He started pulling out the food he'd bought, laying it across the end of the bed like it was a banquet table. "I just wasn't sure what you'd want, so I got a little of everything."

"Oh. Wow. Cody, that's..." Her throat worked, and for a second, he thought she'd trail off again, but then she finished with "That's really thoughtful."

"Yeah, well, the way you ran out of there, I had a sense that maybe you weren't feeling the small-town warm welcome we're known for here in Aspire."

Her lips twitched. "More like the small-town gossip mill."

He grimaced. "Yeah. That's the flip side of the coin, I guess." He snagged a fried chicken sandwich after she helped herself to the pulled pork sliders. "There's nothing like a small town when it comes to neighborliness," he continued. "If anyone's in trouble, the whole town rallies."

She nodded. "That must be nice."

"'Course, on the other hand, if someone comes to town and seems to be a threat to one of their own..."

"Break out the pitchforks." Sierra smirked as she sat cross-legged on the bed while he leaned against the desk.

"It's really not so bad as all that." He wiped a blob of mayonnaise off the side of his mouth with a napkin. "People are just curious about you, that's all."

"Mmm-hmm." Her tone said she was unconvinced. "So what about you?"

"What about me?"

"I guess you're a fan of small towns, huh? For better or

for worse?" She sounded so certain. Like it was a no-brainer.

And maybe that was why the truth slipped out. "I don't know."

She blinked in surprise.

"I mean, it's all I've ever known, you know?" He set the remainder of his sandwich on the desk and brushed his fingers off, wondering where his appetite had suddenly fled to. Snatching a soda, he popped the top and passed it to her.

She thanked him with a smile. "Do you ever think about leaving?"

"Nah." He grabbed the other soda and ran his thumb through the condensation, staring at the line he'd left behind.

Nah. Why did that suddenly not feel like the right answer?

For reasons he couldn't explain, it felt like something was lodged in his windpipe. He cleared his throat. "Well, maybe. Sometimes."

She was watching him closely as she nibbled on her food. "But..."

He lifted a shoulder. "But my family is here. My friends. My life."

She nodded, and he had this sinking feeling that he'd disappointed her. Or maybe...

Maybe he'd disappointed himself with that answer.

"What about you?" he asked. "Where'd you grow up?"

She hesitated, and he realized then that for all their chatting, they'd barely spoken about her personal life. They'd talked about everything but.

"Look, I'm not here to spy on you," he started.

"I know." She said it quickly, taking a swig of her drink and then licking her lips. "I didn't think you were."

"I'm not here to try to make O'Sullivan peace either," he added.

This time she met his gaze evenly. "No?"

"Nope." He pulled out the desk chair and sank into it. "But does that mean I can't even know where you're from?"

She gave a soft laugh. "I grew up in San Francisco. But I haven't lived there since high school."

Slowly but surely, he drew her out of that shell of hers. But they both avoided all talk of Frank and the O'Sullivans as if by some silent agreement.

"So you've really traveled all over the world?" He gazed at her, unable to hide his awe.

She nodded.

"Where's your favorite place?"

She tilted her head to the side and pursed her lips as she gave it some serious thought. "So far, India."

Man, she was adorable when she tipped her head that way. The crinkle on the side of her nose, the little furrow in her forehead. He couldn't take his eyes off her as he murmured, "So far?"

She shrugged. "I'm not done traveling. I love where I'm stationed in Venezuela right now, but I'm not staying there forever." Her gaze met his. "I don't plan on ever settling down in one place forever."

He felt the words deep in his chest like an arrow straight through his lungs. But he managed a nod. "And are you really planning on up and leaving Aspire without even meeting your sisters?"

Her brows came down. "Cody…"

He held his hands up in a show of peace. "I'm not gonna try and talk you into anything. I'm just curious."

"I don't know what I'm doing here." She sighed. "Or how long I'll stay." She rubbed her eyes in a way that made his heart ache. "I don't know anything."

He got up and moved to sit beside her. "Come on. Yes you do. Tell me one thing you know for sure."

She turned to meet his gaze, letting out a soft little laugh as she trailed her finger lightly down the side of his face. "I know I'm really glad you came by."

His insides hitched at the soft huskiness of her voice. "Me too."

"And..." Her lips curved up. "I know if you really want a rematch, it'll have to be cards, because this inn does not have a pool table. I checked."

He laughed. "How do you feel about poker?"

She got up and headed over to the desk. "That depends. How do you feel about losing...again?"

The next few hours flew by too quickly. Poker turned into quite the event, filled with teasing and laughter. They were betting with french fries, which Sierra couldn't help eating.

Cody laughed at her. "You're gonna eat all your winnings and be left with nothing to bet with."

"Not a problem. My pile's only getting bigger," she teased back.

And she was right. Her pile grew quickly. But then Cody had a good run, and she lost one fry after the next until she was left with a piddly pile of cold fries on her napkin.

Before she could lose it all, he called the game and convinced her to go to the coffee shop with him to get out of the cramped quarters for a while. They snagged a table in the very back, away from prying eyes, and over coffee, she finally opened up a little more, telling him about her mother, about the birthday cards she'd found, about the anger that had driven her here…only to find out she was too late to meet her father.

"You're angry with your mother," he said. It wasn't really a question, but she nodded.

"I know she's only ever wanted what's best for me, but I can't help but be mad that she made this decision for me, you know?"

He nodded. "I can see that, for sure." After a beat, he added, "I can also see how coming here and getting hit with all kinds of shocking news about your father's passing and six sisters you didn't know about…" He waited until she looked up and met his gaze before he continued, "I can see how that'd be a lot to take in. How there'd be a whole lot of emotions to sift through…"

"Cody." Her voice held a note of wariness…of warning.

"I know, I know." He smiled. "I promise I'm not trying to convince you of anything. Well, maybe that's not the whole truth."

She arched a brow as she sipped her coffee.

"I'm not trying to convince you to do anything for anyone else's sake," he clarified. "But for your sake, I wish you'd give your sisters a chance."

She started to protest, but he put a hand over hers and she froze, her protest dying on her lips.

"I know them, Sierra. Each of them was lonely and lost and scared and grieving when they showed up in this town. I know y'all started off on the wrong foot, and I know you came here hoping to meet your father, but I think you owe it to yourself to get to know the ones you found. And maybe grieve the one you lost."

Her eyes were bright with unshed tears. "You know, if those sisters of mine did send you as a spy, they're evil masterminds."

He chuckled.

"You're awfully good at this," she murmured.

"Does that mean you'll stick around?" He found himself holding his breath as he waited for her answer. But she paused too long. When he followed her gaze, he saw her watching the high schoolers hanging signs and getting Main Street ready for the next day's festivities, and it sparked an idea.

"Come to the festival," he blurted.

"What?" She blinked at him.

"Everyone goes to it." He gestured to the sign. "I guarantee your sisters will be there, and it'll be neutral ground, and..." He leaned forward, clasping her hand tightly and loving the way she squeezed back. "And I'll be there. I'll have your back every step of the way."

Her lips quivered. "Yeah?"

He nodded. "I promise. You can count on me, Sierra."

She blinked rapidly, and his heart twisted when he realized she was fighting back tears. But she forced a smile as she sniffed, then rasped, "Okay, Cowboy, you have a deal. But you drive a hard bargain."

CHAPTER 17

Cody didn't want to leave her, but after a while, they were both sitting there with empty mugs, and his phone was dinging.

"You're a popular man," Sierra observed, nodding toward his phone. "Is that your friend from earlier?"

His brows knitted in confusion. *My friend from...?* "You mean Bella?"

Her lips pressed together, and Cody tried not to smile. "Why? You jealous?"

"No, of course not. I just—" Her chin jerked back, and her brows lowered.

"I'm teasing, Sierra." He reached across the table and covered her hand with his. They both went still at the simple touch, which somehow felt anything but simple.

The mix of feelings that shot through him were definitely not easy to explain, and he didn't bother to try.

Her gaze was fixed on their hands, but when she lifted her eyes to meet his, he added, "Bella's just a friend. We used to date, but we realized pretty early on that we're just meant to be buddies."

She nodded slowly. "Okay."

His lips twitched with the urge to grin. Did she have any idea how adorable she was? "Okay," he repeated. Then he pulled his hand away, and she gave her head a little shake before nodding to his phone. "So who's been blowing up your phone, then? Your pal Daisy?"

He shook his head. "Daisy's off on a camping trip with her boyfriend, Levi, and his family."

She nodded, and he thought maybe he caught a glimmer of interest, so he added, "Levi's the sheriff in this county, and he's got three kids. All five of them headed to Colorado for the annual Baker family get-together. They camp, fish, roast marshmallows. I'm sure you get the picture."

She nodded, then shrugged. "So…one less sister for me to run into."

He chuckled. She wouldn't admit it, but he suspected she was curious about her family.

"Yeah, well, I hear you already met Dahlia…sorta."

She grimaced, and he burst out laughing.

"Trust me, you'd like Dahlia if you got to know her."

"I'll take your word for it."

"No, seriously. We all felt that way when she first showed up. She's sort of an acquired taste."

"Uh-huh."

He laughed. "Once you get to know her, you realize she's just a mama bear with a side of tomboy and a heart too big for her chest."

She arched her brow. The only sign that maybe she was interested. Cody shifted, not sure how much he should say, then settled for "They didn't have it easy growing up either."

Her gaze softened. "Oh."

He shrugged. "I'll let them tell you about that, but that's why Dahlia is the way she is, I guess."

"And you know her so well because…"

"She manages the business end of things on the ranch." Then he added with a slow grin, "Plus, she just married one of my best friends, JJ."

Sierra chuckled. "Wow, you guys really are one big happy family out there on that ranch, huh?"

He smiled. *There's room for more. You're a part of that family too…*

He bit his tongue. He'd pushed her enough for one day, and her agreeing to go to the festival was a good start.

"Whoever's texting, it seems like they really need you." Sierra pointed at his phone.

"Yeah, this…" He spun his device so it faced her and slid it across the table so she could see the incessant texts from Boone. "This is my new roommate at the bunkhouse now that JJ's off on his honeymoon with Dahlia."

Sierra's smile made his chest feel too tight. "A needy roommate, huh?"

"Nah, just a worried one." Cody laughed at her look of surprise. "But he's got nothing to be worried about. I'd much rather be spending the day with you than the guys I see twenty-four seven at the ranch."

She clasped a hand to her heart. "You say the sweetest things."

He smiled. "But…I should be heading back. I've got to stop at my parents' house on the way home and make sure my dad's doing all right. He's been having an issue with the medication he's on. Nothing serious," he added quickly. "And I promised my adorable little niece and nephew I'd stop by as well to play for a little while."

"Play, huh?" The laughter in her voice made him warm all over.

"Hey, I'm not just good for pool and poker, you know." He leaned toward her and lowered his voice. "I'm also something of a pro when it comes to Candyland."

"You are a man of many talents, Cody Swanson."

He shrugged with false modesty, and she burst out laughing, but she grew serious as they stood and took their mugs to the counter. "I'd better get back to the hotel," she mumbled as they headed to the door. "I've got some more research to do on estate laws, and apparently you have to go take care of everyone..." She paused just outside the door of the coffee shop, her head cocked to the side as she studied him. "You do that a lot, don't you?"

He blinked. "Do what?"

"Take care of people. Your parents, your brother's kids..." She shot him a rueful smile. "Me."

He ducked his head, not sure how to explain. Yeah, maybe his family did rely on him to help out, but when it came to her... "I didn't seek you out because I thought you needed someone to take care of you."

"No?" Her tone was joking, but he heard the real question there.

"No." He leaned in close and pressed a kiss to her cheek, loving the way her breath caught. Heaven knew his heart stuttered at the innocent gesture. "I sought you out because I like spending time with you. A lot."

"Well...good." She backed away from him, a smile tugging at her lips and her cheeks a sweet shade of pink. "Because you're gonna be spending lots of time with me at this festival tomorrow." She narrowed her eyes. "You promised to have my back, remember?"

"How could I forget?"

She flashed him one last smile that made him feel like a king...and then she slipped around the corner, heading back to the inn.

And he did what he'd said he'd do. First he swung by the bar and made sure Boone had a safe and sober ride home, and then he checked on his dad, and had some fun with his niece and nephew. Kit and Lizzy didn't mention Sierra's name, and neither did he.

He supposed none of them wanted the twins to see them bickering.

After that, he headed back to the ranch and found himself thinking about Sierra until sleep dragged him under.

The next day, he woke to thoughts of her, and he couldn't stop grinning, not even when Boone gave him a hard time over it when he finally stumbled out of JJ's bedroom looking worse for the wear.

The two of them went up to the main house to join the others for breakfast before church. With Daisy and Dahlia away, the house was quieter than usual, and Emma excused herself to finish getting ready for church, leaving Cody with Boone and Nash.

For a while, he listened to the cousins as they caught up on family small talk and ranch business, but then Boone dragged him into it when Nash asked about what they'd done with their day off. "The other ranch hands and I had fun. But apparently old man Cody over here doesn't believe in having a good time anymore."

Cody chuckled at the teasing, but Nash shot him a curious look. "I didn't see you around the ranch yesterday. What'd you get up to?"

Cody hesitated but then admitted to his friend that

he'd spent the afternoon with Sierra. He'd thought easy-going Nash, of all people, would be cool about it.

But he was wrong.

"Cody, what were you thinking?" Nash's brows drew together, and his gaze was filled with...disappointment. He was Kit's age and had always been like an older brother, but Cody wasn't a kid any longer—far from it. And he bristled at being treated like one.

"Who I spend time with is my business," he snapped.

"Yeah, but that woman is trouble," Nash argued. "She's trying to tear apart everything Emma's been fighting for, and—"

"You don't know that." Cody shot to his feet as Emma came in wearing her Sunday best. "In fact, none of you know anything about her because you haven't tried to get to know her."

Nash rose, too, ignoring Emma's pleading look and her murmured "Let's just drop it, honey."

"How much do you know about her, huh?" Nash pointed at him. "You may have spent time with her once or twice, but that's not enough for you to really know her."

"I know her well enough," he clipped, surprising himself with his heated tone. He ran a hand through his hair and looked away, struggling for calm.

But for some reason, Sierra's voice was in his head, pointing out that he was always looking after everyone else. He'd never minded...not really. But right now the injustice grated at him. Everyone counted on him to be a good friend and a dutiful son and a doting uncle and a reliable babysitter and ranch hand and the list went on and on.

They relied on him, but not one of them was acting like

maybe he might have a mind of his own. Or that maybe his instincts could be trusted.

No one seemed to consider the fact that maybe he wasn't the bad guy here...and neither was Sierra.

"Cody, you've got to see why this is a problem for us," Nash argued. "If you're spending time with Sierra, she could be using you or trying to learn—"

"You might not trust Sierra," Cody interrupted, turning back to a grim-faced Nash and a worried-looking Emma, "but y'all should trust me by now."

"We do." Emma bulged her eyes, obviously shocked that he would think for one second that they didn't trust him.

"Of course we do," Nash added gruffly.

Cody kept his gaze on Emma. "If you can't give Sierra the benefit of the doubt, try having a little faith in me."

Emma's lips parted like she might speak, but then she shut her mouth and Cody turned to leave, catching Boone grinning at him in approval before he went out to drive to church—alone.

CHAPTER 18

This was a mistake.

Sierra paced the confines of her hotel room, pausing at the window every so often to glance out at the view. If she craned her neck just a little, she could see the festival on Main Street in full swing.

Her belly tumbled with a somersault.

Why did she agree to go?

Her palms grew clammy as she pulled the drapes shut and resumed pacing. They'd all be there, Cody had said. All of her sisters.

Well, not Dahlia—thank goodness.

And not Daisy or April, presumably. But still…

There were plenty of O'Sullivan sisters still here in Aspire, and she'd actually agreed to meet them. Or at least be at the same place at the same time, so…yeah.

She'd have to meet them. Wouldn't she?

Nibbling on her fingernail, she glanced down at her phone, but Cody hadn't responded to her text saying she was having second thoughts. The only text that lit her screen was the last one she'd gotten from her mother, which was basically just a reminder that Frank and his family owed her, which...

Did they?

Maybe he had, but the more she learned about her sisters, the clearer it was that none of them had gotten much, if anything, from Frank.

She shook her head. She couldn't think about her mother and how they'd been abandoned. Not now. She had a decision to make.

Picking up the phone, she hit Call and waited as Cody's phone rang and rang. Where *was* he? She thought about leaving a message, but bailing on someone in a voice mail wasn't her style.

Bailing, in general, wasn't her style.

She caught her reflection in the mirror, and her chin came up. Since when did she take the coward's way out?

She grabbed her leather jacket off the back of the desk chair and headed toward the door.

She'd find Cody, and she'd check out this festival, and she sure as heck wouldn't hide in her room all day.

Of course, a little while later, when she found herself surrounded by strangers in a crowded, blocked-off street, Sierra began to second-guess this decision. Her phone was still silent—no texts or calls from Cody. And she was almost positive she wasn't imagining all the stares and whispers that followed in her wake as she made her way from one stall to the next.

A band was setting up on a stage at one end of Main Street while the far end seemed to be devoted to the local restaurants and bars that had set up a sort of outdoor food court. In between it all were tents and stalls filled with people raising money for local causes by selling trinkets and homemade goods. The volunteer fire department was out in force, trying to gather funds for their operations. She spotted a tall black man with a friendly grin, laughing with a couple kids. They were gazing up at him like he was Superman himself.

Turning away, she kept ambling through the crowd, spotting a few stalls that had games for the kids, then a space at the end that was running dance lessons for the teens and adults.

It was all quite...charming, she supposed.

Or it would be if she didn't feel like a stranger in a strange land.

She looked up from the handmade leather wallets she'd been eyeing to see an older couple watching her. They gave her strained, polite smiles before walking away. "...the O'Sullivan girl," she heard the woman say.

It was like that everywhere she went.

Clearly she was a hot topic in town, and it didn't take a genius to see she wasn't universally beloved.

Which was fine. Just great.

She stuck her hands in her pockets as the sun slid behind some clouds and the warm day turned chilly in a heartbeat.

She shivered...and that was when she spotted them. She blinked a few times when she saw the three blonde women heading her way, one with a baby in her arms and the other two each holding the hand of a kindergarten-aged child.

She recognized them even before she caught sight of Cody beside the smallest blonde with the baby. Three other men followed closely, but it was the women who held her attention. These were...

Oh heck.

She swallowed hard because the whole cluster of O'Sullivans seemed to see her at once.

They stopped walking, and the crowd jostled around them. For one crazy moment, Sierra was sure she heard the opening whistle to *The Good, The Bad, and The Ugly* play as she squared off in the middle of the street while a kids' choir started to sing on the stage behind her.

For a moment, it all felt surreal, like *High Noon* meets *Sound of Music* as she stood there frozen, her expression just as grim as theirs.

Slowly but surely, they started walking again, but Sierra's heart sank as she took in the whispers and the glares as her gaze roamed over the pretty blonde women and the protective men who seemed to huddle around them like she was actually going to start a rumble.

"Sierra." Cody caught her attention, and she turned her gaze to see him giving her that slow, sexy, lopsided smile of his. The one that said he was at ease even if everyone else in this whole dang town seemed to be watching her and Frank's other daughters with unabashed interest.

He picked up his pace, leaving the cluster of wary, glaring blondes in his wake until he reached. "You came."

"Yeah, I..." She forced herself to meet his gaze. To ignore the hostile looks she was getting from...from...

No, they were not her sisters.

Well, they were. But in name only. That didn't mean anything.

She wet her lips, her heartbeat uneven. "I, uh...I tried to call you. I had second thoughts, and..." She shook her head. Dang it. She would not get emotional. "Maybe I was right. I shouldn't have come here."

She started to turn, but he caught her arm. "Sierra, wait."

He was frowning down at her, his gaze so focused it made her feel rooted in place. Grounded and safe even though an emotional maelstrom was circling all around them.

"I'm sorry," he said. "I was at church, so my phone was on silent. And then we headed right here, and I figured I'd see you, and—"

"And I should go." She tugged her arm free.

She was keenly aware of the cluster of sisters who'd come to a stop behind him, a few feet away. These were his friends.

This was his family.

And they were all glaring at her like she was the Wicked Witch.

She took another step back and forced a smile. "This was a mistake." She finally uttered the words she'd been thinking all day.

"Sierra, don't run away." His voice was low and serious.

Her smile faltered. "I can't do this. They don't want to meet me—"

"They don't know you."

"Clearly they know enough," she snapped, then took a breath and continued through a frozen smile, "Everyone's glaring at me, Cody. I've gotta go."

He reached for her hand and tugged her closer. "I'm not glaring."

"Yeah, well, hang around me long enough and you'll get a bad reputation, too, so just—"

Her words were cut off with a gasp when he tugged her closer still, his arm wrapping around her waist as he leaned down and kissed her.

No, kiss wasn't a good enough word for what he did.

His lips crushed hers, yes, but he also worked some sort of magic that made her forget where she was and who was watching. For a moment, she was too stunned to respond, but the bruising force of his lips, the heat of his body pressed against hers, sent a tremor of desire right through her.

Her heart lurched into overdrive as her lips parted on another gasp, and he deepened the kiss with a groan that she felt in her bones, melting her tension and making her heart feel too big for her rib cage. Her hands fluttered before landing on his chest, her fingers curling into his soft, faded T-shirt as his arm around her waist held her tight, taking on her weight as she sank into him.

When he finally came up for air, she was grateful for his support because her legs were definitely not working. Neither was her brain, because all she could manage was "Whoa."

Which made him grin. And goodness gracious, that smile might just be the death of her. It had her heart ricocheting like a pinball in her chest.

He lifted one hand and brushed back a lock of her hair. "*Whoa* is right."

She let out a huff of laughter, and it was only then that she remembered who was standing right behind him.

Who'd just witnessed Cody's kiss.

Her heart shot up into her throat, and her eyes stung with a sudden wave of tears. Warmth flooded through her as she realized what exactly he'd just done.

It had been a kiss—an epic kiss—but also so much more.

That public embrace had been a statement. A declaration.

He'd shocked her silly when he'd told her he had her back the other day. But right now…

Right now he'd proven it.

And Sierra wasn't sure she could remember anyone ever doing anything like that for her.

Her exhale was shaky as she said it again. "Whoa."

CHAPTER 19

If looks could kill…

Cody shifted, trying to block Sierra from view. But it was impossible because they were surrounded by gaping bystanders. So he focused on shielding her from Kit and Lizzy, who he had no doubt were responsible for the burning glares he could feel on the back of his neck right now.

Sierra pulled back a little to glance around him, and her wince confirmed it. "I think you just royally irritated your brother." Her eyes held an impish twinkle when they met his. "At least I'm assuming that handsome cowboy is your brother."

"You think he's handsome, huh?"

Her lips twitched. "Don't worry. He's not as handsome as you, Cowboy."

He let out a huff of amusement. Only this woman could make him laugh when his brother and all of his friends were no doubt planning a myriad of ways to ream him out.

But not right now.

He kept one hand at her waist as he nodded toward the stage, which was in the opposite direction of Kit, Lizzy, and the others. "What do you say we go support the kids' choir until some of the stares stop?"

She let him guide her in that direction, but her murmur was filled with amusement. "You really think everyone's going to forget that their favorite hometown charmer just kissed the Wicked Witch of the West?"

"Wicked Witch, huh?" he teased. "I gotta say, I can't really picture you riding a broom. The bike is way more fitting."

"Because I'm such a badass?" she shot back.

"Because it's faster," he said. "Something tells me you don't waste time when you're ready to get moving."

She didn't have a comeback for that, and Cody shook his head, irritated with himself for bringing up the fact that she didn't stay in one place for long. He'd said it for his own sake. To remind himself that no matter how epic that kiss might have been, this thing between them was only temporary.

But that doesn't mean it's not real.

The thought was heartening, and when they came to a stop in the middle of a crowd of parents—all of whom turned to stare at them—he wrapped his arms around her waist from behind and settled his chin on her shoulder.

The kids were singing a rousing—if off-key—rendition of "God Bless America."

"They're awful," he whispered.

Her giggle made him grin.

"*You're* awful," she shot back. "They're cute."

He ducked his head, pressing a kiss to her neck and loving the way she shivered in his arms. After another minute of listening to terrible singing, she broke the silence between them. "Shouldn't we be…I don't know, making nice?"

He chuckled.

"Wasn't that the point of all this?"

It was. It had been. But now…

"Maybe holding your first meet and greet in the middle of a gawking crowd of townsfolk was not my finest idea," he admitted.

"You think?"

Her tone was so dry he started to laugh. Which was saying something considering some part of him was simmering with anger at his friends' reaction to seeing her. "Maybe we should start by showing you that this town can actually be a pretty great place to spend time." He slid his hand into hers as the choir took a break, leading her toward a row of tents filled with games.

"If you win me a teddy bear, I might just believe you." She winked at him.

He eyed the ring toss game they were standing in front of. "Something tells me you'll be the one winning the teddy bear for me by the end of this."

"Who, me?" She feigned innocence.

"Once a hustler, always a hustler," he shot back.

She laughed as she jokingly pushed him toward the rings. "Come on, Cowboy. It's all going to charity, right?"

He caught sight of Emma and Nash watching him from the funnel cake stand across the way, but he pointedly ignored them. Emma leaned forward to murmur something to Ellie, the town librarian, who shook her head and winced before shooting a curious glance Sierra's way. He shifted his body to block her view.

He knew he'd angered his friends and family with that kiss, but truth be told…they'd angered him too. So he turned his focus to Sierra, and together they pointedly ignored all the stares and whispers, pretending they were in their own little world for the next hour as they challenged each other to games and stood in a long line for too-sweet lemonade.

When the sun started to sink toward the mountains, Sierra let out a sigh. "Look, I appreciate everything you've been doing today, Cody. But honestly, I'm kinda exhausted by…this."

She waved a hand vaguely, but she didn't have to explain. He felt it too. The weight of the stares and the judgmental glares they couldn't seem to escape.

"I'll walk you back to the hotel," he said.

Her smile held a hint of relief. "I'd like that."

The farther they drew from the crowd, the more he felt the tension ease out of her. He wished he could let it go so easily.

"I'm sorry if you're gonna be in trouble with your brother and his wife because of me," she said suddenly.

He stopped short to turn and face her. "I'm not." Her brows hitched up, and he reached out, cupping her chin so she couldn't look away. "I'm not sorry I kissed you, Sierra. And I'm not sorry that they don't approve. I'm just sorry…"

That you're going to leave.

I'm sorry this can't be more than a fling.

He took a deep breath, focusing on those brilliant green eyes and the way her lips quivered even as she tried so hard to pretend she didn't care. "I'm just sorry they're acting like fools."

Her lips twitched up. "I didn't give anyone a reason to like me."

"Maybe not," he agreed, letting go of her chin to stroke

her hair back from her face. "But if anyone should under-stand how hard it is to come here and deal with the past, it's them."

She gave a little nod, her eyes sparkling with emotion.

"And I think..." He winced. "I don't want to be making apologies for anyone, because honestly, I'm disap-pointed in my friends, my brother...heck, I'm disap-pointed in the whole town. But I can see what's happening here, and I know..." He swallowed hard, searching for the words. "I know they're just scared. Your sisters, I mean. You coming here and making threats, it put them on the defensive, you know?"

She bit her lip, and then she nodded.

"They feel like their home and their families are being threatened, so, while I don't like the way they're acting, I'm still standing here asking you to give them a chance."

Her eyes widened slightly.

"I know you probably want to run—"

"I don't run, Cody."

Now it was his time to arch his brows in surprise at the forcefulness of her tone.

She softened it with a smile. "I move around a lot, and I love to travel. But I don't run away. Not from a fight and not from...well, not from something good either."

His lungs hitched like she'd just reached inside and clenched them with her fist. Did that mean...?

Could they possibly have a future?

Hope hung in the air, but he couldn't tell if this was an oasis or a mirage. He took a deep breath and looked away.

It didn't matter right now anyway. What mattered now was Sierra and helping her to make peace with her family. "Give them another chance," he whispered.

She blinked, her head tilted to the side. "You make it sound like that's what they want…"

"It's what I want." He reached out and gripped her waist, tugging her close. "And I think maybe you want it too."

Her eyes searched his, and he saw it—a world of hurt and fear and vulnerability that she kept so well hidden behind that shocking red hair and the leather jacket.

The fact that he got to see this side of her felt like an honor. A right reserved for precious few.

"Okay." She nodded at last, her voice a hoarse whisper.

He leaned down until his forehead rested against hers. "Okay."

She was smiling when he kissed her, and she tasted like too-sweet lemonade and something even sweeter. So sweet it made his heart ache.

When he pulled back, his chest gave a sharp tug when he saw her blushing smile, another hint of the vulnerable woman beneath the tough facade.

"This Friday." He started forming a plan.

She arched a brow. "What about it?"

"Emma's husband, Nash…" He waited until she nodded. "His family has a barbecue coming up. Everyone will be there—"

He stopped with a laugh when she wrinkled her nose.

"Not the whole town," he explained. "But your sisters will be there, plus Nash's family who will, hopefully, be far more open-minded and welcoming. You know what? They will be. I just know it."

He was thinking of Boone, at first, but really Boone got his friendly open nature from his family. Nash might've been acting like an overprotective bear lately, but Cody knew in his gut that Mr. and Mrs. Donahue would

146

welcome Sierra with open arms, as would Casey, their daughter.

"This time I'll make sure everyone knows you're coming," he added. He tugged her close, relishing the sound of her sharp inhale when their bodies collided. "As my date."

Her lips twitched a little before she twisted them to the side in a cute, impish grin. "As your date, huh? You sure you want to do this?"

He kissed her again, slower this time and with everything that was in his heart. "I've never been more sure of anything."

CHAPTER 20

Sierra tried not to laugh as she watched Cody stare at her motorcycle, his arms crossed and a determined glint in his eyes.

"I want to ride it," he said.

"You ever been on one before?"

"Nope."

She eyed his truck, which was parked next to her bike. "What about your truck?"

"We'll come back for it after the barbecue." He shot her a sidelong glance. "It'll give us a chance to bail early if you're not enjoying yourself."

Her stomach roiled with nerves, but she forced a smile because she knew Cody was worried about her.

Right up until five minutes ago, when they'd walked out of her hotel room to drive out to the Donahues', she would have said he had no reason to be worried about her. She'd had a quiet, relaxing week, for the most part. She'd found a lawyer and handed the will over to him, and with that off her plate, she'd spent her days exploring the area. Driving and hiking in the surrounding mountains, and taking day trips to a ghost town and another tourist town Cody had told her about.

He'd been busy with work, but he'd come into town midway through the week for another night of poker and laughs in her hotel room.

And kisses.

Her cheeks warmed just thinking about the way he'd kissed her that night before he'd left. With each new touch and every conversation, she could feel herself growing more and more attached to this man.

And she was almost certain he felt it too. Which was... a little scary, because no matter how today went with her sisters, this town and this cowboy were not a part of her plans.

But more importantly, this town and her sisters were definitely a part of Cody's future, and right now she wasn't sure if she was more nervous about getting to know her sisters or failing to make a good impression and letting him down.

She didn't want to see him at odds with his family. And even though he didn't talk about it much, she knew he was. It was in the tightness around his mouth when he mentioned Kit and the irritation in his voice when he talked about the others at the ranch.

She'd come between him and his family...and that was not okay by her.

"What are you thinking, Hustler?" His voice was gruff as he turned to face her head-on.

She straightened. "I'm thinking...we need to find you a helmet."

He smiled, and after a quick trip to town to get Cody a shiny new helmet, he straddled the bike behind her.

"You ready for this?" she called over the engine's roar.

She wasn't even sure if she was talking about the drive or the encounter to come, but he wrapped his arms around her, his voice low in her ear. "Lead the way, Mona Lisa."

Grinning at the reminder of that first night when he'd just been that handsome cowboy and she'd been some mystery woman, she set out on the road, laughing as he whooped and cheered with every bend and dip in the road.

"I take it you liked the ride," she said when she pulled off her helmet.

"That was fantastic," he breathed.

Her heart hitched when he removed his helmet. With his mussed hair and stubble, it was like he'd been born to ride. He looked way too natural on the back of her bike, and she turned away with a sharp inhale. "Shall we?"

He strode up beside her, his arm brushing hers—a subtle reminder that he was there. At her side.

He had her back.

The thought had her chin coming up, so by the time they rounded the corner of the house and into the Donahues' sprawling backyard, she at least looked confident.

Inside? Not so much.

She murmured to Cody. "I know there's no record player out here, but if there were…"

"Yeah, that record would be scratched all right," he returned with a chuckle.

His laid-back tone helped put her at ease along with his laugh. It also helped that Nash's parents were just as welcoming as Cody said they'd be. His mother pulled her into a hug that nearly toppled her over.

Then Cody's parents came over, and…

"You didn't tell me I'd be meeting the parents," she gritted out through a smile.

"You didn't think you could kiss their son in the middle of a town festival and get out of Dodge without meeting the folks, now did you?" he teased.

But unlike Kit, who watched them from the far side of the yard where Lizzy and the twins were playing, Cody's parents were warm and friendly as they all took turns getting food and drinks at a long picnic table.

Sierra hesitated with a plate full of food in her hands. "Should we...?" She nodded toward a table where Emma and Nash were sitting beside Dex and Rose, their little baby snuggled up in Emma's arms as they all laughed and talked.

"You want to?" Cody asked.

She hesitated a second time, and he gave her a gentle nudge. "Hey, we've got all day, right?"

She nodded, relieved when he led the way toward a picnic table on the far side of the lawn, away from the others.

"For the record..." She paused to take a bite of her hamburger. "That was not me being a coward."

"Of course not!" he said quickly, sounding offended on her behalf.

She grinned. "That was me being strategic."

He scoffed. "Of course. I never doubted you."

She leaned forward to retort but was cut off by two whirling dervishes who launched themselves into Cody's lap. Her heart may have melted a little as she watched him with his niece and nephew.

He was a natural, and they so clearly adored him. "Chloe, Corbin, meet my date, Sierra."

"You're our new aunt!" Corbin shouted.

Sierra started to laugh. "I am. I guess that makes you my new nephew."

"And I'm your new niece." Chloe's chest puffed with pride.

"Want to know a secret?" Sierra whispered, leaning forward as the two little ones gathered close. "You're my *only* nephew and niece."

They looked pleased as punch by this news, and Cody grinned at her. Could he see how much this was a revelation for her as well?

She'd stewed over the fact that she had half sisters but never once thought of what it meant that she was an aunt.

Her. An aunt.

"Don't forget Kiara," Chloe pointed out. "You have two nieces now."

"That I do. But I'm still new to this aunt thing, so maybe you can give me some pointers."

This set the twins laughing as they told her their favorite games, but soon they were running off to play with the other kids.

"You're good with them." Cody watched them run off with an adoring smile.

She shrugged. "I like kids. Always have."

"Yeah, but…" He shook his head. "I don't know. People can like kids and not necessarily be comfortable around them."

She smiled, thinking of all the many days, months, and years she'd spent working in pediatric clinics the world over. She'd made it her mission to get a smile out of every one of them. Their hugs and laughter filled her heart to overflowing. A sudden pining for the orphanage in Venezuela shot through her, but it was interrupted by a panicked shout from Corbin.

"Uncle Cody, Uncle Cody!" He ran up to them with tears in his eyes. "Chloe's hurt! She was eating and we were running, and then she just stopped and started doing this weird thing with her body. Now her lips are blue and—"

Cody cut the child off, shooting out of his chair and gripping the boy's shoulders. "It's all right, buddy. Go get Dr. Dex and your dad. Quick as you can."

Corbin ran off...and so did Sierra. She started moving as soon as she heard the combination of food and running. Like shutters coming down, her mind zeroed in on the problem. She'd experienced enough medical emergencies to find that place of quiet efficiency inside her. She was by Chloe's side in a heartbeat, speaking soothingly to the panicked little girl who stood there clutching her throat with wide, horrified eyes.

"Chloe, honey. It's gonna be okay. You have something stuck in your throat, and it's blocking your airway. That's why you can't breathe. I'm going to get it out for you. Just trust me, okay?"

With calm, sure movements, she positioned the struggling girl, ignoring the other kids and even Cody, who hovered beside her looking just as scared as Chloe.

"What can I do?" he asked.

But she didn't have time to talk to him as she kept up a steady stream of reassuring explanations to Chloe, all while she wrapped her arms around her from behind, clasped her hand into a fist, and positioned it carefully. Then she gave a hard pull, and then another, until a piece of hot dog came shooting out of Chloe's mouth. The little girl gasped, then wailed as she fell into Cody's waiting arms.

"Deep breaths, honey." Sierra rubbed Chloe's back as she sobbed against her uncle.

Pulling her away, Cody gently held her shoulders and repeated what Sierra said, coaching her through some deep breaths until moments later, Lizzy was hurtling toward them.

"Mom!" Chloe started sobbing all over again, raising her arms to be lifted into a fierce hug by her stepmother. She clung like a spider monkey, wrapping her legs and arms around a terrified-looking Lizzy.

"Thank you, God. Thank you." Lizzy closed her eyes, cupping the back of Chloe's head and murmuring repeated prayers.

Kit bounded up behind them, wrapping his arms around them both, looking sick, worried, and relieved. His arms trembled a little when Corbin muscled in on the hug too. He lifted his son onto his hip and bent his head to rest against Lizzy's cheek.

Sierra watched the foursome huddle, her throat swelling with emotion.

"You were amazing." Cody whispered in her ear.

She blinked, relief coursing through her as her mind decided to play mean and run through all the scenarios that could have been. She sucked in a deep breath of her own, trying to calm the chaos inside.

"That really was quick thinking." Rose's husband, Dex, was watching her. She hadn't even seen him appear.

She gave him a polite smile and nodded. "Just doing what I was trained to do."

He cocked his head to the side. "Nurse or doctor?"

"Nurse."

His smile was warm and genuine as he extended his

hand. "I'm Dr. Dex. Nice work, Sierra. Which hospital are you with?"

She squeezed his fingers with a brief shake, then crossed her arms, aware of all the eyes on her as she answered his question. "I've been working with a humanitarian organization in Venezuela. I've been stationed at an orphanage near Bolivar these past two years, but we travel where needed."

He looked impressed by her answer, and so did Rose, who sidled up to him with a genuine smile, cradling their daughter.

Sierra returned it, then started to excuse herself as the rest of Chloe's family gathered around. But no one would let her out of this little love bubble. Emma and Nash had reached them, Emma's face pale with worry as she ran her hand down Chloe's back and checked in with her niece. Nash mumbled something to Kit, obviously asking what had happened, and then his usually reserved, steely gaze landed on her, instantly softening and lighting with gratitude.

Cody wrapped an arm around her waist and kept her put. Escaping this moment was impossible, so she leaned into his side as a teary-eyed Lizzy and a stone-faced Kit stepped up to her.

"Thank you." Lizzy's voice shook as she stroked Chloe's hair and snuggled her a little closer.

"You saved our little girl," Kit croaked, his voice so gruff and low it nearly made Sierra cry.

"Yeah, well, it was all—" *Part of the job.*

She never got the chance to finish because Kit reached out and pulled her in for a bone-crushing hug.

CHAPTER 21

K it leaned against the fence where Cody was making repairs. "So, wait...does Mom know you rode a motorcycle?"

Cody rolled his eyes. "I'm not a child, Kit. I don't need Mom's permission."

Kit arched a brow and handed over a hammer.

Cody sighed. "And no. Mom doesn't know."

His older brother's head fell back as he laughed.

"Have you tried driving it?" Boone called out from where he sat astride his horse.

"Please tell me you'll take a class or something before you do," Nash chimed in.

All four of them were winding down for the day, and somehow they'd all descended on Cody. Maybe they were making up for the fact that they'd been steering clear of him all last week.

Well, not Boone. That guy didn't seem to care much about ranch business or the O'Sullivan sisters. He just steered clear of anything serious.

But ever since the barbecue this past weekend, the

tension had waned. It wasn't gone completely, but Sierra's name no longer caused instant anger at the ranch. Just…caution.

Which was an improvement.

By the time the barbecue had come to an end, Sierra had held a civil conversation with Lizzy and Kit, Emma and Nash, and Rose and Dex. She'd had a smile on her face the whole time, though no one brought up the topic of the will or any potential legal battles.

When they'd left, Sierra had kept that smile in place until they'd rounded the corner of the house. Then with a sigh, she'd slumped against him, letting him take some of her weight as he'd wrapped an arm around her waist and led her to the motorcycle.

Cody was fairly certain he lost his heart right then and there. Something inside him came undone the way she'd trusted him in that moment.

"So, are you seeing her again tonight?" Kit asked.

Cody looked down as he wiped his dirty hands on his jeans. "I don't know yet. We haven't made any plans."

But they had been talking and texting. It'd only been a day and a half since the barbecue, but he already missed her. Texting and talking on the phone weren't enough.

And if he felt that way now, when she was a twenty-minute drive away in Aspire, how would he feel when she took off to another continent?

Nash's loud exhale had him looking up. His friend was wearing a grim expression that made Cody tense. "Look, I think we all feel sorry for not giving Sierra a proper chance."

Kit nodded, looking down at his feet. "If she hadn't been at the barbecue…"

Cody clapped a hand on his brother's shoulder. "But she was. Chloe's okay."

Kit nodded again, but the event the other day had clearly left him rattled.

Nash leaned against the fence as well, and even Boone slid down from his mount to join them.

"I just wish we knew what she was thinking," Nash murmured, kicking the heel of his boot into the dirt.

Cody kept his mouth shut.

"Has she told you what she's planning?" Kit asked. "What'd her lawyer say?"

Cody shrugged, then shook his head. "We've steered clear of that conversation."

"At some point we're not going to be able to ignore the issue." Nash took the hammer from him, returning it to the toolbox before crouching down to inspect Cody's handiwork.

Cody didn't argue. Nash had a point. Taking his time to pick his words, he licked his lips and said, "Look, guys, I think y'all have been ignoring this conversation for a while now." He glanced over at Nash and Kit. "I mean, before Sierra even entered the picture..."

Neither of them tried to protest.

"You're probably right," Kit mumbled. "With April ignoring us and Sierra so hard to track down, I guess we sorta just..."

"Got comfortable," Nash finished. "We made a home."

"All the girls did," Cody pointed. "And that's nice. It's great. But everyone knew a decision had to be made eventually. The will clearly states that the decision must be unanimous. All seven daughters have to agree to keep this place."

Kit gave a reluctant nod while Nash grimaced and continued kicking the dirt.

They all got lost in their thoughts for a while until Boone broke it. "Where'd April get off to, anyway? That girl loved it here. I can't believe she wouldn't want to have a say."

Kit, Cody, and Nash looked at him in surprise.

"Were you friends with April?" Kit asked.

Boone shrugged. "I wouldn't say we were friends, but we were in the same class. I've known her forever."

"She should definitely have a say," Nash said.

Boone kicked at a loose stone and watched it scuttle across the dirt. "She must be going through a tough time with her mom and dad passing like that. And now she's ignoring y'all..."

Kit sighed. "We'll have to make sure April comes home so this can be resolved once and for all."

Nash nodded, turning his gaze to Cody. "And if Sierra is serious about wanting the property..." He sighed, taking off his hat and running the rim through his fingers. "Maybe we could work out a deal to buy it from her, or..."

His expression was tense, and his tone faded like he didn't know how to finish.

"Even if we all pitched in, this ranch is worth more than we could afford," Kit stated the obvious.

Cody shifted, uneasy. He couldn't speak on Sierra's behalf, but he didn't think it would come to that. But then again, if she didn't want to stick around—and she'd made it clear she didn't—then maybe she wouldn't see the point in holding onto the land.

"Maybe your dad could buy the property," Boone offered. "Uncle Patrick has the money."

Nash winced. "Much as it pains me to say it, I don't

want my dad near this thing. Not after the way he behaved when Emma first arrived on the scene. She told him straight that this would never become Donohue land, and I'll back her all the way."

Boone grimaced but nodded. "Yeah, I get it."

They all got quiet again. Cody pushed away from the fence. "Standing around here brooding isn't gonna solve matters," he said. "We need to get April home. And Dahlia and Daisy need to be in on this conversation too."

Nash gave them a lopsided grin. "Dahlia would have our heads if we made any decisions without her."

They all laughed, and the tension eased again.

"At least Sierra's part of the conversation now." Kit shrugged. His gaze met Cody's, and there was more than a hint of regret there. "That's a start. And it's all thanks to you."

Cody brushed his hand through the air, heading to his horse. "Emma, Lizzy, and the others would have come around eventually. They've all been burned by Frank O'Sullivan, but they all know family comes first."

The others nodded, heading back to work. But Cody's own words haunted him as he rode the range.

Family comes first.

It was true the other O'Sullivan sisters felt that way. But Sierra never had siblings. And from what he'd heard of her relationship with her mother, it was far from healthy.

What she cared about most was a continent away. Far from Aspire, far from her sisters…

Far from him.

CHAPTER 22

M ama's Kitchen was bustling with a lunch crowd, and for the first time since she'd arrived in this town, Sierra didn't feel like a spectacle as she sat in her booth and waited for her order.

"Hey, there she is. Hi, Sierra!" Cody's friend Bella waved to her from where she stood in line waiting for a table. It looked like she was with friends, and while they all turned to one another to whisper, there didn't seem to be any malice there, just interest.

Sierra was starting to wonder how much of the whispers and glances these past few weeks were really critical and how much was just curiosity. It was hard to tell if the attention was less negative since the barbecue the other day…or if she was just less paranoid.

The thought had her laughing softly to herself, and she automatically picked up her phone to share the thought with Cody before stopping herself.

The guy's working. Leave him alone.

It wasn't his job to keep her entertained night and day. But even so…she missed him.

She toyed with her fork, smiling when a young waitress brought over her lunch.

She stabbed a fork into her chef salad a little too hard. Dang it. Why did she miss him?

It'd been a day. One full day.

And a morning.

But still. She went months away from her friends and family without so much as a prick of homesickness, yet one day away from Cody and she was pining like a lovesick tween?

This was not okay.

She watched the crowd being seated and the servers and busboys scurrying around as she ate her meal.

Maybe it was because she didn't know many people in this town. Maybe she thought about him constantly because he was a nice distraction from her family issues, and…

She let her fork fall from her hand with a clink as she sighed. Who was she kidding?

She wasn't just thinking about his kisses because she was lonely in a new town. And she wasn't tempted to text him morning, noon, and night just because he was easy on the eyes.

She liked him, plain and simple.

Maybe too much.

And that could only be a bad thing. A bad, wonderful thing that she didn't know how to handle.

Sierra was actually relieved to see one of her sisters walk through the door of Mama's Kitchen. Emma didn't see her at first as she eyed the line at the hostess stand, but when she caught sight of Sierra, her face lit up with a smile that made Sierra automatically respond in kind.

Without thinking it through, she waved her over. "Do you, uh...do you want to join me?"

Emma's brows arched in surprise.

Sierra hurried on, feeling like an awkward kid asking a boy out on a date for the first time. "I mean, if you're here alone, it doesn't make sense for you to wait for a table when I've got this whole booth and—"

"Yes," Emma said with a wide grin. "I'd love to join you. Thanks."

"No problem."

Emma slid into the booth, and for a moment, there was a silence so awkward that they both burst out laughing.

"So..." Sierra drew the word out.

"So," Emma echoed, still laughing as she clasped her hands together on the table.

"What are you doing in town?" Sierra asked.

Like at the barbecue, she couldn't bring herself to talk about the will and the inheritance. Besides, what was the point? Her lawyer was still reviewing her right to a claim, and April was still MIA.

Emma chatted easily about the errands she'd been running, pausing only to order when the waitress stopped by. "I figured I'd swing by the boutique Lizzy works at this afternoon to say hi. Have you been?"

Sierra shook her head and glanced down at her faded T-shirt and ripped jeans. "I'm not sure boutiques are really my thing."

Emma's laugh was so genuine and kind, Sierra was a little taken aback. "Trust me, I get it. My mom and I always question where Lizzy got her keen fashion sense." Emma looked down at her nice but admittedly uninspired white T-shirt and shorts. "It's definitely not genetic."

"Not on the father's side, at least," Sierra said.

For a second, she tensed, wondering if she'd just opened a can of worms by bringing up their father, but Emma just laughed again and shook her head. "Definitely not."

They fell into an easy conversation about Emma's teaching job at the school and how she'd met Nash. But when Emma's food arrived, she fell silent, her nose wrinkling slightly as she clutched the table and sucked in a breath through her nose.

Sierra studied her carefully, and her nurse instincts went on high alert. "Emma? Are you feeling all right?"

"Yes. Er...no. Not really. But it's nothing. It'll pass." Under her breath, she muttered, "It always does."

Sierra tilted her head to the side, studying Emma with a keen eye. She wasn't wearing makeup, and Sierra could see a hint of dark circles beneath her eyes, and her skin was turning a sickly pallor as she eyed her sandwich.

"I came in here starving, but now I..." She clamped her lips together and shook her head.

Sierra leaned forward, elbows on the table. "Emma, what's going on?"

Emma smiled, but it looked strained. "Nothing. I don't think. Just..." She sighed and rubbed a hand over her eyes. "I've been so tired lately. And this past week I'm just..." She looked at the plate with a grimace. "My stomach's been off."

"Have you been throwing up?"

"Only once. It's mostly just nausea, but I don't know what I ate to give me this bug or why it's lasting so long. I suppose I should go to the doctor about it, but I don't want anyone to worry. The nausea comes and goes. Yesterday, I thought I had recovered, but now..." She sighed and rubbed her forehead.

"No fever or headaches? Stomach cramps?"

"Nope." Emma shook her head. "Just tiredness and nausea."

Sierra pressed her lips together, the nurse in her at war with the fact that this was her sister.

Her sister who she'd only just met and barely knew.

But she couldn't not say anything.

Her eyes crinkled at the corners as she leaned a little closer and gently asked, "Do you think it's got to do with your cycle? I know I can feel a little nauseated when I get my period. When are you due for your next one?"

Emma made a face, her cheeks flushing. "I just had it, but it was super light and different to my usual ones. I..." She started playing with her bottom lip, her eyes darting across the table like she didn't want to accept the suspicion she might be feeling. The suspicion that Sierra was growing more and more confident about.

Clearing her throat, Sierra shuffled in her seat and rested her hand on the table, near Emma's plate. "Is it possible...I mean, is there any chance that you and Nash might be...?" She paused when Emma locked eyes with her, silently begging her not to say it...or maybe *to* say it. Sierra couldn't work out what Emma was feeling. There seemed to be a shock of panic coursing over her expression, but it was flicking between that and what seemed to be...elation?

Sierra's forehead wrinkled. "Emma, your symptoms indicate that you could be preg—"

"No." Emma shook her head, her blue eyes wide and glassy as she blinked and then let out a soft gasp. "Not possible."

"Okay."

Emma's brows drew down, and she bit her lip, darting

a glance over her shoulder before leaning forward and whispering, "We use protection."

"Protection isn't 100 percent guaranteed, though. I mean, you can still get—" Sierra's words cut off as someone bustled past the table. They both went stiff as the conversation they were having and the place they were having it in suddenly hit home.

If anyone around them heard one sniff of the word *pregnant*, poor Nash would end up finding out the news before Emma could even take a pregnancy test.

Emma's lips parted, her eyes wild with panic again. "Oh my gosh. It can't be. We have a plan. I've mapped it out perfectly. It's not supposed to happen until..." She shook her head. "It's too soon."

Sierra tried not to smile. She really did. But Emma looked so surprised, and there was that elation again. That hope.

It was really kinda sweet.

Leaning forward again, she rested her hand on Emma's arm this time and asked, "Do you want to find out for sure?"

Emma nodded, clamping her lips shut as her eyes welled with tears. She swallowed hard and then said, "I do."

Rushing out of the booth, they paid at the counter and headed out into the sunny afternoon. Sierra was pumped, ready to march down the street and enter the pharmacy, but Emma caught her arm, yanking her to a stop. "I can't do this."

Sierra's heart sank. "Look, I know it can be scary, but—"

"No, no, not that," Emma said quickly. "If I am...if this is happening...I'll be ecstatic. In shock, maybe, but definitely ecstatic." She grinned, but the expression quickly faded. "It's just..." She bit her lip as she glanced at the pharmacy across the street. "If I go in there and buy a pregnancy test, half the town will know before I make it back to the ranch."

Sierra winced, surprised she hadn't thought of that herself when she'd been so aware of it in the diner. "Yikes."

"Yeah."

"I can go in," Sierra started. She stopped when Emma gave her a look that said "Well, aren't you cute?"

"You think that'll be any less scandalous?"

Sierra shrugged. "I don't care what people say about me."

"Yes, but it wouldn't just be about you." Emma started walking, dragging Sierra along beside her. "Poor Cody would be answering questions left and right about when he's gonna pop the question."

Sierra stumbled in her steps. Emma was kidding. Obviously. But all at once her mind's eye filled with a picture so bizarre it took her breath away. It was an image of Cody on bended knee. Of Cody at her side in front of a church filled with loved ones.

An image of Cody being a natural with kids—*their* kids.

Emma glanced over her shoulder, one hand on the door handle of her car. "I'm thinking my best bet is to head to Wellsprings. You coming?"

Sierra blinked and stuttered to a stop. "Are you sure you want me along?"

Emma laughed. "I definitely don't want to do this on my own."

The whole drive to Wellspring, Emma babbled. She

was clearly nervous as she told Sierra about her five-year plan and how they hadn't meant to start a family until after she'd had a few years of teaching at Aspire Elementary under her belt. They'd done some budgeting and decided to save a little money so Emma could be a stay-at-home mom for the first few years of their baby's life. And then they'd maybe have another one or two kids and she could just do a little part-time teaching or tutoring when the children were in preschool. It was quite the elaborate plan, even going so far as to work out the optimal season to have a baby, which, according to Emma, was early spring so she could be at her biggest during the winter months. Then, when her baby was at its smallest and most vulnerable, the weather would be cold enough to still swaddle comfortably but not the frigid, icy cold of winter, and by the time the baby was crawling around, it'd be the height of summer and the perfect temperature to enjoy the outdoors.

Sierra's eyes bulged as she listened, looking out the window to hide her chuckle.

The whole time Emma rabbited on about this plan, it was obvious how over the moon she was at the idea of an unexpected baby.

When they got to Wellsprings, Sierra insisted on being the one to buy the test, and then they both went into the bathroom of the local diner. Seconds ticked by slowly as Sierra and Emma waited and watched until...

Emma gasped. "Is that...is that a plus sign?"

Sierra grinned. "Sure is."

Emma's jaw dropped, but then a second later, she was squealing as she leapt onto Sierra, grabbing her in a bear hug that turned into a weird dance as they both hopped up and down with excitement.

"Oh my goodness, I can't believe this is happening." She pulled back, her smile watery as she met Sierra's gaze. "Thank you."

"I had nothing to do with it." Sierra laughed.

Emma rolled her eyes, still grinning. "Yeah, but I'm so glad I had a sister to share this moment with. Thank you for that."

Sierra's heart swelled. "It was my pleasure."

And that, Sierra decided, was the understatement of the decade. She wasn't sure she could express just how honored she was to be a part of this moment. To be included in something so personal like...like a real part of the family.

Emma snagged her hand, dragging her toward the car. "We've got to go to the ranch to tell Nash."

CHAPTER 23

C ody was the first to see them coming.

Kit and Boone were still at the stables, but Nash and Cody were heading back to the main house for an afternoon pick-me-up when Emma's car pulled in, and Sierra climbed out of the passenger seat.

Cody's whole body came alive at the sight of her, his heart slamming into action like he'd just gotten a jolt from jumper cables. He picked up his pace, walking even faster when he caught Sierra's hesitation as Emma shut the driver's door, staring at Nash and biting her bottom lip.

Sierra, meanwhile, was taking in the house and the property.

She hadn't had much of a look at the place during her one and only visit when she'd chewed Daisy out. He could only imagine the feelings that were pouring through her now as she took in her father's land.

But as he and Nash got closer to the women, it was Emma who seemed uncomfortable. She was blinking like she was fighting tears, her chin bunching as her lips trembled.

"What the…?" Nash hurried to his wife's side. "Honey, is everything okay?"

Cody stopped short when Emma burst into tears.

Nash looked just as stricken as he rushed over and pulled her into his arms. He glared at Sierra over the top of Emma's head, his tone sharp. "What happened?"

Cody didn't hesitate before coming between them, standing partially in front of Sierra to face off with Nash. "Watch your tone, boss."

Nash held Emma tighter, running his hand down her back to comfort her. "My wife is sobbing in my arms right now, and you're expecting me to watch my tone?" His glare landed on Sierra again. "What did you say to her?"

Cody took a step forward, but Sierra caught his arm. "It's okay, Cody. Just…give Emma a minute."

That had both Cody and Nash staring at Sierra in confusion, and then Nash dipped his head, his lips buried in Emma's hair. "Sweetheart, what happened? You have to talk to me. You're scaring me, darlin'."

Emma wailed something that was muffled against Nash's T-shirt. Cody looked to Sierra in alarm and was shocked to see her pressing her lips together to hide a smile. He gave her a questioning frown, but she shook her head and winked at him.

That's when Emma finally drew away from Nash, lifting her chin to stare up at him. Tears streamed down her face as she blubbered, "We're having a baby!"

Cody's heart gave a surprised jolt, and he could only imagine what Nash was going through right now. The poor guy looked like someone had just decked him.

Glancing at Sierra, he took in her elated grin, loving the way her eyes sparkled. She covered her mouth with her hand, hiding her laughter while Nash continued to stand there gobsmacked.

"Nash?"

Emma touched his cheek, and it pulled him out of the trance. He let out a choking kind of sound that was a mix of laughter and pure shock. "Are you serious?"

She nodded.

"But I thought…"

"I know."

"And you said you had a plan, and—"

"I know! But it looks like God had other ideas." Emma started to laugh when Nash lifted her into his arms. Her feet left the ground in a rush as he spun her in a circle and held her close.

"Emma, my love, my…" He placed her back on her feet, pulling away to gaze at her face, then giving her a kiss that was so passionate Cody and Sierra both looked away.

Cody shuffled closer to his Mona Lisa, leaning across to whisper in her ear. "You knew about this?"

"I guessed from her symptoms and went with her to buy a test."

Sierra looked so happy in that moment, he couldn't help but pull her into his arms, the feel of her so perfect and right and…

What would happen when he had to let go?

He shoved the thought aside. Now wasn't the time to worry about that. This was a time for celebration.

A second later, Emma and Nash broke apart, and Nash hugged Sierra, murmuring something to her Cody couldn't hear, but by Sierra's quick shake of her head and answering laugh, he suspected his boss was apologizing for leaping to conclusions…again.

Then Nash was clapping him on the shoulder. Cody gave him a hug, and then Emma was crushing him with a bear hug, and all four of them were laughing and talking at once.

"But you can't tell anyone." Emma pointed at all three of them. "I'm not ready for everyone in town to know, and when it comes to Lizzy and my sisters—" She gave Sierra a small smile. "—my other sisters, I want to surprise them."

"Surprise them how?" Sierra asked.

Emma grinned. "I don't know. But you're gonna help."

Sierra's brows shot up. "I am?"

"You are." Emma's tone was no-nonsense. Kind but firm, like Sierra was one of her students. "Tomorrow, you and I are going to make a plan."

"Oh, um…" Sierra didn't look nearly as certain about this, but then Nash was wrapping an arm around Emma, and the two of them were lost in their own private little world as they headed inside.

Sierra turned to Cody. "I guess I'm helping to plan a surprise."

He chuckled. "Looks that way." He glanced over at Emma's car. "Also looks like you might be stuck here for a while. You want a ride back to town?"

She nodded, and he caught a flicker of uncertainty as she glanced around.

"How about a tour first?" he offered.

Her gaze met his. "Yeah?"

"Why not? This is your property too."

She nibbled on her lower lip as she nodded. "Yeah, I guess so."

He started to head inside, but she shook her head. "Let's give them some privacy."

"Right. Let's take a stroll around the property, then, shall we?" He offered her his arm, and she giggled.

"Let's."

They didn't get far before they came to the pigs, and Sierra was enchanted. "They are so cute!"

He chuckled.

"I can't believe I'm part owner in a place that has livestock." Her smile was rueful as she turned to look at him. "Not exactly my scene."

"You?" He leaned against the fence beside her. "You should have seen Lizzy when she first arrived."

"Oh yeah?" Her smile was adorable, like she was just waiting to laugh.

So he launched into a story about Lizzy's first weeks here. He told her how she'd called off her wedding and fled here, and how she'd spent weeks wallowing in her bed before Kit finally started dragging her out into the sunlight.

"Poor Lizzy." She laughed.

It was hard not to when you knew how happy Lizzy and Kit were now.

"Yeah," Cody agreed. "I wish you could have seen her tottering around in her stiletto heels."

"I can just picture it." Sierra laughed some more, shaking her head.

"JJ and I couldn't tell if she really loved her heels that much or if she just loved driving Kit nuts strutting around in them."

That set Sierra off even more, and he joined in with her.

"What about Daisy?" she asked. "How'd she meet the sheriff?"

"Oh the age-old tale." Cody grinned. "Girl speeds through town. Boy pulls her over."

She giggled. "Sounds like everyone finds their happily ever after here." Her lips hitched to the side. "I guess I can see why they're so attached."

He swallowed, feeling how loaded that statement could be.

It took everything in him not to ask if she might find her happily ever after here. If she might become attached.

But he had a feeling that would kill the mood in a heartbeat, and he wasn't ready to let go of the sweet, melodic sound of her laughter or see the light in her eyes be dimmed by a conversation that couldn't possibly end the way he wanted it to.

So, instead, he pointed down the hill. "Want to check out the stables next? I bet the horses will be happy to see you."

She smiled as she followed at his side. He pointed out the bunkhouse and the cookhouse, the garage, and the office Dahlia used when she was here running the business side of things.

"Must be nice," she said softly.

"What?"

"Dahlia working here. Emma living in the house with Nash and Daisy. Kit working here, and you." She smiled up at him, but he was almost certain he caught a hint of strain. "Like one big, happy family."

His own smile faltered. It was exactly how he'd come to think of this situation. The only problem was… "I'm not sure where I fit into that."

He hadn't actually meant to say it aloud, but it was so easy to talk to Sierra.

Even now, she didn't pester him with questions, or give him her opinion. She just watched him thoughtfully as she nodded. "I could see that too."

What else do you see? He stopped himself from asking.

Honestly, he wasn't sure he wanted the answer.

Her tone lightened a bit as she nudged him playfully. "I'm not sure how I'd fit in either."

He pretended to be confused. "What do you mean? Every family needs its hustler."

She laughed, and the sound eased every last shred of tension inside him. She slid her arm through his again and tugged him toward the stables. "Come on, Cowboy. Show me your horses."

CHAPTER 24

Cal's Coffee Shop didn't have many customers coming through at this time of day, but each and every one of them knew Emma.

"Hey there, Miss Emma," one of the older men Sierra recognized from her first day in town called out.

"Hi, Norman!" Emma's tone was so cheerful and her smile so wide, Sierra felt like she was walking beside the town's very own Disney princess.

Which makes me...what? Her lips twisted with a wry smile. Probably best she didn't ask.

"Have you met my sister Sierra?" Emma asked.

Norman winked at Sierra. "Not officially. But I hear we have you to thank for saving little Chloe's life."

Sierra blinked in surprise. "Oh. Well, I was just doing what—"

Emma cut her off with a side hug. "She's too modest. We owe her everything."

"Including the ranch?" It was her mother's angry voice she heard in her head, and Sierra clamped her mouth shut. No one had mentioned the inheritance, and while she

knew maybe she should—it wasn't like this was a topic they could avoid forever—she found she didn't want to. Especially not now when Emma was being so warm and welcoming.

"We'll stop by and chat when we're done catching up," Emma promised the older man, and Sierra returned his wave as he walked over to join his posse sitting by the window.

"I'll just take an herbal tea, Jamie," Emma said when they reached the counter.

"Coffee," Sierra said. "Black."

A little while later, they had their drinks and were seated. Emma pulled a notebook out of her purse with a flourish. "Let's do this."

"Do what exactly?" Sierra fiddled with the sugar packets, rearranging the order so the sweeteners were lumped together.

"Surprise our sisters!" Emma rolled her eyes and presumably didn't see Sierra's reaction.

How was it so easy for Emma to say that? *"Our sisters."* And earlier with Norman—*"my sister."*

Like it was so easy to accept that some strange woman with bottle-dyed red hair who rode into town on a motorcycle was now family.

Sierra swallowed hard and took a moment to blow on her too-hot coffee. "What were you thinking?"

"Well…" Emma leaned back in her seat, her expression thoughtful. "First, we need a reason to get all of us together." Her lips pursed. "We'll have to make it at a time when Dahlia can join on a video call. But that means we need a *really* good reason…"

"Me," Sierra said simply. "Tell them you need an emergency meeting to discuss…me."

Emma blinked. "You want me to lie and say you're making threats against the ranch or something?"

Sierra flinched, her cheeks warming. Wasn't that exactly what she was doing? Threatening to take Emma's home?

And yet Emma didn't even look angry when she said it, just thoughtful. "Nah. I don't think that'll work." She reached over and patted Sierra's hand. "Thank you for offering to play the villain, though. That was sweet of you."

Sierra choked on a laugh. *Play* the villain? She *was* the villain as far as these women were concerned.

No, not "these women."

Her sisters.

"Besides, I don't want to stress everyone out or get them all riled up." Emma wrinkled her nose. "That's not a good vibe." Her expression brightened. "But we could still use you as an excuse to gather, just…in a happy way."

Wariness made Sierra shift in her seat uncomfortably. "How so?"

"I'll tell them I think it's high time we thanked you properly for saving Chloe—"

"That's really not necessary," Sierra started.

Emma ignored her. "I'll remind them that we handled your arrival into town all wrong and that you deserve to be welcomed into the family properly and…" She leaned forward, her brows coming down. "And that's true, you know. We really should have handled it better, and—"

"I should have handled it better," Sierra interrupted. "And I'm sorry. I should have said that a while ago. When I showed up at the ranch and met Daisy, I'd just found out that Frank had passed, and…"

Emma leaned over and gave her a hug. "I know."

That was it. *"I know."* Two simple words that spoke volumes.

Sierra patted Emma's back as tears stung her eyes. If anyone did know, it was Emma....and Lizzy and Daisy and Rose and Dahlia and April.

Good grief, she had a lot of sisters.

Emma pulled back, blinking rapidly and clearing her throat. "But this is a happy occasion, so all that is water under the bridge..." She shot Sierra a sidelong glance. "Aunt Sierra."

Sierra laughed. "Aunt Sierra. I like it."

"Okay, so that's how we'll get them all together in one place. But then how do I make the big announcement?" Emma asked, her pen poised over the notebook like Sierra was going to start rattling off a list of baby announcement ideas.

"Um..." Sierra shrugged. "I've never done this."

"Neither have I," Emma sighed.

"Do you want them to walk in and find streamers and a big sign?" Sierra asked.

Emma jotted it down. "Maybe."

"Or we could be baking and have buns in the oven."

Emma giggled. "Just keep mentioning the buns in the oven until somebody catches on?"

"Exactly!" Sierra laughed.

"I could give them all shirts saying Auntie or something," Emma offered. But then she added, "Although that'll take a while."

"Unless we make them ourselves." Sierra took another sip of her coffee.

"That's true. I like the idea of a surprise, though."

"How about fortune cookies?" Sierra waited for Emma to laugh it off, but she gave her a curious frown instead.

"That would be really fun, but where would we get customized fortune cookies?"

Sierra laughed. "We'd make them."

"How?"

Sierra grinned. "I've made them before. It's not hard."

"Where'd you learn how to do that?" Emma eyes widened. "Were you a nurse in China?"

Sierra laughed. "I was, actually, although I wasn't there long. But fun fact: fortune cookies aren't really a thing in China."

"No?" Emma said.

"It's true. But I grew up in San Francisco, and one of the apartments we lived in was in Chinatown, and our school took us on this field trip to one of the factories where they make fortune cookies." Sierra sipped her coffee. "I was a fan, so my mom got me this kit, and..." She shrugged. "The rest is history."

"I love it," Emma breathed. "How are you with dumplings?"

"I can roll and fold with the best of 'em," Sierra shot back.

"That's my girl!" Emma lifted her hand, and Sierra gave her a high five. Then they both burst out laughing.

A second later, though, Emma was back to business, her pen in hand. "Okay, let's figure out the best day and time."

Sierra bit back another grin. Emma was a sweetheart, all right. And Sierra couldn't help but like her. Leaning forward with a nod, she grinned. "Okay...let's do this."

CHAPTER 25

Cody was speechless.

Sierra shifted before him in the door of her hotel room. With a frown, she looked down at her little black dress and ankle boots. "What? Is this not okay?"

He was still speechless.

"You said you wanted to take me on a proper date," she muttered. "Should I change, or—"

"No!" Cody swallowed hard and tried to regain the use of his brain. "It's just…" He let out a harsh exhale, a slow grin spreading across his face. "You look amazing."

"Oh." Her lips curved up with a pleased smile, but it was the hint of pink in her cheeks that made his heart stutter. "Okay then. I'll just…" She gestured back into the hotel room before darting in to grab her purse and leather jacket. "Ready."

"I guess I'll be driving, huh?" he teased as he glanced down at the short hem of her dress.

Her cheeks tinged a pretty pink again, and she dipped her head, looking uncharacteristically bashful. Cody reached for her hand, threading their fingers together, unable to control the smile spreading across his face.

"So, where are you taking me?" she asked when he held the truck door open for her. "Emma said that pizza place on Main Street is good."

"It is," he agreed. "But I thought maybe you might want to get out of town for a change." He'd climbed in behind the wheel before she responded.

"I definitely wouldn't mind a change of scenery." She turned to look out the window as they drove toward the highway on-ramp. "Although, this town is growing on me."

He shifted in his seat, glancing over to steal a look at her profile. Hope curled in his gut like a rattlesnake waiting to strike. He took a deep breath. *"This town is growing on me"* was hardly a declaration that she wanted to settle down here in Aspire.

He shifted his hands on the wheel. "It's a nice place to live once you get used to the small-town vibe."

"Mmm." She toyed with the hem of her dress, and he willed himself not to look.

Good grief, he hadn't thought this woman could be any sexier, and then she had to go and look like this.

"It helps that I'm not getting stares all the time," she said.

Cody blinked, and it took him a full second to remember what they'd been talking about. He tore his gaze away from that dang hem and those long, lean legs. "Yeah, I'd guess you're old news by now."

She chuckled. "I wouldn't go that far. But the stares are now usually accompanied by smiles. And people talk *to* me rather than *about* me these days."

"Good," he said. "I'm glad you're feeling more at home here."

She gave a little snort. "I wouldn't say *at home*, but…" She shot him a sidelong glance. "Yeah, it's…getting better."

He gave her a small smile of understanding. It'd been nice seeing the way she and Emma had gotten along the other day. And while she hadn't exactly ended their tour of the ranch begging to move in, he thought she at least had felt a little more comfortable being on the property.

"So, where are you taking me, Cowboy?" She turned in her seat to face him.

"It's a bit of a trek, but Bozeman has a lot more restaurants to pick from," he said as they merged onto the highway. "If you don't mind the drive."

"Mind?" She sat up a little straighter, her voice getting lighter. "You should know by now that I'm always up for a new town. New town, new state, new country…" She shot him a teasing grin. "I'm game."

His own smile faltered. Of course he knew that. And that was why he'd decided to take her to the city of Bozeman rather than one of the tried-and-true steakhouses in their valley. But still, the hope that had started to form got a swift kick, and Cody had to face the fact that he didn't just enjoy spending time with this woman…

He didn't just like her company and her kisses and the sound of her voice…

He was getting attached. And with each new text, and call, and time spent together, this feeling of neediness only grew worse.

Heck, he was hooked on her, and he was pretty sure there'd be no cure when she left.

"So tell me about Bozeman," Sierra said, her tone light and happy as she went back to taking in the landscape.

She was excited for their big night out, and there was no way Cody was going to ruin it by stewing over the future. And so, for the rest of the drive, he answered her questions about where they were going, and they went through the list of restaurant options.

By the time they arrived in town and he found a place to park, Cody was just as eager for their date as she was. As they strolled down Main Street and stopped to listen to buskers playing music, he found himself laughing and talking more than he ever had with any woman.

Or maybe just ever. Period.

Sierra was just so easy to be around. It was like hanging out with a friend. With his best friend.

She slid an arm around his waist as they listened to a man playing guitar near the restaurant where they were headed, and he pulled her close, amending that last thought.

It was like hanging out with a best friend he couldn't wait to kiss again.

He stole a kiss before they headed into the restaurant, and the dazed look in her eyes when he pulled back made his chest feel two sizes too small.

"What was that for?" she asked softly.

He leaned down until his forehead touched hers. "I couldn't wait until the end of the night."

She smiled. "I'm glad. I want to make the most of every second with you."

He wrapped an arm around her, guiding them inside. Her words clung to him, though, and he found himself stewing over them as they placed their orders and got their drinks.

"I want to make the most of every second..."

She felt it too. He was almost sure of it. This impending sense of doom that threatened to dampen what was supposed to be a fun night.

"Sierra, when you're done working through the inheritance issue..."

She arched a brow when he trailed off. "We're not gonna talk about ranch business on our date, are we?"

"No." He reached across the table and covered her hands with his. "I have no desire to discuss the ranch. But I would like to talk about us."

Her burgeoning smile stopped in its tracks, but she didn't pretend not to know what he meant. There was a sadness in her gaze when she murmured, "You want to know where this is headed."

He nodded. "Don't you?"

She wet her lips and tugged on her hands, but rather than pull them out of his, she flipped them around so she was clasping his hands in hers. "Cody, I really like you."

His heart gave a sharp thud. It was part happiness and part terror because he could feel the "but" that was coming.

She breathed out slowly. "But I can't stay here forever."

"Yeah, no. I know." He swallowed hard, squeezing her hands as he nodded.

She tilted her head to the side, her gaze piercing. "Do you?"

"I get it." He kept nodding, an automatic movement he couldn't control. "You have a career to get back to."

"I do." She bit her lip, her gaze focused on his and filled with warmth and sadness. "I don't want to think about saying goodbye. I know that's selfish of me, but you are the best thing to...to come out of this visit. And I want to enjoy every second."

His throat felt too tight. His chest felt like it was collapsing in on itself. But he nodded. "Yeah. I want that too."

She held his gaze for a long moment, as if to reassure herself that he meant it. Finally she nodded and dropped her gaze to their interlocked hands. "I take my job seriously." She rubbed her thumb over his knuckles. "I decided a long time ago that I wanted to devote my life to taking care of those less fortunate than me. And I know," she said hurriedly, as if he'd been about to interrupt, "there are people less fortunate than me here in America. And maybe one day I'll be content to settle down and tackle the issues on my own doorstep. But the thing is, this country has resources, and it has wealth, and not every country has that and—"

"Sierra," he interrupted gently when her brows drew together in frustration. "I get it."

She blinked at him. "You do?"

He slid his knuckle gently down her cheek. "I do."

"Okay then." She nodded.

He let out a soft, rueful laugh. "Okay then."

"So I have to go," she said softly, her eyes glimmering in the candlelight with what he suspected were unshed tears. "When all this family business is sorted...I have to go."

"Yeah." His voice was so gruff it was barely audible. He squeezed her hands. "I get that too. I just..." He cleared his throat. "I hate it. I hate the thought of saying goodbye to you."

Her lips trembled. "Me too."

"I mean..." He breathed out sharply and looked away

for a moment to gather his thoughts. "I've only just met you, and I already hate it. And I think...I think I'm only gonna hate it more with each passing day." His gaze collided with hers. "Does that make sense?"

"It makes so much sense," she whispered. "Because I feel the same."

"So..." He tried for a smile when the silence grew too long and heavy. "Okay then."

Her answering smile was just as weak. But then she blurted, "Does that mean you don't want to spend time with me, or—"

"No." He said it too quickly, and this time they both did laugh, although the sound was more rueful than amused. "No," he repeated. "I want to spend as much time with you as I can."

She squeezed his hands so tight it might have hurt if he didn't love the connection so dang much.

The waiter arrived with their appetizers, and he reluctantly let her hands go. For a little while, they busied themselves with filling their plates and eating and talking about the food and the wine. But when the waiter cleared the appetizer from the table, Sierra's expression grew serious.

"What about you?" she asked.

Cody stared at her with a blank expression for a moment. "What about me?"

She lifted one shoulder. "Just..." She glanced away, oddly hesitant.

That put him on edge. She was many things, but hesitant wasn't one of them. "What do you mean, Sierra?"

"I mean...I don't want to keep harping on about the future because I know we just agreed to enjoy our time together and—"

"Sierra." He kept his voice low and soft. "What do you mean?"

She wet her lips. "I mean, what about your future? Is it...?" She winced slightly like she regretted asking. "Is it definitely here? Or...in Aspire, I mean?"

"Yeah," he replied automatically, surprise clear in his voice. "Of course."

"Of course," she echoed, a smile on her face but disappointment in her voice.

He leaned forward, needing to explain. "My job is here."

He could instantly hear how flimsy that sounded. He liked his job and found it satisfying, but it wasn't like he had some deep passion for being a ranch hand. Mostly it was just nice to be able to work with his hands and be around people he cared about.

"And my family," he added.

She pressed her lips together, and he thought she might say something, but she ended up just nodding.

He fought the urge to justify his reason. His parents did rely on him. Sure, Kit was around, but he had a family of his own to focus on.

And Kit and his twins, they still relied on him.

They might not need him the way they did before Lizzy came along, but...

"I get it, Cody." Sierra pulled him out of his thoughts.

He glanced up to see her giving him a sad smile.

"If you love living in Aspire, then that's where you should be." She paused, and he found himself tensing, because yet again it felt like she wanted to say something more.

Her shoulders slumped, and she seemed to reconsider, but he leaned forward and reached for her hand. "Say it."

Her eyes widened slightly. "Okay. I guess..." She sighed loudly. "Look, if you love Aspire and want to be close to your family and friends, I get that. I just...I just wouldn't want you to stay because you think you have to. Because..." She winced at whatever she saw in his expression. "Forget it."

"No." His insides churned, but it wasn't with anger. "Finish."

She took a deep breath. "It seems like you feel obligated, you know? Like you think your family and friends can't exist without you, and I just...I just want to make sure you're thinking of yourself, too, when you dream of the future. Not just everyone else."

He held her stare for a long moment as her words sifted and settled inside him.

But his insides never settled. He felt like she'd stirred up something that refused to go back to sleep.

She shrugged, her smile sweet and gentle. "Just think about it, that's all."

"Yeah." He nodded. "Yeah, I will."

"Okay then." She winked. "What do you say we go back to enjoying date night, then, hmm?"

He dipped his chin with a soft laugh. "Speaking of, I happen to know of a place with a pool table nearby. You game, Hustler?"

"Always, Cowboy." She laughed. "Always."

CHAPTER 26

E mma leaned in until her head was right next to Sierra's as she watched her cook. "Are you sure this burner trick is safe?"

Sierra laughed as she stirred the veggies. "It's the only way to get the wok hot enough."

"Right," Emma murmured. "Which brings me to my next question. Where on earth did you find a wok in Aspire?"

"I didn't find it in Aspire. I found it in Bozeman."

"Ah." Emma scooted aside to lean against the counter next to Sierra. "On your date night with Cody."

Sierra shot Emma a sidelong warning look that only made her laugh. "Okay, fine. So you're not ready for the 'let's talk about boys' phase of our sisterly bonding. Got it."

Sierra nearly burned herself on the wok.

Sisterly bonding.

Geez. Emma said it like it was normal. Which, for Emma, maybe it was.

"I can't believe you know how to make all these dishes," Emma said.

"And I can't believe this town doesn't have a single Chinese take-out place," Sierra shot back.

Emma shrugged. "I do miss that about Chicago. But Bozeman has a good food scene, and Missoula isn't too far away either, so lack of ethnic food isn't the end of the world."

Sierra didn't respond. She just peeked at Emma to see if she was trying to be manipulative and convince her to stay in town...or at least reconsider her desire to sell the ranch.

But one glance at Emma's wide-eyed, sweetheart smile and Sierra sighed.

No. Of course Emma wasn't trying to manipulate her into staying. Just like Cody hadn't tried to force the issue.

It was her own mind that was messed up these days. More than ever since their date night when Sierra and Cody had finally discussed the elephant in the room. She'd been replaying their conversation ever since. What he'd said. What she'd said.

What she'd almost said.

"You are the best thing to...to come out of this visit," she'd said.

What she'd almost blurted?

"You are the best thing to happen to me."

She flinched as some oil splattered her hand. *Dang it.* She had to concentrate. She'd been stewing over that conversation for twenty-four hours, but no amount of replaying snippets changed the fact that once her business with this ranch was through, she was heading back to Venezuela.

198

"So where'd you learn to cook like this?" Emma asked. "Your mom?"

Sierra tensed. "Uh, no. I like to take cooking classes everywhere I travel. It's a fun way to learn the language and the culture...and be able to bring some of the culture with me when I leave."

"That's such a cool idea." Emma grinned. She started talking about how her mom taught her to bake and how her grandmother passed down recipes...

Sierra was content to listen. She didn't want to talk about her mother. Especially not with Emma. It just felt wrong when her last phone call with her mom had ended in its usual fashion—with her mother going off on a tirade about Frank's "second family" that he'd left them for.

She wouldn't listen when Sierra explained that he hadn't just left them to go on and make one big happy family somewhere else. He'd actually left a trail of women in his wake. It didn't take her long to realize that that was the worst thing she could have said.

But she'd been trying to garner some empathy for the other daughters he'd left behind.

He'd abandoned all of them without an explanation. All except for April—but now *she* was the one abandoning the family.

Sierra frowned down at the sizzling veggies. No, April wasn't abandoning them. No more than Sierra would be abandoning this family when she went back to Venezuela.

They each had a right to live their lives. Their father's death and his will didn't take away the fact that they were grown women with independent lives.

"Ooh, I think you're burning." Emma sniffed the air, then pinched her nose, obviously battling a little wave of pregnancy nausea.

Sierra quickly pulled the wok from the heat just as the timer went off for the rice. "Looks like we're ready for the surprise party."

Emma swallowed.

"If you're up for it." Sierra brushed a hand down her arm. "Can I make you some ginger tea?"

"That would be lovely, thank you." Emma pulled herself straight, as if talking herself out of feeling a little green. Inhaling a deep breath, she ran a hand over her stomach, then beamed and clapped her hands together like a little kid.

Sierra got the water boiling for the tea, laughing at Emma's sweetness.

"The others should be here any minute now." Emma kept her eye out the window as Sierra steeped the soothing tea.

Sure enough, the rest of the O'Sullivan sisters piled into the kitchen minutes later, and soon the kitchen was buzzing with noisy chatter and laughter as Daisy, Rose, and Lizzy oohed and aahed over Sierra's "olive branch" meal.

That was what Lizzy dubbed it, assuming—and not incorrectly, Sierra had to admit—that Sierra's culinary work was part of her effort to make nice with her new family.

Of course, Lizzy hadn't learned yet that this was only part of the reason.

Having the distraction of her sisters around seemed to help Emma, and by the time she'd finished her tea, she was back to her bright, carefree self.

"Who's calling Dahlia?" she asked when the sisters were nearly through their meal.

"I've got it." Rose grabbed her phone, pulling up

Dahlia's contact info when she gave Sierra an apologetic wince. "I should probably warn you. She might not be…"

"Overjoyed to see me?" Sierra offered in a dry tone.

Rose giggled. "Exactly."

"I can handle it." Sierra winked.

"Brave woman," Lizzy teased. "But I think you're right. If anyone can stand up to the dragon, it's definitely our eldest sister."

"I thought we agreed no one would call her that anymore," Emma chided.

Rose giggled again. "It's okay. I think she kinda likes it."

Daisy nodded knowingly. "She totally does." To Sierra, she added, "See, Dahlia resents the fact that we've all seen her soft underbelly thanks to JJ. Now we all know she's not nearly as coldhearted as she liked to pretend."

"I see…," Sierra said slowly.

"Yeah, so she kinda likes the dragon nickname," Rose continued with an impish little grin. "Makes her feel like she's still a tough guy."

Sierra laughed along with the rest of them.

"Really she's just overprotective," Lizzy explained to Sierra. "Once you get to know her, you'll love her."

"If you say so," Sierra teased. She already sorta liked this woman who was so protective of her family.

It was hard to fault someone who looked after their own.

Emma went around the table handing out the fortune cookies she and Sierra had made that morning. When she got to Sierra, she winked and then handed her a cookie. "Look out, because once Dahlia realizes you're not a threat to her family, you're going to be one of the people she looks out for."

Sierra smiled, but her insides felt shaky.

"Once Dahlia realizes you're not a threat..."

Wasn't she? She hadn't called off her lawyer.

Granted, she wasn't trying to get sole ownership of the ranch anymore—that had been anger and her mother's resentment talking. And maybe a little grief as well.

But she still wanted to be able to sell her portion of this place. Didn't she?

Dahlia's voice filled the kitchen. "So what, this new sister makes one lunch for you guys and all is forgiven?"

Daisy laughed. Rose sighed. Lizzy gave Sierra a little shake of her head that seemed to say, *Ignore her.*

"Be nice, Dahlia," Emma sang out happily. "We're about to have dessert, and we wanted you to be here for this nice moment."

"Yeah, but—"

"Don't ruin it, sis," Rose said so sweetly that Dahlia just grumbled something that sounded like "I leave for a few weeks and they go soft on me."

Sierra wasn't paying attention to the so-called dragon sister, though. Like Emma, she was eagerly waiting and watching to see how the others reacted to the surprise.

"Wait, what's this? Is this homemade?" Lizzy asked as she started to crack open the cookie.

Emma hovered next to the table, her eager anticipation so palpable that Sierra wasn't sure how the others didn't feel her vibrating with excitement as she waited for them to read their "fortunes."

"This year shall bring you joy and laughter," Lizzy read with a grin. "You're going to..." Then her lips parted, her eyes bulging wide before a smile split her face from ear to ear. "I'm going to be an auntie again?"

"Ahhh!" Daisy jumped up so fast, the chair crashed

back from the table, making them all jolt, then burst into laughter. "We're going to be aunties!"

Racing around the table, she only just beat Lizzy to Emma's side. They squished her into a hug, squealing and dancing while Rose sat at the table, brushing tears off her cheeks and looking the happiest of them all.

"Kiara's getting a brand-new cousin." Her voice wobbled. "They're going to grow up together."

"I know." Emma smiled back, her eyes glassing with tears. "We're gonna be baby mamas together."

"Would you stop sitting there crying and go hug her, please?" Dahlia quipped. "You're killing me, Rosie!"

Laughter bubbled out of Rose as she stood from the table and joined in on the group hug. The phone was still in her hand, and no doubt Dahlia was getting a close-up shot of squished hair and wet cheeks.

Sierra remained at the table, and as their shrieks of excitement filled the air, she found herself wondering if *she* was the dragon.

The bad guy who wanted to sell this place. This home.

She did still want to walk away from this ranch…

Didn't she?

And then Daisy tugged Sierra out of her seat to join in on the crazy dancing and hugging and crying and gushing as the girls celebrated Emma's happy news.

"Wait, you knew about this?" Lizzy asked Sierra, tears streaming down her cheeks after she and Emma finally broke apart from what looked like a bone-crushing hug.

"I was in the right place at the right time." Sierra shrugged.

"And she made these cookies so I could surprise you. How cool is that?" Emma beamed, sharing a smile with

Dahlia, who was on the phone, fighting tears and trying to look stoic.

"That *was* cool of you," Dahlia murmured.

Sierra shrugged again.

Rose continued gushing about how wonderful it would be to have another baby in the family, making playdates for Kiara and the unborn cousin. Lizzy started chattering a mile a minute about how excited the twins would be, and Emma had to cut in with a stern warning that this news was still on the down-low…

"For now, at least," she said. "You know how this town loves to gossip, so until I say so, this news is for immediate family only."

Emma turned to smile at Sierra, and she felt her heart ache.

Immediate family only.

That…was her. Sierra swallowed hard, grateful for the interruption when Daisy came over to her and slid an arm around her waist, her voice filled with laughter. "Mark my words, this is how it all begins."

"How all what begins?" Lizzy asked.

Dahlia answered. "The baby wave."

Rose laughed. "That's what our mom used to call it when sisters or groups of friends all started having kids at the same time."

"It's an epidemic," Daisy said with comically wide eyes.

Sierra laughed along with the rest of them when Daisy lowered her voice like she was letting Sierra in on a secret. "Mark my words. Rose and Emma are just the beginning. Soon they're gonna be expecting all of us to pop out little rug rats."

Rose and Emma burst out laughing, and Rose shot

Sierra a cute little grin. "We have to secure our oldest sister a husband first..."

"Oh no." Sierra went along with the teasing and laughter like it was second nature, holding her hands up in defense. "I see what happens when O'Sullivans come to this town."

"Don't try to resist, Sierra," Dahlia shouted, laughing on her end of the line. "The harder you fight it, the worse it is."

"Yup. I think it's safe to say the O'Sullivan women are fated to meet their match in Aspire." Emma nudged Sierra's arm.

Sierra laughed, even though her mind's eye was filling with an image of Cody, and her heart was thrashing around like a wild animal.

She could not be falling for the cowboy...

Or, okay, maybe she could.

She flinched. Okay, fine...she had.

But that didn't mean she was going to give up her life and stay here.

"Don't try to fight it, lady. We all fall for the cowboys in the end," Lizzy laughed.

Sierra forced another laugh in turn. It wasn't like she could deny it. Cody had slipped into her life and made her feel things, want things...

He made her question everything she always thought she needed.

Daisy squeezed her shoulders with a grin. "Like I said...it's an epidemic."

CHAPTER 27

For the middle of the work week, the ranch was bustling like it was a holiday.

Which, in a way, Cody supposed it was. It wasn't every day their foreman and one of the ranch's owners announced they were having a baby.

And even though Cody already knew the big secret, he got caught up in the celebration right alongside Kit, Levi, and Dex.

It seemed Dex and Levi had been curious about what this lunch was all about and were currently out near the stables, listening to Nash explain that this was still hush-hush.

"JJ will have heard by now, I imagine." Nash nodded toward the house. "But other than that, no one else knows, got it? Not until we're ready."

Kit scratched his chin. "What d'you want to bet JJ's next to become a dad?"

Levi chuckled, leaning back against the fence. "Well, there's only two left who aren't daddies." He eyed Cody meaningfully.

Cody held his hands up. "Oh no. Don't look at me."

Nash laughed. "I don't know. You and Sierra have been spending a lot of time together lately..."

Cody scratched the back of his neck. "If you think spending time together is how you become a daddy, then I feel sorry for Emma."

Nash and Levi laughed, and Dex grinned as he shushed baby Kiara, who was just starting to fuss. Levi's kids were at camp, but Lizzy and Rose had come with the whole family.

Kit arched his brows, his expression expectant. "So? How serious are you two?"

Cody eyed his brother with feigned suspicion. "Who wants to know? You, Lizzy...or Mom?"

"All of us." Kit grinned.

Cody jabbed a finger in his direction. "And that's why I'm pleading the fifth."

"Aw, come on." Levi chuckled. "You've watched the rest of us fall for an O'Sullivan woman. You're talking to a group of experts here."

Cody looked away with a laugh. He knew they meant well. They were just having fun. But he didn't want to talk to anyone about his feelings for Sierra. Least of all these men. They all got happy endings to their love stories, and Cody...

Well, he wasn't sure how this was going to go.

All he knew was he didn't want it to end.

But while Levi, Dex, and Nash seemed content to change the topic, Kit was watching him closely. "Seriously, bro..."

"What?" Cody kicked at the dirt.

"Don't you ever think about settling down?"

Cody stared at him, and not for the first time, he

wondered if his brother remembered what his life had been like before Lizzy. After his wife had left him and the twins, he'd been a single dad to two little babies.

"What?" Kit frowned, obviously curious about Cody's silent stare.

Eventually, he scrubbed a hand over his face and shook his head. "It's nothin', Kit." He started to walk away to check on the dogs, who needed to be led back to the kennel for feeding.

Nash fell into step beside him. "Kit just worries about you, you know."

Cody nodded. For as long as he could remember, Nash had been the self-appointed peacekeeper. But Cody wasn't angry with Kit. He was just…

Aw heck, he didn't know what he was.

Frustrated, maybe?

"We all want you to be happy." Nash gave him a good-natured slap on the shoulder.

Cody looked over to see Nash wearing that expression of his. The one Kit called Nash's dad face. He started to laugh.

"What is it?" Nash asked.

"Nothing, just…" He clapped a hand on his friend's shoulder. "You're going to make a great father, you know that?"

Nash grinned. "Thanks, man. And you're gonna make a great husband to some lucky lady."

Cody dipped his head.

"I'm not prying. Whatever's going on between you and Sierra, it's clear you two have feelings for each other. And we all just want you to be happy."

Cody nodded. He appreciated that. He really did. But as he split off from Nash to deal with the dogs, it was Sierra's words from the other night that kept coming back to him. Not even what she'd said but the questions she'd forced him to face.

He *had* been needed around here. For years, he'd felt the responsibility of being a good brother, uncle, son, and friend. But now?

Now he couldn't help but wonder if he was needed any longer. And if he wasn't...

Where did that leave him?

"I just want to make sure you're thinking of yourself, too, when you dream of the future. Not just everyone else."

The words had rattled him then, and they made him antsy now. The dogs seemed to pick up on it, because they were less obedient than usual as he fed them and gave them water.

The words still nagged at him when he headed back to the others, but now they'd reshaped themselves into a question. What did he think about when he dreamed of the future?

Not the future for his parents or his niece and nephew but *his* future.

What did he want?

He'd hoped the conversation would have shifted by the time he rejoined the others, but of course Nash's impending fatherhood was still big news, and everyone was sharing stories of the moment they found out they were going to be fathers for the first time.

Cody couldn't escape when Kit's gaze landed on him. "Come on, bro. You're so good with kids. Admit it—you want children of your own one day."

And just like that, an image jumped into his mind's eye, so clear and pure it nearly cut him down at the knees. He saw Sierra, smiling and laughing, with a kid on one hip and another running circles around her. A little girl was holding his hand, skipping beside him as they walked in the sunlight—a happy family.

The thing was...the kids didn't look like him. Or her. It was a found family. A family for kids who needed a place to belong.

His heart bloomed with a longing so strong and intense he didn't know whether to laugh or cry.

"Cody?" Dex nudged his arm "You still with us?"

Cody rubbed a hand over his chest and dragged his attention back to his brother and friends, who seemed to be waiting for a reply. He cleared his throat, the sound of Chloe and Corbin drawing his attention. He evaded the question with a joking tone. "Who has time for kids of my own when I've got these little monsters to keep me busy?"

Everyone laughed because at that precise moment, the twins spotted Cody and ran to him, shrieking, "Uncle Cody! Uncle Cody!" at the top of their lungs.

His laugh lightened something in his chest as he bent down and scooped them up, throwing one over each shoulder. "Hey, who wants to play some baseball?"

Kit held his hands around his mouth to shout, "Batter up!"

And everyone but Dex jogged out onto the open lawn while Nash fetched the kids' baseball and bat set they kept at the ranch.

"Kiara and I will be the umpires," Dex called out as Chloe stepped up to bat.

"You ready to hit it out of the park, peanut?" Cody shoved a mitt onto his hand.

She jumped to her tiptoes, resting the bat on her shoulder and looking beyond cute. "Ready, Uncle Cody!"

He jogged out onto the "mound," and when he turned

back, he saw Sierra's bright red hair in the kitchen window, a smile on her face as she watched him.

He lifted a hand in a wave and was rewarded with a brilliant smile that made him forget where he was for a moment.

"I'm ready, Uncle Cody!" Chloe pulled him back to the game, and he ducked his head, taking in a deep, steadying breath.

He knew what he wanted, all right.

He wanted that woman. In his life.

Permanently.

CHAPTER 28

Sierra stared up at the beast before her with a furrowed brow. "And you're sure she's all right with this?"

The mare whinnied.

Cody laughed. "I'm sure. Mabel here loves to go out for a long ride."

Sierra shot Cody a sidelong glance.

"A long, *slow* ride," he amended.

She didn't miss the way his lips twitched with barely concealed amusement. And she supposed it was kinda funny. She had no problem whipping around curves on her bike, but the thought of straddling a seemingly docile horse made her twitchy.

Cody came up behind her, so close she could smell his soap and feel the heat from his body—reassuring and nerve rattling all at the same time. His hands settled on her shoulders. "Look, if you're too scared, we don't have to—"

"I'm not scared," she said quickly.

Perhaps too quickly if Cody's snicker was any indication.

Sierra sighed and whirled around to face him. "Is my discomfort amusing to you, Cowboy?"

His smile was slow and so sexy it made her knees weak. "A little. Never thought I'd see my favorite hustler afraid of old Mabel."

She glanced over her shoulder and started to laugh as Mabel looked back at her with big, soulful eyes while she slowly munched on some hay.

A terrifying, bucking stallion she was not.

Turning back to Cody, she arched a brow. "I told you I'm not afraid. Just...respectful."

"Respectful, huh?" His arms wrapped around her tighter, and she shivered with excitement as his head dipped lower, his eyes darkening as his gaze dropped to her lips.

"Respectful," she repeated, her voice far too breathy and her thoughts scattering quickly. "She might look sweet and calm, but that thing could take me down with one bump of the hip, and she knows it."

"Uh-huh," he murmured, clearly not listening. Or if he was, he wasn't buying it. But before she could argue the point any further, he was dipping his head even lower until his lips met hers in a lingering kiss that sent the last of her thoughts flying out of her head.

For several long, delicious moments his lips teased hers, their breath mingled, and the only sound to be heard was Mabel shuffling behind them.

When he finally lifted his head, she murmured, "Poor Mabel. Do you think we scarred her for life with the PDA?"

He grinned and brushed his nose against hers. "Feel any better?"

Sierra laughed, because... "Yeah. I do."

Her nerves had settled, thanks to that slow, sweet kiss. And now when she glanced at Mabel, she found a flicker of excitement at the thought of trying her hand at something new. She smiled up at Cody. "Okay, Cowboy. Let's do this."

He kissed the tip of her nose. "That's my girl."

The words made her belly flutter. *My girl.*

It didn't mean anything. Just a term of endearment. But try telling that to the butterflies in her stomach that took flight and refused to settle.

Cody helped her up into the saddle, and then he took his time explaining where her feet should go and how to hold the reins.

She had a feeling he was taking his sweet time to give her a chance to relax. And soon enough, she did find herself getting comfortable, even laughing when Mabel started to shift around a bit beneath her. She reached forward and patted the horse's long, sleek neck. "Getting impatient, Mabel?"

Mabel huffed.

Cody laughed. "See? You two are already speaking the same language." He took hold of the reins and arched his brows. "What do you say? Want to take a little stroll?"

She nodded, grateful that he stayed by their side, one hand guiding them.

He was doing it to make her comfortable, she knew. He'd told her time and again that Mabel's days of taking off at a gallop were long behind her. So his presence at her side right now was just to put *her* at ease.

And it worked.

She found herself laughing and chatting easily as she got used to the feel of Mabel's shifting weight beneath her. Cody led them on a slow walk around a flat area of land near the bunkhouse, and she smiled and waved back to Boone when he headed past them.

"Looking good, Sierra!" he called out.

She grinned down at Cody. "See that? He thinks I look good."

"Everyone knows you look good, darlin'. On a motorcycle, on a horse, doesn't matter. You're gorgeous inside and out."

She blinked in surprise. Inside and out? She didn't know about that. But he sounded so certain.

He narrowed his eyes teasingly when he caught her staring at him. "Don't go telling me you've got a crush on Boone like every other woman in this town."

She laughed. "Are you jealous, Cody Swanson?"

His sigh was exaggerated and made her laugh all over again.

"Look, Hustler, I know he's handsome and a charmer, not to mention a football phenomenon, but he's nearly a decade younger than you—"

Sierra's laughter cut him off, and he shot her a lopsided grin that stole her breath. "Don't worry, Cody, you're the only cowboy I'm crushing on these days." The admission surprised herself as much as him, judging by the look on his face.

Her heart skittered as a hot flush tore through her.

No one had ever had this kind of effect on her before.

Cody's shoulder brushed her thigh as he turned to face her, squinting against the sunshine as he murmured, "Is that right?"

She nodded, her smile small and shaky. "That's right."

"Well…" There was that slow grin again. The one that made her feel like warm syrup was flooding her veins. "Guess it's a good thing the feeling's mutual, huh?"

"Good thing," she echoed, fighting a goofy grin.

Dang it. How did he always manage to turn her into a silly, flighty girl? That was so not her. She'd never been one for giggles and breathless flirting.

But right now, she had to look away from Cody's dark, heated gaze just to catch her breath.

"What do you say we head up to that grove over there?" He pointed to a thatch of trees a little ways off from the stable and the bunkhouse.

"Sounds good."

And this time Cody let go of the reins and let her handle Mabel by herself as he kept pace with a brisk walk beside them.

When they stopped, he helped her off.

"I think I'm getting the hang of it." She gave him a satisfied grin as he caught her in his arms.

"You're a natural."

They stood there for a long moment, neither pulling away. The sun was high overhead, but the breeze was cool and brought with it the scent of grass and wildflowers.

"A natural, hmm?" she murmured as she looped her arms around his neck and pulled him down for a quick kiss. "You make me feel like I am."

His gaze searched hers, as if he could hear that she meant something by that. Her throat grew tight, and her mouth went dry. She'd never been much on talking about her feelings. But this man deserved to know how much she appreciated it, and how…how she'd never forget it.

Her throat grew even tighter at thoughts of walking away from this…from him.

He kissed her forehead, then her temple, a gentle comforting touch like he knew exactly how she was feeling.

She curled her fingers into the fabric of his T-shirt and clung to his shoulders. "You have a gift, Cowboy. A way of making people feel like they belong. Like..." She swallowed hard and lifted her gaze to meet his. "Like they're at home when you're around."

A muscle in his stubble-covered jaw twitched, and his throat moved when he swallowed. "I make people feel that way?"

She smiled. "You make *me* feel that way. And..."

And no one has ever done that for me.

And I've never felt like this before.

She took a deep breath. "Growing up, it was always just me and my mom. My grandparents were involved, but...but I always knew we'd been abandoned."

He stayed still and quiet, just watching and waiting for her with a patience and calm that was so very Cody.

She wet her lips. "We bounced around all the time. We stayed in San Francisco, but we moved from apartment to apartment, which meant I went to different schools. Anyway, I...I always thought I didn't want a home. I didn't need one, because I'd never really had one where I felt like I belonged..."

Her mind went back to her childhood, and she wished she had the words to explain. She'd never been taken care of. Never been comforted and coddled and surrounded by unconditional love.

Her mother loved her. Her grandparents too. But she'd been the caregiver more often than not. She'd been the one to calm her mother when she was angry. The one to look after her grandparents when they were sick.

She didn't regret a second of it because she loved her family, but...

But she'd never felt like this. Like she was wanted and

like she belonged. Like maybe she deserved to be the center of someone's world.

"I've never been tempted to stay in one place before," she whispered, a little afraid of all she was admitting. But he deserved to know. "I've never met someone who made me feel like..." She swallowed hard. "Like I've come home."

His hands at her waist tightened, and he tugged her close. "I wish you could stay."

And I wish you'd come with me.

She bit back the words. They'd already been down this road. They knew where it ended. So she went up on tiptoe and kissed him with all she was feeling. His answering moan was hungry, his hands sure and demanding as he pulled her against him so they were pressed together from head to toe.

She focused on the feel of his lips, on the way he held her like he'd never let go.

She focused on that and let all thoughts of the future drift away.

There was all the time in the world for heartache...after she left.

But for right now? Right here in his arms...

She was home. She was happy. And maybe...

Maybe even loved.

CHAPTER 29

I *love you.*
The words were on the tip of Cody's tongue when he held her in his arms out by the grove of trees, and they threatened to spill out of him again when he helped her off Mabel in the stables.

But if he let those words tumble out, he wasn't sure he could stop what would come next.

Stay.

Don't go.

He didn't want to go there. Not yet. They couldn't go on pretending like this wasn't going to end, but for today she was here, and so was he. And he meant to make the most of every second.

"So, what's next?" He took her hand and led her out of the stables, back toward the house. "You hungry? I don't have much at the bunkhouse, but I'm sure Emma won't mind if we raid the fridge."

Her small smile when she peeked up at him was filled with mischief. "I actually had an idea…"

"Why did I get a chill just now?" he teased.

Her answering laugh made him warm all over. "Nothing to be scared of, Cowboy."

"Who said I was scared? Just wary, that's all. Something tells me I'm gonna pay for teasing you about being afraid of Mabel."

She arched a brow. "Oh, you figured that out, did you?" She gave his hand a tug, dragging him toward the parking area next to the main house.

"Where are we going?"

She turned around so she was walking backward, still tugging him along, which made him laugh. "Your turn for a lesson in riding." She wiggled her eyebrows. "You, my friend, are gonna learn to ride a motorcycle."

His lungs hitched, and air rushed out of him. Man, she was gorgeous. Not just pretty—although there was no doubt that she was a beautiful woman. But it was more than that. When he looked at her now, her red hair vibrant in the sunlight, her eyes sparkling with laughter, her whole body buzzing with this energy that was so uniquely her…

She was beautiful, yes, but not just in her looks. She was stunning, inside and out. Sierra McNeal was one of a kind.

Unforgettable.

He stopped walking, and she stumbled to a stop as well when he dug in his heels and tugged her into his arms for a quick, crushing kiss.

When he lifted his head, she was breathless and smiling. "What was that for, Cowboy?"

That was a kiss to remember.

That was so you'll never forget me.

"That was a kiss goodbye in case your lessons lead to my demise."

Her head fell back as she let out a loud laugh. "Oh, ye of little faith. I promise you're in good hands."

He grumbled some more just to hear that laugh again, but when they came to a stop beside the beast of a bike, he didn't have to feign nervousness.

Or excitement.

"You're really gonna trust me to ride this?" He scratched the back of his head. "I don't want to hurt your precious baby here."

She nudged him with her elbow. "I trust you. And besides…" She glanced around the open space meaningfully. "This is a safe area to practice in."

"True." He turned to her. "Okay, Teach, where do we start?"

A little while later, he was straddling the motorcycle, and Sierra was watching him with unabashed glee.

"I'm not gonna lie, Cowboy. You look good on my bike."

He chuckled. He knew the feeling. His heart just about burst out of his chest when he'd first seen her on a horse. There was something about seeing the woman he loved showing a genuine interest in his world that made his heart full.

"You ready?" she asked.

"As I'll ever be," he shot back.

He took off, and after a sharp jolt of fear, there came a rush of exhilaration. He let out a whoop as adrenaline blasted through him. But he didn't go far.

"You all right?" Sierra asked when he circled back toward her.

"I'm great." He nodded toward the space behind him. "But I'd be better with your arms wrapped around me."

Her giggle was adorable, and she climbed on. "Start slow, Cowboy."

He nodded as he revved the motor. He'd go slow, all right. There was no way he'd risk her safety. She was the most important thing in the world to him.

The thought had him reaching down to grab her hands and tug her arms around him even tighter. "Don't let go!"

He felt her head on his shoulder as she spoke in his ear. "I'm not going anywhere."

Oh, how he wished that was true. But for now he focused on the sound of her laughter, the feel of her arms, the adrenaline rush that came from trying something new.

When he was done with his lesson, Sierra hopped off and headed straight for the house.

"Where're you going?" he called out.

She turned back with a wink. "I have another idea."

He arched his brows. "Another lesson?"

"More like an adventure," she shot back.

She ran inside and hurried back out a minute later, a big bag hanging from her shoulder. She put the bag under the seat and then playfully pushed him toward the back. "Okay, hotshot. I think you drove enough for one afternoon. The highway is all mine."

"The highway, huh? Where are we headed?"

"That's for me to know and you to find out." Her saucy tone made him grin.

"An adventure," he murmured, echoing her words from earlier.

"Exactly."

He did as she asked, sliding his arms around her waist as they took off down the long winding dirt road toward the highway.

Off on an adventure. He didn't miss the way her tone

was filled with excitement, how she seemed to come alive today as they tried new things and set off for new places.

And this was what life was all about for her.

He could see that.

Heck, he understood it. No, he more than understood it. If he were being honest, some part of him yearned for it —the new experiences, the fresh start, the rush of exploring outside of the tried-and-true.

His mind flitted and circled as he held on to this woman who was leading them down side roads and winding valleys.

Eventually, she came to a stop at a trailhead he'd never seen before. She dismounted, got out the bag, and set off.

"You know where you're going?" he asked.

"Not really." She shrugged. "One of the guys at Cal's Coffee Shop said the prettiest view in all of Montana was up this way."

"Then what are we waiting for?" Cody snagged the bag from her and threw it over his shoulder, taking her hand in his as they wove their way up a rough, uneven trail.

It was a challenging climb, and he eventually had to let go of her hand. The trail narrowed to only allow one person at a time, so he followed her up the steepest part, huffing and puffing more than he felt he should.

Sweat soaked into his shirt, and he wiped his brow with his forearm, wondering how much farther. Sierra still seemed to be bouncing with energy, and he couldn't let on how much his thighs were burning.

But then they reached the top, the path opened up to a lookout point, and his breath was stolen in a whole different way.

"It's amazing," Sierra whispered.

The sun was just starting to sink in the sky, and an orange glow made the valley and meadows below look like something straight out of a painting. Cody dumped the bag on the ground and wrapped his arms around her from behind, nestling his chin on her shoulder. She leaned back against him with a sigh.

"I can't believe I didn't even know this was here," he murmured.

"There's nothing better than exploring and finding a new magical place, you know?"

Her voice sounded dreamy, and he only managed to murmur his agreement because…how would he know? He'd always been intrigued by the world outside his town and this state, but he'd never gone far.

And now…

The thought was there. A hope dangling in front of him, sparkling in the breeze like a mirage.

What if he left?

What if he went with her?

She turned in his arms. "I'm glad I got to see this with you," she whispered. She went up on tiptoe and gave him a soft, sweet kiss. "I've always loved exploring, but I never knew how much better it could be to share it with someone."

He saw the vulnerability in her eyes, felt her yearning the way he did.

He held her close, burying his nose in her hair. They'd made some sort of unspoken agreement not to talk about the future, but right now it was hard not to think about it.

"Sierra, I…" He didn't know how to finish.

I want to go, but I can't.

That was what he should say.

I'm needed here.

That was who he was. His family and his friends were what made him Cody. It certainly wasn't his job. So if he walked away... If it turned out they didn't need him...

She lifted a hand and touched his cheek. "Hey, it's okay." Her smile was sweet and only a little sad. "We've got today, right? We've got this." She turned her head to stare out at the magnificent view. "And this is perfect."

Something settled inside him at the reminder to be in the here and now. He tightened his grip on her, and together they stared out at God's green earth spread out like a gift.

"Thank you for bringing me here," he murmured.

"Don't thank me yet." She tugged out of his arms and headed toward the bag, pulling it open and taking out food and a small blanket.

"You packed a picnic?" He grinned.

"I did. I hope you're okay with Chinese food. I snagged yesterday's leftovers."

"I'm game to try anything." He sat beside her. "But I want to hear all about how you learned to make this and everything you saw when you were there."

She smiled brightly. "Really?"

He nodded. "I want to know all there is about you, Sierra."

And maybe...

Maybe some part of him wanted to hear about her travels and adventures so he could live vicariously through her.

Turned out she was a fantastic storyteller, and she had him in stitches with her stories about her first assignment overseas. And the more she talked, the more he felt himself come alive inside, like he really was experiencing her excitement and awe, curiosity and passion as she roamed the world and took care of people who needed her help.

"You really are amazing, Sierra."

The sun was sinking lower in the sky, and the reddish-orange glow made him feel like there really was magic in the world as he pulled her into his arms, kissing her senseless as they basked in the last rays of light.

"I will never forget this day, Cowboy," she whispered, touching his cheek with a smile that made his heart full.

"Neither will I."

His voice was husky, and in his mind, he added, *I'll never forget* you.

CHAPTER 30

Sierra was still on cloud nine.

She actually found herself humming as she got ready for the day. *Humming.*

She was *not* a hummer.

But apparently Cody had this effect on her. She didn't know how long had passed when she blinked in front of the mirror and realized she'd just been standing there daydreaming. Reliving Cody's kisses, his smiles, the way he'd held her as the sun sank low in the sky.

With a rueful huff of amusement at her own ridiculously giddy state, she snatched her room key and headed for the door. She grinned as she raced toward the lobby, waved at Tom, the weekday manager, and hurried out the front door and into the sunshine.

She turned toward Main Street and tipped her face up to soak in the warm rays.

What a glorious day.

And she was honestly looking forward to it. She'd told Lizzy she'd swing by to see the boutique, and after that, she'd promised to have lunch with Rose and Kiara. And maybe if Cody got done with work early—

"Sierra!"

She stopped short on the edge of the inn's parking lot, her heart falling before she even fully registered what was happening.

But of course, she'd recognize her mother's voice anywhere, and when she saw her climbing out of a rental car in the parking lot, the smile she couldn't help wearing all morning suddenly faltered and fell.

Guilt followed swiftly on the heels of this overwhelming disappointment.

She shouldn't be upset to see her own flesh and blood. This was the woman who'd raised her, for heaven's sake. All their differences aside, she loved her mother, and her mother loved her. It was just...

"Sierra, come help me with my bags." Her mother waved her over to the car.

Sierra dutifully did as she was told, forcing a smile into place. "What are you doing here? You didn't say anything about coming to visit."

"It was a last-minute decision." Her mom handed her a bag from the trunk and arched a brow in a look that oozed disapproval. "Thought I better come check on my daughter. You've been acting strangely, and a mother knows when something is off."

"I told you, I've been busy trying to—"

"I know what you said," she interrupted with a dismissive wave. "But I can hear it in your voice."

"Hear what?" Sierra followed her mother toward the lobby, struggling to keep up with the brisk pace.

"You're letting them get to you," she muttered.

They stepped in the cool, dark lobby and waited for Tom to finish his call.

"I don't know what you mean," Sierra whispered.

"Oh, please." Her mother's look was frustratingly patronizing. "You've always been too much of a bleeding heart. Always taking care of others rather than worrying about yourself."

Some part of Sierra wanted to remind her mom that she'd taken care of *her* all her life. But she'd left that resentment behind when she left home and started her own life.

"It's plain as day what's happening here." Her mother's tone turned sharp and bitter. "That family is taking advantage of you."

"What? Ma, no—"

"Don't try and deny it. I can read between the lines. Those...*women*"—somehow her mother made *women* sound like a curse word—"are making you feel sorry for them. Making you think you have some sort of loyalty to them—"

"Well, they are my sisters."

"They are *not* your sisters." Her mom's cheeks splashed red, her gaze scorching. "That man was no father to you, and his other children have no place in your life."

For a moment, Sierra just stared, her lips parted in shock at her mother's rage.

She should have been used to this anger. She'd spent her childhood trying to soothe it and her adult life either steering clear or walking on eggshells to avoid it. But this was different. It wasn't her mother's typical woe-is-me, self-righteous anger at the lot she'd been given. This seemed personal. Like she was genuinely angry at the O'Sullivan sisters. But for what?

For simply existing?

"Ma, Frank's daughters..." She stopped and started again. "My sisters shouldn't be punished for the sins of their father. They have just as much right—"

"No!" her mother snapped. "*You* are the oldest. And he didn't abandon the others."

"Yes he did. He left *us*," she shot back. "*All* of us." *Except April*, she supposed. But her mother didn't need to know the details. "Look, it doesn't even matter anymore. He's dead."

Her words seemed to echo off the lobby walls now that Tom had ended his call. His jaw clenched as he peered at the computer screen like he was trying to decipher an ancient text and fool them into thinking he couldn't hear every word they were saying.

Sierra took a deep breath and lowered her voice so only her mom could hear. "Frank's gone, Ma, and no inheritance is going to change what he did to me or you or any of my sisters. It won't bring him back or answer any questions."

Her mother eyed her for a long moment, pursing her lips as she blinked and then inhaled a delicate sniff. But rather than respond, she turned to Tom. "I called earlier about a room?"

Sierra sighed, her shoulders slumping while Tom made the arrangements. When they were done and her mom's bags were put away, they headed back outside, agreeing it was too nice out to stay indoors.

Sierra automatically headed toward Main Street, but her wariness grew to full trepidation the closer they got. She was starting to be familiar with the locals, and if they ran into one of the O'Sullivan sisters, she didn't know what she'd say or how to explain the icy woman beside her. The cold vibes coming off her mother as they clipped along the street were enough to give the sun a run for its money.

"Let's hop in here." She directed her mom into Cal's, quietly praying one of the tables in the back corner would be empty.

"I guess." Her mother sighed. "It's not like there are any other options in this town."

Sierra bit her tongue. She was actually starting to like it here. Not that she wanted to make it her permanent home…

No matter how tempting a certain cowboy made that seem.

She didn't. She couldn't.

There were kids in Venezuela counting on her.

Cal's was nearly empty when they walked in—not even Norman and his coffee crew were there—and Sierra let out a breath of relief as they ordered. But she'd sighed too soon, because no sooner had they sat down than Daisy burst in, a whirl of flowing material and exuberant smiles.

She spotted them immediately, in spite of Sierra's attempts to hide in the back corner.

"Hi there!" Daisy waved and bounced over to their table, her blonde curls dancing. "You have *got* to be Sierra's mother. Look at you two!" She pointed between them. "The family likeness is striking. Oh my goodness, what a treat." She took Sierra's mother's hand and pumped it, holding on to it as she sat at their table.

"Um, Daisy, this is actually not a great—"

"Oh, how rude of me. I'm Daisy, Frank's third oldest… no, fourth?" She pursed her lips and then grinned. "No, I was right. I'm third in line when it comes to this wild family."

For a second, Sierra feared her mother had suffered a

stroke. She stared wide-eyed and tongue-tied for so long. "You're...uh, you're one of them?"

If Daisy noticed the slight sneer and the rude way she'd said "them," she didn't let on, smiling and laughing and regaling Sierra's mother with the story of how she'd first come to town and the way she'd met her boyfriend, the sheriff, and...

And Sierra couldn't believe it. Her hard-as-nails, bitter, jaded mother was actually warming up to Daisy.

Sierra watched in awe as the whimsical woman charmed her mom like some con artist.

But, of course, she wasn't a con artist, she was just... Daisy. Charming, sweet, lovable Daisy. And her mother was just as hopeless in the face of her charm as Levi, his kids, or even Sierra.

All three of them were soon laughing and chatting easily enough, but Sierra tensed all over again when Daisy looked at her phone and winced. "Ugh, look at the time. I promised Mikayla we'd hang out this afternoon, so I'd better scoot." She got up and then bent over to give them both air kisses next to their cheeks. "See you soon, Sierra! Jessica, such a pleasure to meet you."

"You too." Sierra's mother smiled.

Daisy grinned and whirled out with the same bizarrely cheerful energy she'd brought in.

The following silence felt deafening.

But then her mother broke it with a light sigh. "She's a sweet girl."

"Mmm."

Her mom's eyes narrowed. "Are they all like that?"

"Uh, no. Not really. But they're all nice and smart and...and unique. I haven't met two of them yet, though, but I imagine they're just as kind."

Well, maybe not Dahlia. But Cody spoke highly of her and seemed to think her match with JJ had been made in heaven, and honestly…

If Cody thought she was great, that was enough for Sierra.

Which was…alarming.

"Why are you frowning like that? What aren't you telling me?" Her mother nudged her elbow.

"Nothing, I just… I was just thinking of someone."

Her mom arched her brows in a silent question, but Sierra quickly changed the topic. "I know you only met Daisy, but I'm guessing that's enough for you to see that Frank's daughters aren't the enemy here, Ma."

Her mother looked troubled, her brow furrowed like she wanted to protest. But eventually she dropped her gaze to the coffee mug in her hand and sighed. "I suppose you're right. It's just…I hate to think of him having other families, that's all."

Sierra nodded. "I know."

"After the way he abandoned me." Her voice shook, her eyebrows dipping together. "Abandoned *us*."

The questions she'd been stewing on but hadn't wanted to ask couldn't be contained any longer. "Ma…did he leave you or us?"

Her mother's head snapped up. "What?"

"I mean…" Sierra shrugged. "You've told me so little. I think it's time I hear the full story."

There was a pleading to her voice that Sierra hated, but her mom softened, the look in her eyes growing distant and glassy.

"We were high school sweethearts."

Sierra stopped breathing for a moment, afraid that if she so much as uttered a sound, her mother would stop.

But she continued in a low voice, "I was a junior, he was a senior, and we connected over the summer. I fell desperately in love with him, and my junior year was the best one I'd ever had. We spent every moment we could together, and I thought after he graduated that he would find a college nearby and we'd spend the rest of our lives together. Or if he chose a school far away, we could do long-distance for a year, and then I'd join him. We'd eventually get married, and…" She laughed bitterly. "I had it all mapped out, so confident that my dreams would come true."

Sierra sighed, her insides churning. "But let me guess. You got pregnant, and he dumped you."

Her mother stared at the table, shaking her head. "He broke up with me right after prom. Told me what we'd had was fun and beautiful but couldn't go beyond high school. He had bigger plans for his future. Plans that didn't include me." She blinked, her chin trembling as she rasped, "I was heartbroken."

"Did he know about me?"

"I didn't even know about you at that point." Her mom let out a fractured laugh that made Sierra's heart bleed.

"I found out after he left." She sniffled, then snatched a napkin and quickly dabbed her nose. "I didn't tell him because…well, because he left. He left me. I was hurt and angry and wounded. I didn't want him coming back out of obligation, and…and so I made sure he couldn't be your father. I left his name off your birth certificate. I…I put *unknown*. Because I didn't know the man who walked away from me. The Frank O'Sullivan I fell in love with disappeared the day he left me crying on my porch steps! He didn't even look back when I called his name and begged him to stay with me." She huffed, and Sierra could see it. That pride that had kept her mother strong in the face of every problem.

The pride she'd inherited.

"You didn't want him coming back for me and not you," she whispered.

Her mother looked away. "He found out about you when you were four. Bumped into one of his old buddies from high school, and they got chatting. He worked out that you must be his."

Sierra swallowed. "Did I ever…? Did he ever…?"

"You never met," she clipped. "I had my parents run interference, and they told him he wasn't wanted. So he started sending cards with some birthday money, and…" She grunted. "A handful of cash. What was I supposed to do with that?"

A jolt of surprise ran through Sierra. "He sent money? Why didn't you tell me? What did you do with it?" The words snapped out of her, probably harsher than she meant them to.

"I put it into an account and spent it on the things you needed. But it was hardly the child support you truly needed. I bought you shoes and school supplies. It wasn't much, Sierra. When I think about the fact that he *owned* a ranch, it makes my blood boil." Her mother sniffed. "He could have done a lot more if he'd wanted to."

Sierra bit her tongue, stopping herself from pointing out that her mom had kept them on the move constantly. How was he supposed to track them down? And he'd had no rights, so how was he supposed to fight for her?

Although… Sierra's eyes stung. He could have fought for her. He could have tried harder and done more. He could have sent child support, gone through the courts for visiting rights.

Why didn't he do that?

She kept her gaze on the table.

"He wouldn't have been a good father to you, Sierra," her mother whispered. "I was afraid he'd come into your life and then leave again, and I didn't want you to go through that heartache. It nearly destroyed me. You were the only thing keeping me steady. I had to be strong for you, so I was. But I couldn't bring that man back into my life. I couldn't taint yours with his broken promises." Sierra nodded. Her gaze was still on the table, and she saw her mother's hand come into view to cover hers. "I'm sorry."

Sierra nodded again. She couldn't bring herself to say, "It's okay," but she appreciated the words. They sat in silence for a long moment until Sierra finally shook off the wave of regret and anger.

Man, she was so tired of being angry.

So she straightened and met her mother's gaze. "Tell me about him."

"What?" Her mom's eyes widened.

"Tell me something nice. Tell me what he was like in high school. Tell me..." She took a deep breath, her thoughts inexplicably flying to a certain cowboy with the slow, easy smile. "Tell me what it was like when you first fell in love."

CHAPTER 31

Cody answered on the first ring, even though there was no privacy to be found in the ranch's office where he, Kit, and Boone had congregated after their morning chores.

"Hey, Sierra," he said quickly before she even had a chance to speak

"Hey, Sierra," Kit said behind him, his voice high and singsongy like they were still children.

Cody swatted him upside the head, making Boone crack up.

"Hey." Her voice seemed a little shaky. "Do you have a minute to talk? I tried calling you on your cell phone, but it just went straight to voice mail, and I'm kind of desperate to get this off my chest, so I called the ranch. Is that okay? I—"

"Of course that's okay." He kept his voice soft and sweet, hoping to soothe whatever was upsetting her. "Sorry about my phone. I forgot to charge it last night, and it died about half an hour ago. What's up?"

Sierra's sigh was heavy. "My mother's in town." And then she started talking. And talking. And talking.

He stuck a finger in his ear to tune out Kit and Boone's banter as Sierra filled him in on her mother's arrival and the conversation they'd had about her father.

Finally.

It seemed a crying shame to Cody that her mother hadn't told her anything about her own father all these years.

But Sierra was clearly relieved and excited, and maybe a little shook up, to finally have some image of the man in her mind's eye.

"See the way he's hanging on her every word?" Kit was saying behind him.

"Oh yeah, he's done for, all right." Boone laughed. "Poor guy."

Cody rolled his eyes and turned his back on them, not wanting to miss a single word. It wasn't like Sierra to open up like this. Or...it hadn't been like her when she'd first arrived. But the more they got to know each other, and the more she trusted him, the more she let him in.

And the more he got to know her, the more he loved her.

So yeah. Maybe Boone had a point.

Cody was done for. He'd lost his heart to this woman, and there was no getting it back.

"That's great." He smiled after she'd finished, wishing she could see his face. Wishing he could brush his fingers down her cheek and pull her in for a hug. "I'm happy for you."

"I'm happy for you," Kit said in a high voice.

Cody ignored him.

"Is that your brother?" Sierra asked.

"Uh…"

Her tone was light and amused. "Tell Kit I'm on my way to see Lizzy at the boutique right now, and if he doesn't stop teasing you, I'm gonna tell his wife."

Cody snickered, then repeated her words, making Boone double over with laughter.

Kit immediately held up his hands in surrender, his eyes wide with feigned innocence. "I didn't say nothin'," he drawled.

Sierra started laughing on the other end.

Boone winked as he walked past Cody to the office door, clapping a hand on Cody's shoulder as he went. "I like this one. She's a keeper."

As if Cody didn't know that.

"Yeah, yeah, she's cool," Kit admitted. But he made no move to leave and give Cody any privacy.

"Brothers," Cody muttered with a weary sigh.

"Tell me about it," Sierra laughed. "Try inheriting six sisters at once."

"Yeah, okay, you got me beat." He dipped his head to hide his no-doubt goofy grin. The last thing he needed was to give his brother even more of an excuse to tease him for being a fool in love.

"Thanks for listening," Sierra said.

"Anytime." Cody shifted from foot to foot as her silence grew.

"I think… I wanted to tell you…"

His stomach twisted with apprehension. "What is it?"

"I think I'm going to take off for a few days."

"Oh."

When she started talking again, her voice seemed rushed. "I've been having so much fun spending time with you, Cody, but the truth is, I came here to meet my father.

And that's not going to happen, obviously. But my time here is limited, and I know I'd regret it if I don't try and get some more information about this man. I want to head to where he last lived and see if I can find someone who knew him recently and can tell me a little more about him. It's not that I want to leave you. I just—"

"Sierra," he cut in as gently as he could. He was all too aware of Kit's eyes on him, and the fact that Nash had just walked in, so he lowered his voice. "I get it. I do."

"Oh." She let out a shaky breath, and now his heart seemed to twist into a knot as well as his gut. He already ached with missing her, and she hadn't even left yet.

"Thank you," she whispered.

"Don't thank me. I know why you came here. And I know…" His jaw ticked as emotions coursed through him. "I know you have to go."

She was quiet for a moment. He suspected they were both thinking about her final departure, not just her short trip to find out more about her father.

"I won't be gone long. Heading to the last place he lived seems like a good place to start. Maybe I'll even find April if I actually set out and look…"

"Maybe," he agreed.

The silence felt heavy, and he hated it. He didn't want to say goodbye. Not even for a short trip. And soon enough he'd be saying goodbye forever.

The thought was crushing.

"Is your mother going with you?" he asked.

"No. She has a job to get back to."

"Gotcha." He was nodding, trying to keep his voice even while his insides were shredded.

"Cody, we gotta go." Kit tapped him on the shoulder.

"We can talk later," Sierra murmured.

"Yeah. Okay." He hung up, but for a second, he couldn't turn around and pretend everything was okay.

Their time together was already short, and now he was going to lose whole days while she went off on an adventure.

Alone.

Or...not alone.

He blinked and took a deep breath, his chest expanding as a new idea sparked inside him. "Boss..."

Nash turned to face him. "What's up?"

"Do you think I could take off for a few days?"

"You sick?" Kit asked. "You never have time off."

Cody shook his head. "Sierra's going on the road to find some more information on Frank, and...I want to go with her."

"Dude," Kit snickered. "You're so whipped."

"Shut up," Cody muttered, never looking away from Nash. "I know we're shorthanded without JJ, but Boone's here, and we got that new kid coming tomorrow. I can show him the ropes, make sure he's good to go and—"

"Cody," Kit interrupted, and his joking tone had faded to one far more sober. "I thought she wasn't sticking around for long. Just how serious are you getting?"

Cody didn't answer. He suspected he didn't have to. It was likely obvious to everyone already.

Nash's brows drew down, his expression clouding with concern. "It's nice of you to want to do this for her—"

"It's not *for* her." Something leapt inside him as he realized the truth of this statement. He'd spent most of his life doing everything for others. Worrying more about what his family and friends needed and wanted, and never stopping to ask what he wanted for himself.

Kit's brows were arched in surprise when Cody

glanced his way before turning back to Nash with a grim expression of his own. "I'm not asking for time off for Sierra's sake. The woman is stronger than most anyone I know. I'm asking for me. Because my time with her is limited, and I want to be there while I can."

Both men seemed stunned speechless as they stared at him.

Irritation flared, the same choking sensation he'd been experiencing ever since the first night he met Sierra.

No, maybe before that. Maybe he just hadn't noticed it before.

He hadn't wanted to.

"Look, Nash, I never ask for favors. I never call in sick unless I'm puking my guts out, and I'm the first to cover when you need an extra set of hands."

"Yeah, I know that," Nash started.

He turned to Kit. "I'm always there when you need me, and I'm the one to take care of things for Mom and Dad."

"No one's arguing that, Cody." Kit's tone was quiet, filled with concern.

Cody's hands clenched and unclenched as he tried to fight this surge of anger—no, resentment. He was always putting others first, and just this once he wanted to be selfish.

Because she'd be leaving, and he'd stay here, and he'd be doing it for them. For all of them. All the people who counted on him.

Because they needed him…

Didn't they?

"I hope you know we don't take you for granted around here," Nash murmured. "We appreciate what a loyal ranch hand you are." His brows knit together. "If we've made you feel like that—"

"No," Cody said quickly. Because he knew he was appreciated. He knew he was loved.

But are you needed?

It was a nagging voice in the back of his head. It was his own thought, but he heard Sierra's voice in there too. Kind and sweet…and brutally honest.

"You don't take me for granted." He looked at his boss. "But I guess I'm just saying, after all these years of not asking for anything…this is me asking for something I really want."

Kit continued to stare at him like Cody was a talking fish as Nash scratched the back of his neck, then shrugged. "Yeah, okay. You're right, Cody. You never ask, so this must be important to you."

He nodded. "*She's* important to me."

He shot Kit a sidelong glance, but Kit didn't mock or tease.

Cody supposed if anyone knew what it was like to have a woman come along and become the sun around which your world orbited, it was these two.

And that was him. He was drawn to Sierra in a way he couldn't explain. She lit up his life and made him feel whole inside. Like a piece of the puzzle he hadn't known he'd been missing.

"Then you should go." Nash nodded.

"Thank you." He breathed out the words and shot his boss a grateful smile.

He was itching to tell Sierra the news.

They were going on another adventure.

A smile tugged at his lips as dialed up the motel to ask for her room. He couldn't wait to tell her. He couldn't wait to go.

CHAPTER 32

S ierra eyed Cody standing next to her motorcycle. She took a deep breath to settle her fluttering belly.

Would the sight of him ever get old?

Highly unlikely.

"Where to first, Hustler?" he said as he sauntered toward her. He caught her by the waist and gave her a too-quick kiss before stealing her bag from her to stow it.

"Why? You impatient to get on the road?" she teased him. "Don't tell me you're getting the travel bug, Cowboy."

He shot her a lopsided little smile. "Must be contagious."

I wish. She swallowed the words. After he'd called to tell her he was coming along for the ride, she'd made a promise to herself not to talk about the future.

It would be on her mind—no doubt his too—but he hadn't once tried to guilt-trip her into staying, and she wouldn't try to sway him to leave. The fact that he wasn't trying to make her stay made him that much more lovable.

It showed he understood her. He respected her.

And she'd do the same for him. She might not love that he felt like he had to stay for the sake of his family and friends, but she could respect it. She'd seen enough of the bond he shared with the others at the ranch, and with his parents and niece and nephew.

He wouldn't be Cody if he didn't feel a sense of loyalty and obligation toward them.

"Well?" He turned back after stowing her gear to see her standing there staring like an idiot.

She gave her head a quick shake. "Well, we know he and his wife were in Bozeman for the last year of her life, so they could be close to the hospital. I'm assuming he and April stayed there after she'd died." She pursed her lips as she thought through everything her sisters had told her when they'd gathered for dinner at Rose's house the night before...

Like the surprise pregnancy reveal party, they'd dialed Dahlia in, and Sierra had explained to them all what she was setting out to do.

"You want to find out more about our father?" Dahlia sounded angry at first, and Rose and Daisy shared a funny look Sierra hadn't been able to decipher.

"I didn't even know his name until a few weeks ago," Sierra said with a helpless shrug. "I didn't know he'd been sending cards. My mom only just told me there'd been money inside each one, like maybe..." Her voiced had trailed off, stolen away by the other women's stares.

Did she sound as pathetic to them as she did to herself?

But Rose cut the silence. "I get it, Sierra." She glanced around. "We all do."

"Of course we do," Dahlia agreed in that same snappy

tone. "He's a mystery to all of us, and it's only natural to want to know about your family. But what I want to know is…what does this mean regarding your potential lawsuit against the ranch?"

"I…" Sierra started and stopped, painfully aware of her sisters' eyes on her as she floundered for words.

Emma's were hopeful, Lizzy's held a hint of fear, Rose looked calm and knowing, and Daisy was giving her a sweet little smile like no matter what she said, Sierra was still welcome at this table.

"I dropped the idea of trying to grab the whole thing for myself right away." The words tumbled out quickly. "I would have told you that when you'd called the motel, Dahlia, but you steamrolled right over me."

There was a beat of silence, and then Daisy burst out laughing. "Of course she did. That's what Dahlia does best."

Everyone shared a laugh, but they were waiting for her to continue.

Sierra shifted uncomfortably. "I still don't think… I mean, it still seems nuts to me that Frank wants us all to agree, though."

There were a few nods—of understanding or agreement, she wasn't sure.

"I don't know what he was thinking." Sierra's brows lowered with a frown. "I guess that's one of the reasons I want to try and get to know him. To understand why he abandoned us all when he was alive but is forcing us to come together after his death like we're…like we're…"

"Family?" Emma suggested. She and Lizzy shared a knowing little smile that made Sierra swallow hard.

"Yeah. Exactly," Sierra mumbled.

There was a brief silence that felt kinda…nice as

Emma, Lizzy, Daisy, and Rose gave her affectionate grins that said they understood completely.

But then Dahlia spoke up. "So, I guess the question, then, is do you want to be a part of this family?"

Sierra stiffened. "It's not that simple."

"Isn't it?" Dahlia shot back.

Sierra's chest tightened. Was it? Was it that simple? She either wanted into this family or she didn't?

She pressed her lips together, her thoughts straying to Cody, wishing like heck that she could talk to him and figure it out. But the thought of him brought a rush of frustration she couldn't hold back. "Does being part of this family mean you're obligated to do what they want you to do?" she asked.

The words hung in the air.

"Shouldn't family mean that you can go anywhere and do anything, and they'll always have your back?" Sierra realized her hands were shaking as she reached for her water glass and took a big gulp, trying to calm this rush of emotions. "I'm honestly asking," she said, her gaze scanning the others, meeting their surprised stares. "I've only ever had my mom and my grandparents," she admitted. "So I guess I don't know what it means to be part of a family." She shrugged, feeling like the worst disappointment. "I'm sorry."

A heavy silence fell, and it was Dahlia who broke it tersely. "Don't be sorry."

Sierra's head snapped up in surprise.

"You're not wrong," Dahlia said. "Family means unconditional love. It means..." She trailed off, and they all heard a sniff, then "I'm fine, JJ. Stop fussing."

All four of the sisters looked like they were smothering smiles.

Sierra arched a brow at Daisy, who leaned forward to whisper, "Dahlia's only just figured out that she has emotions. It's like watching a baby bird learn to fly."

Sierra bit her lip to stop a laugh.

Then Dahlia let out a sharp exhale. "You're not wrong, Sierra. We just don't want to lose our home. I don't think any of us ever expected to have this, and...and we don't want to lose it."

Sierra nodded. "I get that. I do."

"But, seeing that you're not trying to steal it out from under us..." Dahlia's tone lightened with a rueful humor. "I'd say that's progress."

Sierra was rewarded with smiles all around, and she felt like a gigantic jerk for not clearing that up right away.

"Now." Dahlia cleared her throat. "Here's what I know about Frank O'Sullivan..."

Sierra was brought back to the moment with a start when Cody tugged her into his arms. He brushed some hair out of her face and tipped her chin to meet her gaze. "I lost you there. Where'd you go?"

Her lips parted, and for a moment, she thought about telling him all about the dinner and what had been said. But there'd be plenty of time for chatting on the road. And honestly, this newfound need to tell Cody every little detail of her life was unnerving.

She'd never felt the need to share before, but with him...

Oh heck. With him everything was different.

She smiled as she reached past him for his helmet. "Dahlia did some digging, and April's grandparents on her mother's side live in a town about two hours north of

Bozeman. I say we start there and see where that takes us."

"Yes, ma'am." He grinned, taking the other helmet she offered him.

"They're in Coleville," she said. "Do you know it?"

"I do." He paused while adjusting his helmet. "Hey, how much of a hurry are you in to get there?"

The glint of mischief in his eyes made her heart thump wildly. "Funny, I was going to ask you how much of a hurry you were in to get back."

He strode past her to the bike, calling over his shoulder, "You up for a little adventure along the way?"

"Always." She grinned as she hurried to keep up.

She had a side adventure in mind as well, but she couldn't wait to see what he had planned.

CHAPTER 33

Cody barely took in the scenic setting around him. He was too busy watching the awe that transformed Sierra's face.

"This is so cool," she exclaimed.

He slung an arm around her shoulders and breathed in the scent of her shampoo as he teasingly murmured into her hair, "You're so cool."

"Well, that's a given," she shot back. "But this..." She spread her arms out before her to take in the lush green canyon with the dilapidated remains of old structures. "This is amazing. Like...like the past is right here."

He nodded. "It's kind of a trip, right?"

She turned to him. "Are all ghost towns like this?"

He tipped his head from side to side. "Nah. Some are what they call living ghost towns. Basically a tourist trap to teach kids about regional history. They're fun, though. We can totally go to one of those, too, if you want."

She smiled and kindly didn't point out his gaffe.

When were they supposed to plan some big trip to

another ghost town when her time in Montana was almost up?

"But this..." He gestured ahead of them, where the remains of an old schoolhouse tilted sideways, the windows long gone and pieces of an old stove rusting in the stream beside it. "This is the real deal. The last remnants of an old mining village."

"Wow. It's crazy to think that this was once a bustling little town." She rested against his side. They were both tired out from the hike up here, and he heard his own stomach growl.

She clearly heard it, too, because she grinned up at him. "Guess we should start heading back. We've got a long hike and then another drive ahead of us before lunch."

"Speaking of lunch," he said slowly. "I've got another surprise."

A little while later, Cody was regretting many decisions.

"You want to quit, Cowboy?" Sierra teased as sweat trickled down his forehead and he sniffed.

He eyed the sauce-covered burrito before him with renewed determination. "I'm gonna finish."

Sierra laughed as she took a big bite of her own meal. "I can't believe there's a legit Mexican restaurant tucked away up in these mountains."

"Hey, people like Mexican food everywhere," he rasped.

"Just not necessarily spicy." Her tone held more than a hint of laughter.

And he deserved every bit of it for declaring that he could handle whatever she could when it came to spice. "Tell me, Hustler, were you always a fan of spicy food, or was it an acquired taste?"

"Always." She shrugged. "But I developed more of a tolerance for the high heat when I started traveling."

He went back to his food, which was delicious...when one got past the burning tongue.

"I wonder if I got that from my dad," Sierra blurted.

She looked a little embarrassed when he glanced up in surprise.

"It's just...my mom hates spicy food, so maybe..." She wrinkled her nose. "I guess I'm reaching, but for some reason, I feel like it would give me some closure if I could feel a sort of connection to the man." She looked down. "I know, it's silly—"

"It's not. It's human nature to want to belong. To be a part of something bigger."

Her lips hitched up on one side. "A caveman instinct to fit into the tribe?"

He arched a brow as he dug his fork into the food. "Hey, no one wants to be the weak straggler who gets picked off by the predator, and that's a fact."

"I'll take your word for it, Cowboy." She smirked. "Something tells me you know way more about the ways of the wild than I do."

"Maybe. But you know way more about the world outside Montana." He didn't actually mean to bring it up, but he couldn't hide the hint of wistfulness in his voice.

She caught it, too, because her head tilted to the side. "Are you ever curious...to explore, I mean?"

He nodded. No point in denying it. "Yeah. I think some part of me has always been curious. But it was just never in the cards, you know?"

She nodded, and the silence stretched. But before it could get awkward, she smiled and leaned forward to rest on her elbows, pushing the plate with its last few bites out of her way. "You ready for another adventure?"

"What do you have in mind?"

She beamed as she unfolded a tattered piece of paper that had been tucked in her back pocket. "Now, if you don't want to go…"

He lit up at the sight of the flyer. "Are you kidding me? I was dying to go to this concert when the bands were announced, but then JJ went and got married and decided to have the world's longest honeymoon. I didn't think I'd be able to get the time off to go. But then…" His voice trailed off as he caught the skeptical look in her eye.

"Seriously? You knew about this? It's all heavy rock, and they're kinda obscure bands. I only know the headliners, and that's because I love—"

"Zombie Town," he finished, a smile spreading across his face. "Me too."

"No way." She leaned back in her seat with a suspicious little smile. "I pegged you for a country western boy."

He lifted a shoulder. "I don't mind country now and again, but I love Zombie Town."

She turned back to the flyer, obviously unconvinced, like he was just saying this stuff to win her over. It made him want to laugh that she didn't believe him. Oh, how he was going to surprise this woman.

She pointed out the location, and he refrained from telling her that he was well aware of where it was. He'd been to this outdoor music festival before. It took place every summer and always got lots of attention because of the rowdy crowd. But since the stage and the campgrounds around it were in the middle of a rural area with nothing else nearby, no one threatened to shut it down.

Sierra bit her lip. "It's out of the way…"

A sense of urgency hit him hard, and he leaned forward to catch her hand. "I thought we agreed there was no rush on this trip."

She smiled and nodded. "You're right. April's grandparents will be there, and I…I want to make the most of our time, you know?"

He nodded. He definitely did know. That was his plan too. They couldn't extend this adventure indefinitely, but he planned to make the most of every second.

CHAPTER 34

Cody had never been happier...even as his current home tried to fly away.

"I don't think they gave us enough stakes," Sierra laughed as she looked up from the sleeping bag where she sat to see the tent wobbling wildly in the wind.

He grinned. "It'll hold."

"That's right, I forgot. I'm with an experienced camper." She leaned back on her elbows, the remains of their makeshift lunch of chips and beef jerky abandoned between their sleeping bags.

"Yes, ma'am."

She narrowed her eyes teasingly. "I'm gonna guess you were a Boy Scout."

"'Course I was," he shot back. "My mom was the town's scout leader."

She burst into giggles that made his grin widen. "I can totally imagine that."

The wind picked up, and they both glanced to the left corner, where the tent did look a little loose. "I'll fix it," he said.

"No rush." She smiled brightly. "We've got a little time before the next band goes on."

"Just so long as we find a good spot in time for the headliners," he agreed with a nod.

She shook her head. "I still can't believe you like Zombie Town."

"You didn't believe I liked yesterday's headliner either, if you'll recall." His tone was smug, but he couldn't help it. He still grinned every time he thought of her gaping shock when he'd burst out singing along with the chorus last night, knowing every word.

Honestly, it had been like that since they'd arrived at the campground the afternoon before. They'd bought this well-used tent and some sleeping bags at a thrift store in a neighboring town and then joined the rest of the concertgoers for a whole lot of singing and dancing. And throughout it all, he and Sierra kept surprising each other.

He'd seen a whole new side of her when she'd started dancing, the carefree, youthful part of her she kept so well hidden. Then last night, they'd stayed up late in their little tent, telling each other stories from their lives, stealing kisses, and sharing secrets until their voices turned to whispers and sleep stole over them.

He'd woken to find her snuggled against his side this morning, both still in their respective sleeping bags—but they'd managed to seek each other out in the night despite that.

For a long while, he'd watched her sleep, his heart aching at the vulnerability and softness he saw in her features and marveling at the way she trusted him.

Then she'd woken, and in seconds she was filled with that vibrant energy that was so very Sierra. She'd shot up, announcing that they needed to explore while the rest of the campers were sound asleep.

And so he'd followed her on a morning walk around the grounds, then on a drive into town for breakfast.

The seconds and minutes and hours seemed to be flying past, and they both knew it couldn't last. None of it.

Zombie Town was the last band of the night, and tomorrow morning they'd set out bright and early for the town where April's grandparents lived.

Maybe Sierra's mind was heading in the same direction, because she sprang to her feet. "Come on, let's go find a good spot."

Cody paused to fix the tent, and then they were on their way, threading through the crowd hand in hand.

"I can't believe it's taken me six years to come back here," he admitted.

She shot him a grin. "I can't either. It's so close to you."

"I know, I just… I guess I didn't have anyone to go with." Even now, he couldn't imagine his friends or family enjoying this. The only reason he'd come last time was because one of the summer ranch hands had talked him into a day trip. The guy had since moved on, and Cody was once again the only hard rocker on the ranch.

Sierra's expression turned coy. "So, what are you going to do without me when I'm gone?" She nudged him with her hip. "Admit it, you're gonna miss me. You're gonna be sooo sad and never leave the ranch again and—"

He cut her off with a kiss. After a second of shocked rigidity, she sank into him, her lips curving up in a smile when he drew back from the kiss. "What was that for, Cowboy?"

"Just getting in all the kisses I can." The band started to play—a local band, more country than hard rock, but right about now, Cody welcomed the slower, softer music as he held Sierra in his arms. He leaned down until his nose grazed hers. "Because you're right. I am gonna miss you, Sierra."

She wrapped her arms around his neck, and together they started swaying in time to the music, their bodies in sync as if they'd been moving together for decades and not days. She kept her gaze straight ahead so she was looking over his shoulder when she whispered, "I wish I didn't have to leave you."

His heart leapt with hope, even though he knew very well it was hopeless. Still, he found himself saying the words he'd promised himself he wouldn't. "Then don't. Don't go." His arms tightened around her waist as she glanced at him in surprise. Some part of his mind was telling him to stop, to not pressure her when he knew very well why she had to go. But that reasonable part of his mind was drowned out by the crushing emotions that filled his chest at the thought of letting her go. "Stay with me, Sierra."

"Cody, I…" She wet her lips, her expression pained.

And he knew what she was going to say. Of course she wouldn't stay here just for him. He started to look away, but her hand came up and caught his cheek, forcing him to look at her.

"I shouldn't have teased you about me leaving," she murmured. "I guess I'm just…I'm a little tired of avoiding the elephant in the room, you know?"

He nodded. They'd been dancing around the topic of her leaving for days now, and she was right. Avoiding it wasn't making it go away, and it wasn't making it easier. His jaw worked, and his voice was too low when he croaked, "I shouldn't have asked you to stay."

Her expression was unbearably sad. "Cody, when I said I don't want to leave, I meant...I meant I don't want to leave *you*."

His grip on her tightened, as if he could hold her tightly enough that he'd never have to let her go. "Then don't." He hated the desperation that tinged his voice. "Don't go if you don't want to. I'm sure your work can find a replacement, and—"

"Cody, I meant I want you to come with me." She said it abruptly, and the vulnerability in her eyes took his breath away as surely as if she'd just punched him in the gut. Her throat worked as she swallowed. "I know I shouldn't ask... I know I don't have any right..."

"Sierra," he started slowly, his heart aching.

She wanted him to come with her. She wanted to be with him as much as he wanted to be with her.

She lowered her hands from his neck to his white T-shirt, and her fingers curled into the fabric as she held on to him. "I've seen the way you light up when I talk about my travels. I see the hunger in your eyes when you ask me about different countries and cultures and languages..."

"I'm curious, sure," he admitted. "I've always wondered what it would be like to travel."

Her eyes brightened with a hope that made him flinch. He didn't want to crush it, but couldn't she see? "My life is here, Sierra."

Her eyes dimmed as she nodded. "I know. I just... Just think about it, okay?" Her lips hitched in a sad little smile. "And trust me when I say that seeing you on the road like this, trying new things and having adventures..." She went up on tiptoe and kissed him hard. "It's like watching you come alive, you know?"

He was speechless, because...yeah. He did know. He'd

felt more alive these last few days than he ever had in his life. Heck, since the day he first met her, he'd felt it starting —an old curiosity turning into something living, breathing…undeniable.

Just as undeniable as she was.

She cupped his face as she moved back to meet his gaze. "I won't pressure you, and I won't make you feel guilty. All I ask is that you consider what I said, okay?"

He nodded, incapable of speech.

"Now." She let out a sharp exhale, and her smile widened, rueful and sweet. "What do you say we go back to enjoying our time together, huh?"

He nodded again, unable to resist an answering grin. "What do you have in mind?"

"Only God's gift to music festivals everywhere," she said as she took his hand and tugged him toward the long line of food trucks nearby.

"And that is…?"

"Funnel cake," she shot back with a beaming grin.

He laughed, letting her drag him along behind her.

He'd enjoy every second of their time together, no doubt about that. But her words just now had started his mind buzzing about potential futures he'd never let himself consider.

"Just think about it," she'd said.

As if he was even capable of thinking about anything other than a life with Sierra McNeal.

CHAPTER 35

The feel of Cody's large, calloused hand pressed against her lower back was the only thing keeping Sierra grounded.

Her breathing felt too shallow as she waited uncomfortably in the Gardiners' foyer. April's grandfather had opened the door, his face a mask of surprise when Sierra stated who she was and why she was there. Then he'd ushered them inside and told them he'd get his wife and be right back.

Maybe Emma had been right. Maybe she really should have called first.

But it was Lizzy who'd suggested she just show up, on the off chance that April was lying low in their basement or something.

Sierra took in the thickly carpeted living room to her right and the kitchen that lay straight ahead. No sign of April, just lots of framed photos of a happy family.

Her father's family. His last one, anyway.

Her stomach did a flip as she caught sight of Frank O'Sullivan smiling at her from a framed photo on the wall, his arm around a tall, dark-skinned woman with a warm smile, and a tween with braces grinning between them.

April.

The girl had golden-brown skin and rich black hair. She definitely didn't look like the rest of her sisters, but the longer Sierra stared at the family portrait, the more she thought she saw of Frank—the strong jawline, the tenacious look in her eyes. Sierra's gaze darted between the girl and her father as she tried to find more similarities.

"You okay?" Cody murmured.

"Yeah, it's just weird, that's all."

He nodded. She appreciated the fact that he didn't try to comfort her or deny just how bizarre this situation was. She'd never been fond of denial, which was probably why she'd gone and made things tense between them by asking him to leave with her.

But…whatever. She couldn't think about that now. What was done was done. And the worst that could happen was that Cody didn't come. Which he'd never planned to do in the first place, so really, she had nothing to lose.

"Sierra?"

An elderly woman's voice had her looking to the staircase to her left. Mr. Gardiner was escorting his wife down the steps. They both seemed kinda…frail, and the nurse in her wondered if it would be inappropriate to address the fact that they might want to relocate to a single-level home.

Not now, though. Because right now they needed to have a very awkward conversation.

"I'm sorry to intrude, Mr. and Mrs. Gardiner," she started, glancing between them and noting the family

266

resemblance. Their daughter looked so like them, as did their granddaughter.

"Oh, please, call us Billy and Myra." Billy smiled, and suddenly he didn't look so old...or so frail. "That's what everyone calls us. Even April."

"Never could get her to say 'Grandma.'" Myra shook her head with a wry smile.

"Is April...uh...?" Sierra looked around them as if the girl were hiding behind the curtains or under the couch. "Has she visited you lately?"

Myra's face fell. Billy's too. They exchanged a quick look, and then Myra sighed. "We were going to ask you that." She gestured toward the living room. "Please, have a seat."

Cody followed Sierra to the couch and sat by her side. It was almost embarrassing how comforting his presence was. She'd gotten so used to being the strong one for her family, so used to taking care of herself when she was on assignments abroad. Now here she was, ready to weep with relief when Cody's thigh brushed hers and he intertwined their fingers in his lap. It gave her the strength to delve into the delicate topic at hand.

"This might come as a bit of a shock, but I'm actually..."

"Frank's daughter?" Myra offered gently when Sierra hesitated.

Sierra blinked in surprise. "You...er, you know about me?"

Myra and Billy exchanged looks again, and Billy nodded. "We didn't at first. Neither did our Loretta. She was Frank's wife for nearly two decades before she...she passed." He choked out the last two words, showing how much the loss still hurt him.

Sierra nodded.

"He told Lori about his other daughters early on in their relationship," Myra was quick to clarify. "And they agreed they'd tell April when the time was right."

There was such sadness in both their faces, Sierra felt like she knew how this ended. "There was never a right time, was there?"

Myra shook her head. "Lori got sick when April was in middle school. She fought the cancer with all she had, but for the next five years, it was all they could do to keep her healthy."

"She'd have good patches. For a little while." Billy's voice was strong...until it faded again. "But the cancer would always come back."

"It took a toll on April and Frank." Myra forced a smile, running a hand down her husband's back.

Sierra felt tears stinging the back of her eyes for people she'd never even met. "I can imagine."

"Anyway, they didn't want to add more to her plate, so they kept waiting until Lori was well, but...she never did get well. All the way well. Healthy enough to handle a conversation so heavy."

The grief on their faces was heartbreaking, and she gripped Cody's hand like a lifeline.

He squeezed right back, a silent *I've got you.*

"Did April ever find out?" Sierra asked. "About us, I mean. Her half sisters."

Another long look between the couple, and then Myra licked her lips and slowly explained, "She did...but not in the way anyone would have liked. After her mother died, she couldn't settle. Neither could Frank. They were torn up. We thought maybe moving house might ease the pain. They could start somewhere fresh. Frank didn't mind the idea so much, and they thought they'd move up near us for a while until April decided what she wanted to do with her future. She only just managed to graduate from high school. With all that had been going on, it felt like a miracle. College was beyond what she could cope with, so we were all just giving her time. But then..." Myra's voice trailed off, so Billy took over.

"She found Frank's...documents. A folder of official papers, you know? His will. I'm sure he intended to talk to her about it, but she was so confused, so hurt by the lies, that..."

Sierra held her breath, waiting for the last of it.

But it didn't come. Billy covered his mouth with trembling fingers while Myra dipped her head and sniffed.

Sierra's heart felt a pierce of pain. She'd been shocked to discover those cards and her mother's secrets, but she could only imagine the betrayal and shock April had felt finding out like that, especially while coping with the loss of her mother.

"She was angry with him," Billy finally managed. "And angry with us for keeping his secrets for so long."

Sierra nodded slowly. That she could definitely understand. "And you don't know where she is?"

"She took off. Left a note and nothing more." Myra swallowed, and then her chest started to shake. Gripping Billy's arm, she choked out the rest. "Frank went after her, but he...he...he—"

"The accident wasn't his fault," Billy butted in. "Some fool ran a red, and there was nothing anybody could do."

"We managed to track April down and tell her the news. I was so worried. I begged her to come home, but she couldn't face her daddy's death too."

"So, you haven't spoken to her since?" Sierra asked.

"Oh, she checks in on occasion." Myra's smile was wan. "She knows we'd be beside ourselves if she didn't. But that poor girl went through so much." She rubbed at her eyes wearily.

Sierra pressed her lips together. She didn't even want to think about the guilt April must have felt on top of all the other emotions if Frank passed before they could make amends. All Sierra could hope was that she didn't know Frank had died coming after her. She didn't need that baggage as well.

"I think she's just trying to escape all the memories. She doesn't want to be here, or in Bozeman, or back at the ranch either." Billy's face was etched with sadness.

With a start, Sierra recalled the purple room on the ranch's second floor. The one with bunk beds and…

April's bedroom.

She'd known that logically. Emma had said so when she'd given her the tour. But now April wasn't just some hypothetical someone. She was a real young woman with a boatload of baggage, and the poor thing must know by now that her house—her childhood home—had been overrun by the sisters she never even knew existed.

Sierra winced, and apparently her distress was obvious, because Cody let go of her hand to wrap an arm around her shoulders.

"We'd hoped you'd come to tell us you'd found her," Myra admitted.

"No, we haven't, but…" Sierra said, her voice hoarse. "But we *will*."

She said it with such strength and confidence, she nearly shocked herself. Cody went still beside her.

"We will?" he silently asked.

She could practically hear his thoughts, and the idea

that they were so bonded she could read his mind made her smile as she reached a hand out to Myra, who clasped it eagerly. "If there's one thing I've learned since meeting Frank's other daughters, it's that we're a stubborn bunch."

Myra choked on a laugh. "I don't doubt that. Comes from the father's side, I'm sure of it."

"And if you met Emma and Lizzy, Dahlia, Daisy, and Rose…" She grinned as she pulled back and leaned into Cody's strength. "When I tell them what you just told me, they'll be as committed to finding April and bringing her home as I am."

"That's good," Myra said, her eyes sparkling with tears. "We'd appreciate that."

"April might be the most stubborn of you all," Billy said. "But she's not as tough as she thinks. She needs friends and family around her at a time like this. She needs to find her way home."

Sierra nodded, her throat thick with tears.

"Find her way home."

Maybe that was what she needed too. What they all needed.

And with Cody's arm around her like this, she could fool herself into thinking she'd found it already.

Billy got to his feet so quickly, Sierra looked up in surprise. "I've got something that belongs to you. To you and your sisters…and April when you find her."

Sierra nodded as he ran off, leaving Myra to give them a bright smile. "Can I get you kids some lunch before you go?"

It felt almost churlish to refuse because she looked so eager, so when Billy returned, he found them eating crust-less ham and cheese sandwiches and drinking pop in his kitchen. Billy set a box at her feet. "We were hoping to give it to April when she returned, but it's only right that you and the others have a chance to go through Frank's belongings as well. And if you find April…" He trailed off with a look of such concern, Sierra reached out and touched his arm.

"We will find her."

He nodded. "Please make sure she sees this too."

Sierra nodded.

Myra stood, taking Billy by the arm and leading him out to a side hallway. "We'll give you a moment of privacy."

Sierra looked to Cody, who gave her an encouraging nod.

Swallowing hard, she opened the box. Tears sprang instantly to her eyes, and Cody was at her side before she could even blink.

"You all right?" He knelt beside her chair, his gaze so warm with concern and affection it made her want to cry even more.

With a trembling lower lip, she nodded. And together they opened the box even farther, revealing Frank's things. The old box was stuffed with everything from books to journals, the high school yearbook from her mother's old school, a stuffed yellow ducky and a bright pink porcupine, plus a handmade puppet that looked like a beloved school project from years ago. Deeper down lay some folders of paperwork, and against one side sat a stack of vinyl albums.

She pulled one up and gasped.

"No way," Cody breathed.

"He liked Zombie Town?" she whispered.

He lifted a shoulder. "It is an older band…"

She started to laugh, fresh tears flooding her eyes. "I guess I really am his daughter, huh?"

Cody's smile was sweet and beautiful as he brushed her tears away with his thumb. "At least we know he had good taste in music."

She let out a watery, breathy giggle, and he stroked her back as she sorted through the other contents. There was too much for her to sift through in one go. She wanted to pore over the yearbook, taking her sweet time to study every photo and spot her parents together. Plus, it also felt wrong to be looking through Frank's things alone, without her sisters.

"We'll have to find a way to get it back to the ranch," Cody murmured. "I bet we can have them courier it."

As he pondered how they were going to get it back, Sierra kept digging until her fingers brushed a book at the very bottom. It was black and looked like any other journal. Why she was fascinated by this one in particular, she wasn't sure. Maybe because it looked newer than the rest. Maybe that meant it contained the last words he ever wrote.

She drew it out of the box with a shaky sigh, flicking through the pages. "His writing looks a little like mine too."

"Is that a daily journal or something?" Cody tipped his head. "Maybe it'll give you some answers."

"And maybe help April find some closure." She frowned at the leather book in her hand. "If we can find her."

"We will," he said. When she didn't answer, he spoke with soft determination. "*I* will."

She glanced over at him in surprise.

"I know you'll be leaving soon, but I don't want you to

273

worry. I promise I'll help Emma and the others track her down. I'll make sure no one lets any more time go by with April unaccounted for."

Sierra nodded, tears sliding down her cheeks now. "How did I get so lucky to meet such a good man on my very first night in Montana?"

With a gentle grin, he tugged her into his arms and let her cry on his shoulder. "I'm the lucky one, Sierra. You changed my life just by coming into it." He kissed her temple and stroked her back as confusing emotions poured out of her, along with grief at the goodbye to come. "You woke me up from a deep slumber, Sierra McNeal. And no matter where you go, I'll never forget that." He lowered his voice and held her tighter. "I'll never forget you."

She nodded against his shoulder. It wasn't much, but it was the most he could give her. A place in his memories.

Meanwhile, he'd forever have a place in her heart, and she well knew it.

"Come on," Cody said after a long while. "Let's get out of their hair and get this search for April underway, hmm?"

She nodded, pulling back with a tired sigh. They needed to find a place to stay for the night. They needed to courier the box back to her sisters, and then they needed to figure out a plan for finding April.

Sierra had limited time before she was needed back in Venezuela, but she was determined to use every spare moment she could searching for her little sister.

CHAPTER 36

Billy and Myra's leads were slim. April's grandparents had some suggestions about cabins and second homes of some of her friends, but it still felt like a shot in the dark. Cody was all set to help Sierra start making phone calls and mapping out a plan.

The clock was ticking, and with each hour that passed, the seconds seemed to beat even louder in his mind.

Sierra was leaving soon. He had to get back to work, and their limited days were going to be spent on what felt like a fruitless hunt in the dark for a girl who didn't even want to be found.

They couriered the box and found a place to stay, ordering lunch and taking a quick break before starting their search. They were both quiet as they sat in the hotel room, nibbling on room service fries and staring at the inane show playing on TV. Cody had lost the storyline within minutes, his mind too crowded with the look on Sierra's face when she pulled out that vinyl, and the tears on her cheeks as she wept for a father she never knew.

She'd be facing a lot of questions when they finally got

back to the ranch, and Sierra didn't want to show up without her sister in tow. But how would they find her?

And if they did, how would they convince her to come back with them?

They couldn't be out here forever, a thought that was both a relief and a stress. The end of this trip meant the end of their time alone together. He'd be back at work, and she'd focus on April and her sisters until she had to leave for Venezuela.

The fries turned cold in his mouth, and he sat back from his plate, leaning against the pillows and glancing at Sierra, who was perched on the other bed looking just as glassy-eyed as he was.

"Hey," he whispered and waited until she looked at him before tipping his head with a smile. "C'mere, Hustler."

Her face split with a grin, and she climbed off her bed, joining him and snuggling against his chest.

"What are we watching right now?" she murmured, giggling into his shirt as the woman on screen let out a dramatic wail and started ranting at the inept concierge.

"I have no idea." Cody chuckled, reaching for the remote and plunging the room into silence.

All that remained was their breathing, a unified intake and outtake as his chest rose, making her head rise and fall with it.

Pressing his lips against her red hair, he breathed her in and murmured, "I could get used to this right here." He pulled her a little closer, nestling his arm behind her back as she let out a contented moan.

"It's moments like this where I just want to freeze time for a little minute, you know?"

"I do." He kissed her hair, then trailed his lips along

her forehead, shifting so he could reach her nose, then her cheeks and the edge of her mouth. He kissed her smile and let out a groan when she pressed herself against him, deepening the kiss and making all else fade away.

She felt like home—warmth, comfort, peace. More than anything in the world, he wanted her to feel the same way, to be the home she wanted to return to. Every day, preferably. But he'd take whatever he could get.

Pulling back, he gazed down at her, smoothing back her colorful hair as she smiled up at him.

Her eyes turned serious, her mouth hitching up on the side. "I'm sorry you're being dragged into all of this. I doubt you want to spend your last few days off work searching for April, but it's something I've got to do."

"I know." His voice was low and husky. "I don't care what we're doing, as long as I get to spend my time with you. I don't want to waste one second, because we're running out of them faster than I'd like."

She ran her hand up his side, curling her fingers into his shirt and pulling him close again. "I wouldn't want to be doing this with anyone else."

"Sierra, my—"

His phone dinged, and he rolled his eyes. Perfect timing. He was ready to ignore it, but then it dinged again.

They shared a knowing grin. "Sorry," he muttered. They'd been going in and out of reception for the past few days, and whenever he was in range, his phone tended to blow up with the texts and calls he'd missed.

He went to silence his phone, but the message on the screen made him go cold.

. . .

Kit: Dad's in the hospital. Broken wrist and sprained ankle. Call me.

"Cody?" Sierra sat up, gripping his shoulder. "What is it?"

He frowned as he replied to his brother's message with a phone call. To Sierra, he said, "Kit just told me my dad's in the hospital."

"What? What happened?"

But before he could respond, Kit answered. "Hey, brother. Where are you right now?"

"Uh...about two hours north of Bozeman. What happened?"

Kit sighed. "He was trying to clean the gutters by himself."

"What?" Cody dropped his head into his hand with a groan as Kit continued. Turned out he'd fallen off the ladder. "He got a nasty bump on his head, his arm is in a cast, and they've braced his ankle too. He's looking kind of banged up, so Dex and Mom took him to the hospital in Bozeman to get fully checked out. He's getting a CT scan. The works."

"I should have been there," Cody groaned. He said it softly, but both Sierra and Kit heard him.

"He knew you were coming back soon. He could have waited or asked the neighbor's boy or—"

"Kit, I do the gutters for him every year," Cody snapped. "I should have been there."

"Cody," Sierra started.

He ignored her. "Are they still at the hospital?"

"Last I heard," Kit said. "I was gonna head there after Lizzy gets home so she can watch the kids."

"I'll go." Cody shot off the bed, grabbing his boots and shoving them on.

"You're supposed to be taking a few days off," Kit murmured. "I'm only calling to keep you informed. I'll go help Mom and make sure she's okay. We both know how she gets overwhelmed with the insurance stuff and—"

"And I can handle it," Cody cut him off again. He didn't point out that he always had. He always did. This was his job in the family. Reliable Cody who knew the insurance information and had the numbers for the neighbors so they could make sure the cat got fed.

This was what he did. And look what happened when he'd forgotten his role and took off like some carefree teenager.

He hung up with Kit and turned to Sierra. "I've got to get going." He winced. "Sorry about this."

"You don't have to apologize for anything. Of course we'll go and help your parents." Sierra jumped up, pulling on her own boots and gathering their stuff.

Cody's hands shook as he struggled into his leather jacket and checked the room for anything they might have forgotten.

"Hey." Sierra touched his arm, her brows knitting together with concern. "You know this was an accident, right? These things happen. It's not your fault."

"I know that." His words were coming out snappy and strong. He cringed, not liking the sound of his voice.

"You can't blame yourself for this," she added gently.

Too gently.

It wasn't like Sierra to tiptoe around a topic. "Just say what you're going to say," he sighed.

She looked sheepish, like she'd been called out, but with a shrug, she admitted, "I just don't like seeing you taking all the responsibility on yourself. I know you feel like you should have been there, but it's not your job to take care of everyone else."

"Sierra, I'm not like you," he clipped. "I can't just... walk away." He saw a flicker of hurt in her eyes, and he snapped his own shut with a curse. "I'm sorry, I didn't mean it to sound like—"

"No, you're right." She nodded, looking to the floor and obviously avoiding his gaze. "I walked away from my mom when she needed me. But I guess I realized that if I didn't leave, I'd never have my independence. And what's more..." She moved so she was standing by the door. "I realized my mother would never stand on her own two feet if I were always there supporting her."

Irritation flared. "My dad isn't like your mother. He's an independent man—"

"Yeah. So independent he insisted on doing a job alone when he could have asked for help—"

"From me."

She threw her hands up in frustration. "From anyone! Cody, I may be new to Aspire, but even I know of at least three able-bodied men who'd have come running to help if he'd just asked."

Cody scowled, rubbing a hand over the back of his head. He knew she didn't mean to, but her whole argument was making him feel off-center.

No...useless.

He was useless if he wasn't needed. Couldn't she see that?

"I don't have a career, Sierra. I don't have a driving passion for business or a charity that gives me purpose. All I have is my home. My family. The people who depend on me." He took a step back, hating the look of sadness in her eyes.

It was way too close to pity for his liking.

"That's who I am." He pointed at his chest.

"I know." Her voice held a world of sadness and so much resignation it could make a man bleed. "I know that about you. It's why you'll never come with me. And the ironic part? It's also what I love about you, Cowboy."

She opened the door with a sad smile. "Come on. We'd better check out and hit the road if we want to meet your folks at the hospital."

CHAPTER 37

Sierra had a feeling that if she'd let Cody drive, they'd have reached the hospital in record time. As it was, as soon as she parked her bike, he jumped off the back and started running for the sliding glass doors. She struggled to keep up with him, dodging patients and medical staff as they made a beeline for Mr. Swanson's room.

She paused in the doorway, watching Cody rush around his father's bed and give his mother a hug.

"Cody." She clung to his shoulders, whispering his name in obvious relief. "You're here."

"Are you okay?" He held her shoulders, studying her face as if she were made from porcelain and not sturdy flesh and bone.

"We're doing okay." She gave him a shaky smile that contradicted her words. "Don't you worry now, darlin'. Your father's gonna be just fine."

"Dad." Cody shook his head, gazing down at the hospital bed. "What were you thinking?"

His father huffed and looked away, his poor beat-up face black and blue on one side. He must have hit that ground pretty hard. Sierra winced and edged into the room, the nurse in her wanting to offer any kind of comfort or aid.

"I've been cleaning those gutters most of my life."

"Not lately," Cody argued.

"They needed doing, and I wasn't about to wait around for you. I shouldn't have to."

"Dad, I'm happy to do it. You know that."

"You shouldn't *have* to. I wanted you to enjoy your time away, not be worried about coming back to serve me like I'm some incapable old man."

"Oh stop." Mrs. Swanson touched his shoulder with a gentle smile. "You're getting old now, and there's nothing you can do about it. You know if I'd been home, I would have put a quick stop to your nonsense."

"I should have been there." Cody sighed. "You wouldn't have bothered if I'd come over like I normally do on the weekends."

The usually cool, calm cowboy ran a hand through his hair, looking frustrated beyond anything Sierra had ever seen. And the worst part was the anger all seemed to be directed at himself.

Sierra frowned, reliving their brief conversation in the hotel room and wishing she could make him see. He didn't have to be everything to everyone.

Her heart hurt as she realized he probably wouldn't believe her when she told him that. He *wanted* to be everything for everyone, and he couldn't. That was what killed him the most. He couldn't split himself all these different ways, and the idea that she was just another burden in his life made her stomach sink.

Crossing her arms, she stayed on the edge of the room while Cody and his parents discussed the details of the accident and the care they'd received so far. He sat and helped his mother make phone calls to the insurance company.

Sierra moved closer to the bed and held Mr. Swanson's hand. The poor man looked miserable but still managed to give her a stoic smile.

"Can I get you anything? How are your pain levels?"

"I'm all right. This old man will heal up." He lifted his cast and winced.

Sierra smiled and poured him a glass of water. "Yes you will. But you need to take it easy."

"I hate that I'm getting old," he muttered.

"Even young people fall off ladders, sir." She winked at him.

He paused to stare at her. Then his eyes lit with a smile, and he started to chuckle. "Oh, I like you."

She grinned back at him.

"Yeah, I think you should stick around, young lady."

Her smile faded, and she swallowed, unable to respond. Instead, she handed him his glass of water and stole a quick glance at Cody. He was watching her now, the pain on his face unable to miss. He knew just as well as she did that there'd be no sticking around.

The thought of letting him down tore at her heart.

The thought of telling Cody's parents that she would be breaking her son's heart shattered her.

But there was no other way.

She couldn't stay here, and after what just happened to his father, there was no way Cody would be ready to high-tail it hours away to a remote village in Venezuela.

CHAPTER 38

All around Sierra, emotions were bubbling to the surface.

The box, which had arrived only two hours before, sat on the ground next to the ranch's large kitchen table, and its contents were scattered in front of them.

As soon as the courier had dropped it off, Emma sent out a group text. The sisters were there in record time, standing around the box, holding their breath. In the end, Sierra let out a sharp huff and pulled the box toward her, ripping off the tape and snapping back the flaps.

All of the sisters were dealing with seeing the evidence of Frank's life in a different way.

Emma couldn't seem to stop sorting and piling loose papers, while Daisy stared at a pile of photos they'd unearthed with a dazed look in her eyes. They were snapshots of Frank—one of him laughing, a guitar in his hands while a pretty girl leaned her head on his shoulder. It was Daisy's mother. There was one with Frank carefully holding his twin daughters when they were still newborns. There was another of Emma with blonde pigtails and a baby Lizzy sitting on her father's knee.

Rose sniffled and held Kiara tightly to her chest, stroking the pink porcupine while Lizzy paced in circles around the table, making Sierra dizzy.

Dahlia's sighs could be heard occasionally from Emma's computer screen as she, too, processed the contents of the box.

The journal was the only item they hadn't opened and gone through yet.

The men had given them their privacy. "Sister time," Kit had called it as he'd given Sierra a wink on his way out the door.

He'd been especially nice to her since she and Cody had returned from their trip. His parents too.

She wasn't sure what they all made of the fact that Cody had taken off on a wild-goose chase with her, but if anything, they all seemed to approve of her more now than ever. They definitely didn't seem to resent her, as she'd feared they might.

What with her being the big bad biker chick who'd taken off with their responsible son and all.

But no. They'd all been treating her like she was one of the family. Not just the latest O'Sullivan sister but like a member of their family...the Swansons.

She shook her head and then dipped it to study her hands.

She'd had nearly two days to process what she'd learned from April's grandparents, and the others needed time to catch up. And on top of that...

Sierra was just plain exhausted.

She'd felt depleted ever since they'd gotten back from Bozeman late last night. The hospital had been a blur, and she'd only been in the way as Cody handled the release forms, the doctor's questions, and the insurance.

He really was good at being responsible. So calm and steady. So loyal and smart and organized...

Her sigh had the others turning to look at her. Lizzy stopped her pacing to rest a hand on Sierra's shoulders. "Thank you for going there. Have I said that yet? I don't know what I've said today. It's all just..." She shook her head, looking frazzled. Even her hair was out of place, something Sierra wasn't used to seeing.

She gave her sister a kind smile and nodded. "I'm okay. It's a lot to take in, but..." She licked her lips and shrugged. "It's good to get to know him this way."

A sad silence followed her simple statement, and they all nodded.

"I wish I could have known him better," Rose whispered. "I never thought I needed that connection, but now..." She shook her head. "I always thought he was this coldhearted man incapable of feeling. Some jerk who walked away and never thought about us."

"He sent us the cards every year," Daisy murmured. "He thought about us."

"I couldn't humanize him," Rose whispered. "I wanted him to be horrible, because it made it easy to not miss him or pine for him."

Emma started sniffing, blinking, and swallowing like she was fighting a wave of tears. Lizzy moved to put an arm around her shoulders.

"I want to find April. She was the one daughter he stayed with. I need to hear stories about him. I want to know what he was like, if he had regrets or..." Rose pursed her lips, struggling to get the words out. Daisy rested a hand over hers and gave it a little squeeze.

"Me too." She smiled at her younger sister.

Sierra ached for the love that swirled between her siblings. She could feel their pain, sense their desperation to connect with this man. "I wish I could have done more," she blurted. "I would have done anything to have found her at her grandparents' house. I don't know how we're going to track her down, but I don't think it'll be easy, and…" She sighed, guilt ravaging her as she stared at the floor. "And I can't… I mean, I have to…go." She ended her sentence in a breathy whisper that she was sure most of them didn't hear.

But she couldn't say it again. Mostly because some part of her had been nagging her to stay. It'd been trying to convince her that she could start a life here.

But…but that wasn't who she was. It wasn't what she wanted. Not now, at least.

Maybe someday she'd be ready for a stable home and would really, truly want to put down roots. But she knew better than most what it was like to stay in a situation for someone else's sake. To base your life around someone else's dreams and not your own.

She'd done that with her mother when she was young and had resolved never to do it again.

And the thing was…

She might be able to change her mind, to form some sort of compromise, if she really believed Cody belonged here and that he truly wanted to stay. But she'd meant what she'd said at the music festival.

He'd come alive in front of her eyes with each passing second of their adventure. And she'd seen him go back into hiding the moment they arrived back in Aspire.

The sermon at last week's church service had been about hiding your light under a bushel. She was no biblical scholar, and she wasn't totally sure what it was about, but as they'd traveled, she'd thought about that sermon. Lines from it kept coming back to her.

Cody had so much light to shine, and he was holding himself back trying to do what was right.

"You okay, sis?" Emma tipped her head, the look of compassion on her face enough to unravel Sierra on the spot.

Sierra's head snapped up. "Um…what?"

The others exchanged worried glances, and then Dahlia spoke up. "Okay, if no one else is gonna say it, then I will. Let's change the subject for a minute and get an update on this whole Sierra-Cody thing. Are we still worried about that?"

Sierra stiffened. "Why? You worried I'm gonna be a bad influence or something? Take him away from home like some—"

"No!" Emma cut her off with obvious surprise. "No, no, no. That's not what Dahlia meant."

"Dahlia, remember that little talk we had about tact?" Rose cooed sweetly, smiling down at her baby girl while talking to her older sister. "Now's a good time for it."

Daisy rolled her eyes with a huff. "Dee, explain what you meant to Sierra, please, so she doesn't pull an April."

"We definitely don't need two runaway sisters," Lizzy agreed.

Dahlia groaned. "All right, I'm sorry. That came out wrong. I didn't mean we were worried you'd get together. We're worried you won't."

"I'm not worried." JJ's face appeared on the screen, his sweet smile hidden by a beard that was bushier than ever. Rose giggled. "You do you, new O'Sullivan sister. And we'll all just keep our noses out of it. Won't we, babe?"

Dahlia sighed dramatically. "I suppose. But honestly, according to Kit and Boone, that guy is head over heels, and none of us have ever seen Cody in love, and it just seems to me that—"

"That it's none of our business." Daisy winked as she interrupted her older sister. "Isn't that right, Dahlia?"

"Fine," Dahlia muttered.

"We don't want to intrude," Rose started.

Emma leaned forward, her expression all maternal concern. "But if you did want to talk…"

Lizzy patted Sierra's shoulder as she commenced pacing. "What Emma's trying to say is we're here if you need us."

Sierra was speechless. Her throat was achingly tight, and her eyes stung. But all she could manage was "Thank you."

There was a brief silence, and then Dahlia muttered, "All right, let the poor girl angst in peace. Let's get back to our father's stuff. Someone read me that journal. Rosie, there might be something in there that'll make us feel like we can get to know him better."

Emma reached for the journal and opened it with a determined nod. She flicked through a few pages, drinking in the writing the way Sierra had when she first touched it. Then she skimmed a few pages, paused, and then read a little more.

"Uh, I kind of meant *read it out loud to everyone*." Dahlia snickered, but her amused grin quickly fled when Emma started to sniff and then whimper.

"I don't think I'm the right choice for this…"

She handed the journal to Daisy, who flicked through the pages with her thumb. "You know what? I'm gonna start at the end, which is…" Her face went pale, and she wet her lips. "Two days before he died."

Sierra was almost certain she wasn't alone in only being able to process bits and pieces.

He wrote about a fight he'd had with April. He wrote about the will, about how she'd found out.

…and now I've lost her as well. I should have told her the truth from the start. I've let her down. I've let all my girls down. What I wouldn't give to tell them how sorry I am. There are no words to express the depth of my regret, and I wish there was more I could do to make amends.

The ranch is my home. <u>Their</u> home. I'd give anything to see all seven of my daughters together. To tell them how sorry I am. To tell them how they lived in my heart even though I wasn't man enough to be there for them.

The ranch is all I have to give, but it's not enough. I've spent too many years ignoring the call of my heart, but I have nothing left and nothing to stop me. No matter how long it takes, no matter what it costs, I will bring my family home.

A long, somber silence fell, and Daisy passed the journal to Rose, who then handed it to Lizzy. It was a loud, violent sob from Dahlia that finally ended the silence as the sisters at the table took turns looking at his handwriting and reading his words.

"I always thought he forgot," Dahlia whimpered through her tears.

They could hear JJ comforting her softly in the background.

"I thought he was heartless." Lizzy stared at the journal.

"I thought he was dead." Sierra shrugged when the others looked her way in surprise. "It's true. My mom was always so vague about who my father was and what happened to him, I thought she was making things up, like when she tried to convince me Mr. Gato, my cat, had gone to live with a nice country family."

"You didn't believe her?" Rose asked.

Sierra winced. "I saw Mr. Gato get hit by the car."

"Ouch," Daisy muttered.

"He wanted us to have this ranch." Emma stood from her chair, staring at each of them. "He wanted all of us here...together."

The sisters exchanged a look that included Sierra and made her heart feel too full.

"He wanted this to be our home," Sierra said.

Rose reached over and squeezed her hand. "Or a home base."

Daisy winked. "I don't think our father or any of us want anyone to stay here out of obligation."

Sierra had thought she was out of tears after crying herself to sleep the night before over Cody. But this had her welling up again as she nodded. "I made a decision... about the ranch." She didn't stop to think it through, just spoke from her heart. "My vote will be that we keep it. As our home." She smiled at Rose. "A home base. As a place where we're all welcome. But..." She arched a brow. "Only if April agrees."

Dahlia seemed to understand right away. "It's her house. Her childhood home. She's the one who actually had Frank in her life as a father. Whatever she says goes. Agreed?"

The sisters started nodding, Emma being the last to join them.

Sierra shot her a sympathetic smile. She was the one who actually lived here with Nash. If April wanted to sell, it would hurt Emma the most.

But like the sweet soul she was, she eventually whispered, "Agreed."

"Me too." Lizzy nodded.

Daisy and Rose echoed right after.

"Right," Dahlia said in a take-charge tone even Sierra was starting to be familiar with. "Then the next step is to find her. No more procrastinating or making excuses."

Emma nodded. "We have to find her and bring her here."

Sierra looked around the table at her newfound sisters. "We have to bring her home."

CHAPTER 39

Boone's voice was as booming as ever when Cody
returned to the bunkhouse after a long day getting
caught up at work. "Welcome back, stranger!"

Cody winced. His head had been throbbing all day,
and no amount of aspirin seemed to make a difference.

"I didn't see you get in last night," Boone continued,
following in Cody's wake as he headed into the small
kitchen to grab a drink. "How'd the big trip go?"

"Fine," Cody muttered.

He should have known that wouldn't be enough.

"Did you and Sierra make any progress?" Leaning
against the doorframe, Boone gave him that lopsided smile
that all the girls seemed to swoon over. "What do the kids
call it these days? Oh, did you 'define the relationship'?"
Boone used air quotes, clearly amused by himself.

Cody slammed the refrigerator door shut.

He didn't want to talk about their road trip, and he
definitely didn't want to talk about Sierra. His thoughts
and emotions were still all over the place, having gone

from the best time of his life to crashing back to reality with one call.

Now he wasn't sure which way was up. All he knew was he never should have let himself fall so hard and so fast for a woman he'd known from the start could only be temporary.

"Okay, fine. If you don't want to talk about Sierra, then how'd the mission go? Did you two find out anything interesting about Frank?"

That had Cody turning to face Boone. "Actually, we did get some information…"

Boone listened with a myriad of expressions ranging from open curiosity to an uncharacteristic frown. "So April just…took off?"

Cody nodded. "Her grandparents are worried about her, so Sierra promised we'd find her."

Boone's grim expression was a little alarming. Not because Cody wasn't also worried about April—of course he was. He loved the O'Sullivan sisters like his own family, and to think that one of their own was who knew where and grieving by herself made his gut twist into knots.

But Boone didn't typically get twisted into knots about anything, so far as Cody knew. "Boone, you all right?"

"Yeah, I'm just…" He huffed, his gaze distant as he crossed his arms and leaned back. "I don't like the idea of April being all alone like that."

Cody's eyes narrowed. "You were the same age, right? Same grade?"

"Yeah," he murmured.

"But not friends?"

Boone shifted, his lips pressing together. "We didn't hang in the same crowd."

Cody nodded. This wasn't a surprise. He didn't have much of a recollection of April, but the image he had of her wasn't exactly the cheerleader and football player sorts who made up Boone's circle of friends.

"But I'm pretty sure she always liked me. I'd catch her staring sometimes." A fond smile stretched across his face as he shifted in the doorway, his feet shuffling until he caught Cody's amused stare. "I mean...she's not my type, so nothing ever would have come of it, but she was a cute, nerdy little thing when I knew her. It was kind of sweet, I guess."

Cody's brows arched, but he kept his mouth shut. Man, he wished Sierra was here. She'd be teasing Boone to no end about having a crush on her little sister, which he'd no doubt deny. All the ladies loved Boone, and April was obviously no exception. It must go to the guy's head a little. How could it not?

"I think I remember who she used to hang out with. Before she moved, I mean. Maybe I should ask around, see if her old friends from Aspire have any ideas where she might be."

His expression was so earnest, Cody had to hide another smile. This was definitely a side of Boone he'd never seen before. "Yeah. That would be great, man. I'm sure her sisters would appreciate that."

Boone nodded, tucking his hands into his pockets. "Yeah, okay. Cool. I'll see what I can find out."

Boone headed out the door, then turned back. "Hey, you going up to the main house? Emma invited all us ranch hands up for dinner tonight. Said something about celebrating prodigal sisters...whatever that means."

Cody ran a hand through his hair, his insides torn in two. He wanted nothing more than to see Sierra. Especially after the way they'd left things last night. The hospital had been too hectic to talk. He'd been busy handling paperwork, and Sierra had leapt into action to take care of his mother, who looked frazzled after such a fright, and his father, who wouldn't stop grumbling about old age and wonky ladders.

They'd barely spoken when they'd headed out, and on the motorcycle, there was no chance to do anything more than share an occasional shout over the wind.

So yeah, he wanted to see her, but he had no clue what to say.

"Cody?" Boone prompted.

Cody blinked and took a deep breath. "I think I'm gonna stay in tonight, but tell Emma thanks for the invite."

Boone eyed him a moment longer, but he didn't argue. "Okay, man. Get some rest."

Cody slumped against the kitchen counter. Rest was probably exactly what he needed. He'd barely slept last night, even though he'd been asleep on his feet when he'd stumbled into the bunkhouse.

But how could he sleep after the way they'd left things?

He'd dropped her at the inn, exhausted and bleary-eyed. "I should get some rest," she'd mumbled.

He'd opened his mouth to say…what? He still didn't know. It wasn't like he'd wanted their epic road trip to end on such a sad note. But what else was there to say?

In the end, he'd settled for cupping her face, kissing her gently…and letting her go.

"Good practice," he muttered to the empty kitchen.

Because letting her go was exactly what he had to do. And he might as well get used to it.

CHAPTER 40

Sierra had never been much of a churchgoer. Not because she didn't like church but because she tended to move around so often, she'd never found a community that felt like her own.

But Emma, Daisy, and the others had been insistent that Sierra join them for church this morning, and for the lunch gathering that inevitably happened at the ranch after. So Sierra was trying to hurry out the hotel room door when her phone rang.

"Hey, Ma." She put the phone on speaker and got back to sifting through the contents of her closet for an appropriate sundress. "What's up?"

When her mother hesitated, Sierra stiffened and turned to frown at the phone. They'd talked only the day before, and Sierra had filled her in on all she'd learned about Frank. It hadn't been an easy conversation—she supposed her mother had a lot to digest.

"Ma, is everything okay? Are you sick or—"

"No," her mother said quickly. "It's nothing like that. I

just... I've been doing a lot of thinking lately. Ever since I came to visit you in Montana, really..."

Sierra stepped toward the phone and took her mom off speaker. "What's up?"

Her mother's sigh was loud on the other end. "I spent so many years being angry."

Sierra kept her mouth shut. This was hardly breaking news.

"I'm sorry." Her mom's voice caught at the end.

Sierra blinked. "What?"

"I'm sorry I spent all those years blaming Frank. Hearing what you said he wrote in his journal, his regrets and his mistakes. He...he didn't always have it easy. I knew that. His family life was rotten, and if you and your...your sisters want to hear more about that, I can fill you in."

Sierra nodded. "Yeah, I'm sure we'd all like to hear more. Maybe we can call you when we're all together."

Her mother went silent for a long while. "I know I depended on you...probably too much. And I'm sorry for that too. Meeting Daisy and hearing about these new sisters of yours...I guess I'm starting to understand just how selfish I've been, wanting you all to myself."

"Well, who could blame you?" Sierra's eyes stung with tears, but she forced a light tone. "I am pretty amazing, after all."

Her mom laughed as Sierra had hoped she would. "Does that mean you forgive me?"

Sierra wet her lips, struggling for the right words. Her mind called up Cody and his feelings of responsibilities, Frank and his regrets, and then her sisters and their newfound family. "I...I don't think there's anything to forgive, Ma. It's not always easy to know where to draw the line, you know? And I think...I think we're all just doing the best we can."

Her mother sniffled, and Sierra's chest tightened. "You were in a tough spot, but I never doubted for a second that you loved me. And that's not something every kid can say."

"Yeah, I do love you, sweetheart. And if you want to know more about Frank and spend more time with your sisters...I'm okay with that too."

"Thanks." Tears blurred her vision, and she let them fall as she wrapped up the call with her mother.

Placing the phone on the bed, she checked the time and gasped.

"I can't be late to church!" Swiping away her tears, she checked her reflection in the bathroom mirror, then ran out the door, making it just before the service began.

Emma waved her over to join her and Nash, with the rest of the sisters and their families in the pews in front and behind her. Sierra was surrounded.

Rose leaned forward to whisper, "Glad you made it."

Then the music began and they were singing, then laughing as some jovial parishioner went over the notices before the pastor was speaking and none of them could talk for a while. Sierra glanced around her, not totally able to settle until...

There. Her gaze found Cody, and he was staring right back at her. His lips hitched up on one side—a small, intimate smile that made her insides settle and her chest warm.

It's okay, his smile seemed to say. *We're okay*.

Her answering smile felt tremulous. They weren't okay, not really. Not after the way things had ended the other night. If she'd had any hope at all that he might have a change of heart and take a leap of faith to be with her, their trip to the hospital and the tense silence that followed killed it.

He'd made up his mind. He was staying.

Which was fine, she told herself as she turned to stare straight ahead. It wasn't like he'd made her any promises.

She'd known from the start that this was how it was bound to end, just…

She shifted uncomfortably in her seat as she recalled her parting promise to her mother.

Just a little sooner than they'd expected, that was all.

She tried to clear her mind of all thoughts of Cody as she listened to the minister and enjoyed the choir. But this was easier said than done. She couldn't seem to stop sneaking glimpses of Cody, who looked more handsome than ever in a buttoned-down shirt and his hair neatly groomed. He was even clean-shaven for once.

He looked a far cry from the disheveled, carefree guy who'd ridden on the back of her bike and roughed it in a tent during a chaotic rock concert.

She liked this side of him, too, though. The clean-cut, dutiful son who never missed church and who'd undoubtedly be at the lunch afterward, chasing after his niece and nephew.

She forced her gaze back to the altar.

It would be a heck of a lot easier to leave if she didn't like this side of him so much. But his loyalty and big heart were all part of what made him Cody, and that was who she'd fallen in love with.

Love.

This was love.

She pressed her lips together and took slow, steady breaths. If this was how her mother had felt for Frank when he'd left her for college, she could sort of see why her mom had been so angry. So hurt.

To feel this way and not have it returned would be heartbreaking.

She peeked over at Cody.

Did he feel the same?

She thought so.

She hoped so.

But even if he did, it didn't change things. Did it?

The service was coming to an end when Cody's father was mentioned. Everyone in the church prayed for his quick recovery, and the pastor made an announcement that a sign-up sheet was posted out front to make sure the Swansons had meals delivered daily until he was up and on his feet again.

The service ended, and Sierra turned to Emma. "That's nice of the community to take care of the Swansons like that."

Emma grinned. "That's one of the perks of being in such a small town." Her smile turned rueful. "Gossip is the downside, of course. But to my mind, a few nosy neighbors is an easy cross to bear when it means you're surrounded by folks who'll be there for you when you need them."

Sierra nodded as they fell into step behind Nash. Rose, Dex, and Kiara were ahead of them, and Sierra heard Lizzy's brood follow noisily behind them. When they all poured out into the sunshine, they found Daisy's family already waiting.

Daisy had her arms looped around the younger of her boyfriend's kids, and the daughter, Mikayla, was firmly fixed at her side like they were joined at the hip.

"Are you coming to lunch, Aunt Sierra?" Ronnie asked.

"Of course she is," Daisy replied before Sierra had the chance.

"She has to come," Lizzy added, because apparently steamrolling people ran in the family. Sierra smirked at the thought.

But then Lizzy added, "We still haven't figured out where we're going to start looking for April and who's gonna go after her."

Emma frowned. "That's true. We need a game plan." She smiled at Sierra. "Looks like you're coming to lunch for a strategy session whether you like it or not."

"I'm happy to go to the ranch with you all." Sierra shifted from one foot to the other, her hands flailing a bit. "But unfortunately I'm not sure I'll be able to help much in the search for April."

All of her sisters were watching her with expectant looks that made her belly twist and turn with guilt. "You see, my leave from work is almost up," she started haltingly. "I tried to mention it before, but…" She faltered and looked at the ground, not wanting to take in their expressions. They were no doubt disappointed and angry that she was abandoning them. "I promised my mom I'd spend some time with her in San Francisco before I took off again, which means I have to go tomorrow."

It had seemed like the right decision when she'd been on the phone with her mom. The two of them had a lot to work through, and she didn't want to leave for Venezuela without spending some quality time together.

But now guilt was rippling through her. In being a good daughter to her mother, she was leaving her sisters in the lurch.

Emma wrapped an arm around her shoulders. "Sierra, if you have to leave, we understand."

"I promised April's grandparents we'd find her," Sierra started.

"And we will." Lizzy nodded firmly.

Rose and Daisy joined her, their heads bobbing in unison.

"Being part of this family means being part of a team." Emma smiled. "You promised we'd find her, and we will."

"Yeah, but I feel like I should help." She eyed them all in turn. "Emma, we all know you ought to be resting." Sierra arched her brows meaningfully, and the others snickered. "And the rest of you all have families who need you—"

"And so do you," Emma pointed out.

"Don't worry." Daisy leaned forward and gave her arm a little shake. "Dahlia will be coming home soon."

"And between the five of us, we'll make sure it gets done," Rose added.

Sierra nodded, but her guilt and hesitation must have been obvious because the others shared a look.

"Sierra, if you have to go tomorrow, then you should. Really," Lizzy said firmly.

And loudly.

Loudly enough, it seemed, that anyone could hear.

"Sierra..." Cody's low voice startled Sierra, and she whirled around to see him right behind her. His expression was grim, but his eyes were filled with pain. "You're leaving tomorrow?"

CHAPTER 41

Cody shouldn't have been shocked.

He knew she was leaving. That was always the plan. But as he backed away from Sierra, whose eyes were wide with horror at having him overhear the news like that, he couldn't shake this sickening sensation.

His insides dropped like he was on a roller coaster, and his head spun, like she'd just pulled the rug out from under his feet.

"Cody," Sierra rasped. "I was going to tell you..."

He wet his lips, his gaze darting everywhere but only finding sympathetic expressions from his friends and family.

Kit, who'd been at his side when they'd approached the group of sisters, actually hissed as he winced. "Bro..."

But Cody just shook his head, backing away.

"Cody, wait," Sierra said as he kept moving.

He held up his hand to stop her, then said to the group at large, "I'll see you guys at the ranch for lunch."

He wasn't sure if he was relieved or disappointed when Sierra didn't follow.

It was probably for the best. He needed a moment to collect himself. To remind himself that this was always the plan.

She'd never intended to stay, and he'd never considered leaving.

Not seriously, at least.

Sure, there might've been a moment or two when they'd been on the road that the thought of going with her had flitted through his mind. But then he'd come back to reality.

He ignored a text from Kit as he climbed into his truck.

It wasn't like he could avoid Kit or Sierra for long. And Lord knew the O'Sullivan sisters wouldn't let him brood for more than a minute without sticking their noses into his business.

He let out a humorless huff of laughter at the thought of all the well-intentioned prying he'd face when Sierra was gone.

No, he couldn't avoid Sierra or her sisters, but he could at least have the drive back to the ranch to get his head on straight.

First, he had to stop at his parents' house, though, to make sure they were settled in after the drive home from the hospital. He stayed for a while, adjusting the pillow under his father's elbow, helping his mother empty the dishwasher, and insisting on a list of groceries he'd pick up when he came back to town later.

After a fair amount of fussing on his part, he was shooed out the door by his father, who needed a nap.

"We're fine, Cody. Really." His mother patted his hand when she walked him back to his truck. "Your dad will recover and be back to his stubborn self in no time."

Cody nodded and kept walking to the car, but his mom

placed a hand on his arm. "You know that's what caused this accident, right?" Her brows arched. "Your father's stubbornness is at fault. Not you."

He bit back a groan. What had Kit told her?

"Your brother seems to think you're taking the blame on yourself," she told him.

Cody made a mental note to smack Kit upside the head.

"You know we appreciate all you do for us," his mother continued. "And even if Kit doesn't always remember to say so, he'll never forget the way you were there for him and the twins."

Cody stuck his hands in his pockets and rocked back on his heels. "I know, Mom."

She hesitated, looking like she might say more, but in the end, she just smiled and went up on tiptoes to kiss his cheek. "You drive safe back to the ranch, you hear?"

"Yes, ma'am," he murmured.

He silenced his phone when it gave another ding to signal a text, but soon the silence in the cab of his truck went from soothing to irritating. He didn't want to be stuck alone with his thoughts.

He flipped on the radio, and a heavy metal band was playing. Not Zombie Town, but a band that sounded similar enough that it had him snapping off the radio again with an irritated growl.

Was this what it was going to be like after she left?

Would he see her and hear her everywhere he went?

He gripped the steering wheel harder as he willed his mind to stop obsessing and his heart to stop aching.

It wasn't supposed to be this hard to let her go.

His mind went back to that first night they'd met at the pub in Wellspring. The flirting, the banter, the epic kiss…

It had been the most fun he'd had in...maybe forever. He'd felt like he'd come alive, and maybe he'd been a fool to think he could keep spending time with the woman who made him feel such joy and not get attached.

Maybe he'd been an idiot to think he could date Sierra and not lose his heart.

The drive back flew by in a blur, and once at the ranch, he avoided the main house and went straight to the bunkhouse to change. They were busier than ever with work these days, and try telling the cows and horses it was Sunday.

They didn't care.

So he did what he always did on Sundays. He picked up the slack and did the chores so Nash could spend time with his wife and Kit could be with his family.

Even Boone and the others had taken off for the day. Boone to spend some time with his family in town, and the others...

Well, he wasn't sure what they got up to on their time off, but they definitely deserved a break from the hustle of ranch life.

It wasn't like he was avoiding the main house, he told himself as he fed the pigs. This was what he always did on Sundays after church. And he wasn't avoiding Sierra either. He just needed a minute, that was all.

"I see I've got some competition for your attention, Cowboy." Sierra's husky drawl had him turning to find her leaning against the pigsty fence, her lips hitched in a little smile but her gaze focused on him like a laser.

"Yeah, well...they get almost as hangry as you do if they don't get fed on time."

Her huff of laughter made him smile.

Man, he was gonna miss that laugh.

She cocked her head to the side as she pushed away from the fence and moved toward him. "So...you're not avoiding me, then?"

"Of course not."

"Mmm. 'Course not," she echoed, disbelief written all over her pretty features.

"I had chores to get to."

"Uh-huh."

His heart gave a sharp tug, and his tone was harder than intended when he added, "Life on this ranch doesn't just stop because you're leaving, Sierra."

She flinched but recovered before he could even open his mouth to apologize. "I know that. I don't expect it to."

His gaze searched hers. What did she mean by that?

By the sadness in her gaze, he thought he knew, and it made his insides rebel. "I'm not saying I'm gonna forget you." His voice was too gruff.

She turned her head, but not before he saw that her eyes were shiny with unshed tears. "I wouldn't blame you if you did."

"Well, I won't."

She acted like she didn't hear him. "I meant to tell you I was leaving early." She dragged her gaze back to meet his. "I didn't mean for you to find out like that."

He shrugged, and the gesture felt like the worst sort of lie. As if he didn't care.

As if finding out she was leaving hadn't gutted him and left him hollow.

"Not a surprise," he mumbled. "I never thought you were gonna stay."

She opened her mouth and then closed it. Finally, she nodded. "Right."

"So what time are you leaving?"

Her throat worked, and he watched her nibble on her lower lip as her gaze lifted to meet his. "I need to check out by ten, so I'll probably hit the road right after that."

He tried not to let it show, but he was sure she saw it. The hurt. The pain.

"I need to spend some time with my mother," she said. "I can't just leave for another six-month stint without working things out with her and—"

"I get it," he interrupted.

And he did. That was the worst of it. He understood the need to put family first.

Heck, wasn't that exactly what he was doing?

Shame mingled with his hurt and his heartache. He reached for Sierra and tugged her close. "I'm sorry."

"For what?" she murmured into his shirt. Her tone was aloof, but her fingers clung to his shoulders, and he felt the shakiness of her breaths as she rested against him.

"I don't mean to make you feel guilty for leaving." He kissed her forehead, then her temple. "You're not doing anything wrong. I just…"

He couldn't finish. If he kept going, he might just say too much.

He might beg her to stay.

He might promise to go with her.

But he couldn't do that. His life was here. And hers was there.

She tugged back, pulling out of his arms just as the back door to the main house opened in the distance, and the sound of laughter and chatter drifted out to meet them.

"I should get back." She tipped her head toward the house. "My sisters and I have a lot to discuss before I take off. I just wanted to tell you that I don't…I don't expect you to remember me or…" She wet her lips. "I just want you to be happy, you know? And you made it clear your life is here, so you should make that life. You should find someone and start a family of your own. Because you deserve that." She sucked in a breath before forcing out the rest. "You deserve every good thing."

His heart felt like it was being ripped in two. Was she really telling him to move on?

Did she actually think he'd just forget the way she made him feel? Did she think she was that replaceable?

He had half a mind to tell her she was a fool if she thought he'd move on. But he didn't want to make her feel guilty for leaving, and admitting she was leaving him miserable and brokenhearted wouldn't help anything.

"Sierra, you coming?" one of her sisters called out.

She backed up a step, a question in her eyes.

He nodded. "Okay then."

She nodded as well, her throat working. "Okay then."

CHAPTER 42

S ierra eyed her reflection in the hotel room mirror.

She looked like garbage. Scrubbing a hand over her scratchy eyes and swollen nose, she turned to glare at the luggage on her bed.

Funny how at home she'd started to feel here in a hotel room.

She was a little sad to be checking out. But it wasn't leaving the hotel room that had kept her up crying all night long.

It'd been Cody.

More particularly, the way they'd left things.

"I don't expect you to remember me."

Had she really said that? The thought of him moving on killed her. But she'd meant it when she'd said she wanted him to be happy.

And he deserved the sort of love Kit, Nash, and the others had found.

Still, she couldn't leave letting him think *she* was going to move on. She couldn't just walk away—not this time. If there was any chance that he might be open to a long-distance relationship, she had to try, even if it meant going down on her knees to beg.

She could do that.

He deserved that.

With her new resolve, she grabbed her bag and headed down to the inn's lobby to check out.

It was early, but Cody got up at the crack of dawn to work. She'd find him on the ranch, say what she had to say…and then she'd go.

With a sniff, she said her goodbyes to the staff and headed to the parking lot.

And then she stopped short. "Cody?"

In the dim light of the rising sun, she saw his long frame leaning against her bike, a cowboy hat casting his features in shadow. He straightened when he saw her and took off his hat.

He looked…

She strode toward him.

Well, he looked horrible, plain and simple. Though she suspected she looked even worse, not that she'd know it by the way he looked at her.

He cupped her face in the palms of his hands when she got close. "I couldn't let you leave without a proper good-bye, and I just had a feeling you might cut out early, so I've been here since five, watching that door like a hawk."

She swallowed hard, but it was no use. Tears were already trickling down her cheeks. "I was going to stop at the ranch to see you."

His lips hitched up. "Well, now you don't have to."

She nodded, lifting her hands to hold his. "Cody, I…I didn't mean what I said yesterday."

His brows arched.

"I mean, I did…and I didn't."

His eyes held a hint of amusement. "I'm glad we cleared that up."

She let out a huff of laughter, and they both dropped their hands, wrapping their arms around each other like it was undeniable. They couldn't be this close and not hold on.

She'd been a fool to think she could just let go and walk away. "I do want you to be happy," she whispered, her voice watery and thick. "I really do. But the thought of you moving on…"

"Shhh." He kissed her soundly when she started to cry. "I don't want to move on."

"But—"

"You make me happy." His voice was low and gravelly as he pressed his forehead to hers. "You are my happiness. And you make me feel alive. That's what I came here to say to you. I'm not ready to say goodbye, and I have no plans to move on. Not ever."

Her heart burst into frantic flight. "But I have to go…"

"I know. And I need to stay."

She let out a sigh that held all the hope she'd started to feel. "Yeah."

"But let's not say goodbye, okay?"

She pulled back to meet his gaze. "Do you really want to do the long-distance thing?"

"Phone calls at all hours, texts, and emails. It's…." His brows drew down, and his expression turned determined. "I know it's not ideal. But I'm not ready to say goodbye. Not for good. And even if our connection won't be physical, just hearing your voice…reading your words…that'll keep me going."

Her heart felt like it was trying to escape her chest, it was beating so hard. "It'll keep me going too."

"Okay then." He kissed the tip of her nose. "This is not goodbye."

The sound that escaped her was somewhere between a sob and a laugh. "Okay then. Not a goodbye. Just a...see you later."

"I'll text you before you even leave the parking lot." His eyes were starting to dance with laughter, despite the sadness that still lurked there.

She took a deep breath, finally able to breathe fully, because she felt it too. A new lightness. A sense of hope.

It still hurt to be leaving, but this wasn't the end for them.

"I'm gonna miss you, Cody Swanson. But I know I'm gonna see you again."

"That's right." He tugged her close and kissed her with such hunger, she knew she'd be feeling the heat of his lips against hers until they met again. "And the next time I see you, you're gonna tell me all about your adventures."

Come with me.

Have adventures at my side.

She swallowed back the request. He didn't want that, and she couldn't force it.

"And when I see you again, you'll tell me all about what's been going on at the ranch and in this town."

"Oh, sweetheart, don't think you're gonna escape hearing all the local gossip from your sisters while you're gone." He smiled, and she had this sense that it was for her benefit. He was lending her his strength. "They've got your number now, and the O'Sullivans are nothing if not persistent."

She smiled, reveling in his warmth that seemed to wrap around her. "And the Swansons?"

"We're known for our patience." His voice was quiet

and serious. "I hated what you said about moving on. I won't forget you, Hustler. Not for one single second that we're apart. You understand me?"

She nodded. "I feel like I'm taking you with me in some ways. Whether you like it or not, you're gonna be hearing all about my time on the road."

"I'm holding you to that." He smiled against her lips.

A few kisses and one long embrace later, she finally urged herself to step away.

It was hard. Maybe the hardest goodbye she'd ever said in her life. But she was smiling through her tears as she finally climbed on her bike and gave him one final wave.

Sierra felt Cody's eyes on her as she drove out of the parking lot and through Main Street one last time before hitting the highway.

The sun was rising high in the east when she zipped back to San Francisco.

Her mind called up Cody's smile, his sparkling eyes, and the way he'd whispered, "See you soon, Hustler," just before letting her go.

No, she wasn't heading home. She was heading to her mother.

But once her assignment in Venezuela was done, and before her next assignment came through...*then* she'd be heading home. She'd head back to Aspire and spend time with her sisters on the ranch.

And she'd enjoy every second with Cody.

Because she still wasn't sure how it had happened, but like it or not...that cowboy was her home.

CHAPTER 43

C ody rubbed at his eyes and tugged his bandanna up over his mouth as he led his horse back toward the stable.

August was prime fire season in these parts, and the smoke was so thick he couldn't make out the mountain range that normally lined the horizon to the west.

Two weeks since Sierra had left, and the whole landscape at the ranch looked totally different.

It would look even more different when she came back for another visit.

February, she hoped. That was what she'd said the last time they'd had a video call. But their reception had cut out before she'd been able to give him any more details.

He looked around the range, trying to capture an image that he could describe to Sierra when they talked.

She always loved hearing about his days on the range. The more mundane the better, it seemed.

According to her, she liked to be able to picture him during the day, to imagine what he was doing. So she ate up every last boring detail he provided, and he did the same.

By now, he knew all the kids she worked with by name. He knew their illnesses and what their prognosis looked like. Heck, just this morning he found himself worrying over little Aliana's fever.

He slid off his horse and took the reins.

Maybe this was what it meant to be in love. Their worries became yours. Their joys were yours as well. That was what it meant to share a life.

The moment he stepped into the stables, he knew he wasn't alone. He heard a high-pitched laugh and felt his own lips hitch up at the corners despite himself. Seemed Lizzy had come to visit Kit.

Sure enough, he spotted her perched atop a low wall near the far end of the stable, Kit leaning against her, their voices low and their faces split with grins.

Cody looked away. He was happy his brother was so in love. He was happy for Lizzy and the kids too.

But that didn't mean it wasn't painful to see a couple actually sharing a life together, not just *talking* about their lives.

"There he is," Lizzy called out.

Cody looked over to see her hopping off her perch and heading his way. She held a small paper bag in her hand. "Here." She stuck it out, and he took it with a curious grin. "I promised your mom I'd bring you some of the cookies they got from Mrs. Mapleton."

"Thanks," he said. "You didn't have to do that. I was gonna stop by to check on them after I got done with work."

"No need." Lizzy smiled brightly. "I had off at the

boutique today, so I took the twins by to see your parents. Your father's doing great."

"Oh. That was nice of you to check in on them."

She tilted her head to the side and peered up at him, her smile filled with understanding. "You're not the only one who cares about your parents, you know."

He frowned. "I never said that."

She patted his arm in a soothing gesture as she walked toward the stable doors. "I know. I'm just reminding you. Now, I'd better go save Nash from the twins before they tie him up and use him for roping practice." Lizzy shook her head with feigned exasperation as Kit chuckled.

"They've done it before," Kit said.

Cody started to laugh too.

"It's not funny." She tried to frown, but her lips were fighting a grin. "Poor Nash has to learn not to be a pushover or his own kid is gonna run circles around him."

Cody nodded toward the house. "Want me to watch the little demons for a while?"

"Nah." Lizzy turned and paused in the doorway. "I know you love them, and they adore you, but you don't have to be their babysitter all the time. They say it takes a village, and we definitely have that here in Aspire."

With that, she turned on one of her ridiculously high heels and headed toward the house.

Cody looked at Kit with his brows arched. "Why do I get the feeling Lizzy is trying to teach me a lesson?"

"Probably because she is." Kit's smile widened with pride. "And my wife is about as subtle as a sledgehammer."

Cody chuckled. He couldn't deny that. "Yeah, well, what was she going on about Mom and Dad not needing me, and that stuff about the twins?"

Kit's expression shifted to one far too sympathetic for Cody's liking. It almost bordered on pitying. "You really don't know?"

Cody shrugged, shifting uncomfortably. For two weeks now it'd been like this. Everyone treating him with kid gloves and making weird comments and giving him these sympathetic smiles.

"They're worried about you, bro." Kit looked away as he added under his breath, "We all are."

"You're worried about me? Why?"

Kit turned back to him with an exasperated huff. "Why? How about because you've done nothing but mope and brood ever since Sierra took off."

"I have not," he muttered.

But he had. And he knew it. He was trying his best to find this new normal, but it wasn't easy. Nothing was the same. He couldn't take off for a ride without wondering what Sierra would say or do if she were with him. He couldn't fall asleep without thoughts of her crowding out his mind.

He couldn't even go about his daily work chores without wondering how he'd describe it all to her when they got the chance to talk.

"I'm fine," Cody muttered when he realized Kit was still watching him with that knowing expression.

"You are many things, Cody Swanson...but you are not fine."

Cody rolled his eyes and turned his attention back to his patient horse. "I miss her, that's all. But that's to be expected, right? I'd like to see how you'd be acting if Lizzy was living half a world away for the next six months."

Kit followed him to the stall. "You'd never see such a thing. And do you know why?"

Cody didn't answer.

"Because I'd never let Lizzy go from my side for that long."

"Uh-huh." Cody kept his attention on the horse, trying to swallow down his irritation. "And who would be looking after the twins if you took off after Lizzy, huh? Me and our folks?"

"No, dummy. I'd take 'em with me."

Cody shot him a baleful look.

"Fine, then I'd go down on my knees and beg Lizzy to stay."

Cody paused in brushing down the horse. "And you'd be okay with that?"

"Okay with what?"

"Forcing a wild stallion to be fenced in?"

Cody didn't turn around, and for a long moment, Kit stayed quiet. "No, I guess I wouldn't."

Cody just huffed. He'd made his point.

"But, Cody…"

Cody didn't have to turn around to know his brother was running his hands through his too-long hair. There was something he wanted to say, and he wasn't saying it.

That was annoying.

"What?" Cody finally prompted, curiosity winning out as he whirled around to face his older brother. "What is it?"

Kit winced, which put Cody on edge, defensive before his brother even began to speak.

"Cody, it's just that…you don't have kids."

Cody blinked. "So?"

Kit scratched the back of his head with a grimace. "So it's not apples to apples is what I'm saying. If Lizzy ran off to Venezuela, I'd have my kids to think about…"

Cody understood what his brother was getting at, and the words landed like a blow. "So, what? You're saying I'm not needed around here?"

His brother opened his mouth. Then he clamped it shut. And then, with a sigh, Kit shrugged. "Yeah, I guess that is what I'm saying."

Cody stumbled back a step, the words a jarring jolt to his solar plexus. "Thanks, man. Thanks a lot."

"Look, I did need you. After Natalie left, and I was alone with the twins, I needed you, and you were there for me, and I'm not sure I'll ever be able to repay you for that."

Cody looked away. He and Kit were close, but neither of them was the type to talk about emotions, and this was so not what he'd thought he'd ever hear. "You don't have to repay me," he muttered. "I love those kids."

"I know you do. And I know you love Mom and Dad, and everyone else in this little world of ours. Everybody on this ranch and in this town knows you'd go to hell and back if we needed you to. You're our rock, Cody. You always have been, and you always will be."

Cody turned away, the words causing the most confusing mix of emotions—a surge of relief that he was appreciated and needed…

And maybe more than a little hint of resentment at the same time.

"But we love you too," Kit said, his tone uncharacteristically serious. "You're not the only one who gets to give in this family. Sometimes you gotta let other people step in."

Cody scrubbed a hand over his face, but he didn't respond.

"Lizzy and I can look in on Mom and Dad, and when

we're too busy with work and kids, we'll make sure someone else in the community can step in."

Cody's jaw was so tight, he couldn't speak if he tried. His mind was whirling, and his heart was aching.

He missed Sierra something fierce. But this was his world. His home. What would he even be if he wasn't reliable Cody? If he wasn't the dependable brother and son, and the doting uncle?

You'd be Sierra's partner, a voice in the back of his mind pointed out.

"The kids and Lizzy love you." Kit cleared his throat. "I love you. And that's exactly why we don't want to hold you back. Just like you wouldn't ask Sierra to stay for your own selfish reasons...we don't want you to stay for ours."

A long, heavy silence fell, but Cody didn't turn around, and he didn't speak.

He had no idea what to say.

"Just...think about it, okay?"

Cody heard Kit walking away, but he still couldn't bring himself to speak.

CHAPTER 44

S ierra wiped away a trickle of sweat as she knelt down
to help little Eduardo with his crutch. "I think if we
adjust it just a little..." The crutch clicked as it slid into
place.

Eduardo beamed up at her as he tested it out. "Gracias,
tía!"

Sierra smiled, still loving the way every child in this
place called her "auntie" no matter how long they'd
known each other.

This village was even worse off than the one they'd
been to before, and she'd escaped the stuffy clinic hoping
to find a breeze outside on her break.

Instead, she'd found a blistering hot sun.

Their last village had been in the mountains, and she
found herself missing the shade and the wind now as she
eyed the flat terrain that surrounded their temporary
clinic.

One of the senior doctors came out of the makeshift
office, his face red and beaded with sweat. He spotted her

and walked over with a weary smile. "I see you had the same idea."

"I don't think it's any cooler out here," Sierra murmured with a sigh.

"Well, the sun will be sinking soon, so that'll give us some respite." The doctor frowned back at the tent. "What I wouldn't give for a handyman to fix the fans."

She smiled. It was an age-old gripe. As a charity organization, they were almost always saddled with well-used, often shoddy equipment and no one who knew anything about fixing it.

"Maybe someone in town can tell what's wrong?" she offered.

The doctor tugged at his collar. "Maybe."

They stood in companionable silence for a while, watching as some of the local kids played soccer in the neighboring field.

The parents in this rural area seemed to think they didn't need any medical help, unless the case was severe, but they were quick to bring their kids in for check-ups and vaccinations, so Sierra had become familiar with most of the children in this village.

A couple waved, and she waved back.

"Ah, the nurse smiles," the doctor said beside her.

Sierra turned to him with a questioning frown, and he laughed. "Sorry, it's just…a few of us have noticed that you haven't exactly seemed thrilled to be back. You're not sorry you returned, are you?"

Sierra shook her head quickly. She wasn't sorry. The moment she'd seen the kids and had gotten back to work, she'd known she'd made the right choice. It wasn't easy to be so far from Cody, but she couldn't deny the sense of purpose her work gave her. "It's not that I'm sorry to be here…"

The doctor waited for a moment, but when she didn't continue, he nudged her arm. "Dr. Lewis thinks you're homesick."

She shot him a sidelong look. "You and Dr. Lewis spend too much time talking about me."

He laughed. "Guilty. But if it's true…that you're homesick, I mean…" He shot her a knowing look. "There's no shame in admitting it. We all run into this now and again."

"I know." And she did. More than once, she'd been the shoulder to cry on when one of her coworkers struggled. Between the stress of what they did and the distance from home, it wasn't uncommon for workers to wrestle with bouts of homesickness.

"I want to be here." Sierra said slowly. "But leaving was harder than usual this time."

It felt good to admit it to someone. And when the doctor waited silently for her to continue, she found herself spilling the story of how she'd gone and fallen in love during her time off.

"Ah," he sighed when she was through. "Long-distance relationships are difficult."

She nodded. That was putting it mildly. They'd been doing the best they could to keep in touch, and she looked forward to their video chats with the eagerness of a kid at Christmas.

But they always felt too short, no matter how long they lasted. And more often than not they were cut off, due to poor reception, far sooner than she liked.

His texts kept her going throughout the day, and their calls and photos back and forth gave her hope that she could make it until February.

And then what? She could already feel a sense of excitement and sadness, and she could picture it all too clearly. A too-brief trip that was at once heaven and hell as they enjoyed each other's company and braced themselves for another long stint apart.

Not for the first time, she wondered how other humanitarian nurses and doctors did it. And couples in the military…how did they stand the separation?

Was it fair to ask Cody to keep waiting for her?

Her phone dinged, and her heart leapt with joy. For now, at least, they were together. And when she lifted her phone and found a picture of Cody's eyes, crinkled at the corners, his bandanna pulled up and his hat tilted low, she burst out in a laugh.

The photo was titled, "Fire Season."

She started to type back but realized she was being rude. "Um, sorry. Do you mind if I…?"

The doctor waved her off. "Go on. Get in contact while you can. I hear our next stop has even worse reception."

Sierra winced as she hurried off to find a place where she could get a decent signal.

Cody answered on the first ring. "Howdy, Hustler."

Her heart melted. "Hey, Cowboy."

"How's Eduardo doing with his new cast?"

Her heart skipped and leapt. How had she ever gone this long without a partner? Someone so close and dear that he was a best friend and so much more, all in one sexy, irresistible package?

"He's doing all right. How'd Chloe's dance recital go?"

And they were off, chatting and laughing, and pretending with all their might that this was okay. That this was good.

That this long-distance relationship was enough…
And that it could last.

CHAPTER 45

I t never ceased to amaze Cody how Sierra could still be beautiful even when the screen froze while she was mid-speech.

He took a deep breath to hold back a curse as he waited for the connection to return. When it did, he'd missed something she'd said.

"… but I'll survive. It was only a minor b-burn."

"A minor…" He leaned closer, squinting at the screen as if that could somehow make her words clearer. "Did you just say burn? Are you hurt? What happened?"

He couldn't make out her garbled response, but her smile put him at ease. And then…

Then she was gone.

The call ended with a blip that made his stomach sink.

Again.

He scrubbed a hand over his face, this needy ache in his chest unbearable. It wasn't just an ache. It was a hole where his heart should be.

What if she needed him? What if she was in trouble?

He'd never know, and even if he did, he was too far away to get to her.

What kind of boyfriend *was* he?

A terrible one, that was what.

"Hey, man, you coming to the barbecue at my uncle's or what?" Boone stuck his head into Cody's small bedroom. His hair was wet and sticking out at odd angles, like he'd just gotten out of the shower and run his hands through it.

"Yeah, I'm coming," Cody murmured.

Though, truth be told, he was not in the mood for a big family barbecue, even if he loved every person who'd be there. He'd rather…

Oh heck, he'd rather be with Sierra, even if it was chatting on a video call with a bad connection.

But since he knew from experience that they wouldn't be able to reconnect anytime soon, he might as well go to the gathering.

He'd promised Chloe and Corbin, after all. And his parents wanted to come as well, and someone had to make sure they got home all right if they stayed too long. His mother had horrible night vision.

All the reasons he should go had him throwing on a clean T-shirt and heading out just as Boone was sliding on his boots. "I'll drive us over."

Nash's parents might live on the neighboring land, but it was still too far to walk, so they both climbed into Boone's truck and made the short trek to the Donahues' property.

The party was already in full swing when they arrived.

They spotted Nash's sister, Casey, and her husband climbing out of their truck when they parked.

"I'm gonna go say hey to my cousin." Boone jumped out of the truck and bounded over for a hug.

Cody was slower to follow. The sounds of laughter, music, and loud voices only made his bad mood worse.

Maybe coming here was a dumb idea.

But Boone had already taken off, and he didn't relish the thought of trekking back to the bunkhouse on foot... and then he couldn't escape if he wanted to because he was spotted.

"Uncle Cody!" Corbin shouted at such a loud decibel, it seemed like half the party turned to smile and wave at him.

Cody forced a grin as he waved back, and then he bent down to catch his nephew, who was barreling straight for his knees. He swooped him up and planted him on his hip in one quick move. "Hey there, pardner," he drawled.

Playing cowboy had become Corbin's new favorite game. He and his sister were forever chasing Cody around, pretending he was the cattle they were rounding up.

But at least he never let them rope him like poor Nash.

The thought had him smiling in earnest as Corbin filled him in on all he'd missed at the party so far...which, in all honesty, didn't seem to be much.

"My friend Sawyer is here!" Corbin shouted suddenly, interrupting his own long-winded monologue as he wriggled out of Cody's arms and shot off to see his friend.

Cody found himself eyeing the gathering, feeling a little like that guy from *Groundhog Day*. The Donahues threw these parties regularly, and the crowd was always the same, aside from the newest addition of O'Sullivans over the past year.

He spotted Emma chatting happily with her in-laws,

looking radiant and not on the verge of throwing up for once.

He wondered if she and Nash would tell his folks today or if they still meant to wait.

Meanwhile, Dex and Rose had joined Boone, Casey, her husband, and the summer ranch hands, who all seemed to be taking turns trying to make little Kiara smile.

He spotted his parents and went over to kiss his mom on the cheek and give his dad a pat on his good shoulder, checking in to make sure everything was all right. But after assuring him they were just fine and on the mend, they went back to talking to Nash's grandparents, and Cody found himself...lost.

Well, not literally. He'd worked for the Donahues before Nash brought him over to the O'Sullivan's ranch, so he knew this property like the back of his hand. And he was closely acquainted with every person here.

Most he'd known his whole life.

Which meant this was home, right? This was where he belonged.

But still he found himself wandering through the crowd—at the party but not a part of it. He knew he should be happy here. Before Sierra came along, he'd always loved these events.

What had happened to him that he felt so restless now?

And suddenly, out of nowhere, Sierra's voice was in his head, clearer than it had been on that dang video call. It was something she'd said to him after he'd whispered in awe about her adventurous spirit. She'd just spent hours regaling him with travel stories.

"Ah, but that's the beauty of adventures," she'd said. *"It makes coming home that much more satisfying."*

Was that true?

He reckoned maybe it was. Right now he knew for certain he was taking all this for granted. He had so many blessings in his life, and he ought to be more grateful.

But even standing here amid his loving family and friends, on land he'd worked with his own bare hands...

He still felt that hollow ache. He still found himself wondering what Sierra was doing right now. What she was seeing and who she was meeting.

He found himself wishing he could see it all with her and not just hear about it on their calls.

The thought made him antsy and too irritable for small talk, so he smiled and nodded at the friends he passed as he made his way to a picnic table on the outskirts of the Donahues' lawn.

He wasn't sure how long he sat there, watching as Daisy, Levi, and their kids showed up to join the fun. Listening to the laughter as Lizzy told his parents some story, no doubt about the twins and their antics.

He watched Kit chase the twins around the yard as they squealed and pretended to be scared.

He heard the music when it started and watched as Emma and Nash started to slow dance, quickly joined by Rose and Dex, then all the other couples.

He loved each and every one of the people here, but sitting here on the outskirts, it was hard not to feel a bit like an outsider. They'd all found their people. They'd created families of their own.

He was staring off into the distance when Chloe spotted him sitting on his own and ran over to join him. "Uncle Cody, what are you doing?"

"Nothing, Peanut." He smiled at her. "Just thinking, is all."

She tilted her head to the side. "Can I think too?"

He grinned. "'Course you can. I'd love the company."

Chloe climbed into his lap and made herself comfortable as she'd done so many times before.

Cody sighed as he wrapped his arms around her, settling his chin on top of her head as they both watched her parents dance while Corbin raced around the makeshift dance floor with his friends.

Chloe sat in silence for a while, but when she broke it, she cut right to the chase. "Why do you look so sad, Uncle Cody?"

He took a deep breath, as if that would help ease this throbbing pain in his heart. "I miss my friend."

"Mmm." Chloe sounded far too wise for her years as she nodded knowingly. "Uncle Cody, is Aunt Sierra your best friend? My mommy says she is."

He nodded, his chin brushing against her fine hair. "Feels like it."

Chloe shifted to face him. "Then you should go play with her."

"She's too far away for playdates." His lips hitched up in a sad smile.

"Do you love her the way Daddy loves Mommy?" Chloe looked at him seriously.

His heart stuttered at the direct question, but the answer was so obvious there was no denying it. "Yeah. Yeah, I really do."

Chloe went quiet for a minute. "I learned about Venezuela, you know. I asked Grandma if she could show me a picture on a map, and then we watched a video about it. Do you want to go there one day?"

He shifted. Did he want to? Want didn't seem like a strong enough word. "I'd love to, but…"

"But what?"

He opened his mouth, ready to answer with his standard "I'm needed here," but as he watched the scene play out before him—the happy families all together, looking after one another...

They didn't need him sitting over here on the sidelines feeling miserable. Heck, they didn't *want* that.

They wanted him to be happy just as much as he wished that for them.

His gaze met Chloe's as the tight ache in his chest started to lighten, a flicker of hope making it ease. "What if...what if I did go?"

He wasn't really asking Chloe, but she answered all the same. "I'd miss you."

His lips twitched at her honesty. "What if you knew I would come back to visit, and you could always call me?"

She pursed her lips. "I can call you anytime?"

"Yep." He nodded.

"Will being over there make you happy?"

"I think so." He started to smile as he pictured Sierra there and him working alongside her. Working together, traveling together, seeing new things and learning about new cultures. His heart started to pick up its pace as excitement took hold. His mind's eye filled with an image of Sierra. His love. His woman. That excitement turned to longing and a love so deep it felt unending.

Would going to her make him happy?

"Yeah," he said gruffly. "Yeah, it definitely would."

"Then you should go."

"Yeah, I think I should."

Chloe grinned and then leaned forward to wrap her arms around him and hold him tight.

He squeezed her back. "You know what, Chlo-Chlo? That's exactly what I'm gonna do."

CHAPTER 46

S ierra heard kids' voices outside her little exam room, and though her break was almost at an end, she couldn't stop staring at the calendar in front of her.

She held two pages up as her eyes scanned the days, then lifted a page to glance at the next month.

It wasn't like she was counting the sleeps until this stint was over, necessarily. She was just…

Ugh. Okay, yeah. She was counting.

She dropped the calendar pages with a sigh. This was the pits. She didn't want to be unhappy here. In many ways, she loved this place. She'd had so many rewarding interactions with patients and had learned so much about the culture and the language.

She'd spent every free second doing what she loved while traveling—learning about the country and meeting new people.

It was everything she loved about her job and the whole reason she'd chosen to return to it. She should be satisfied, dang it. She should be grateful to have the life of her dreams.

Except…

Except she missed Cody so much it physically hurt. And that sense of something missing was with her even when she was doing what she loved.

Maybe she'd been an idiot to think long-distance could work. She'd thought they could make it, but the last few calls had been so…unsettling.

Cody had been quiet and distant.

Or…maybe he hadn't. Maybe it was just the poor connection.

Or maybe he was tired of seeing his girlfriend on a screen rather than in person.

Could she blame him?

No. She definitely couldn't. Maybe it was time to bring it up. To give him an out…

The thought had tears stinging the back of her eyes. But she knew deep down that this situation wasn't fair to him. She couldn't ask for a commitment when she'd chosen to leave.

But she didn't want to have this conversation with the terrible connection they had. She didn't want to have this conversation at all, but she could only imagine how much harder it would be to try and have a real heart-to-heart when their voices kept cutting in and out.

Which meant…

Her gaze went back to the calendar.

Which meant they'd have to have this talk when she returned.

Which meant five more months of waiting and hoping and missing and—

"Sierra?" Gabby, one of the other nurses, stuck her head through the flap that gave Sierra and her patients some semblance of privacy. "Dr. Green needs you outside."

She shot up, glad for the distraction. "Did we get another shipment of supplies?"

Sierra didn't wait for an answer as she hurried to follow Gabby to the exit.

"Something like that." Gabby grinned.

Sierra shot her friend a curious look, but Gabby was staring straight ahead as she led the way outside. Sierra followed her into the bright sunlight and squinted as her eyes adjusted to the bright beams that backlit the Jeep her boss had driven into the parking area.

The doors opened, and for a second, Sierra was certain she was hallucinating.

She took a halting step forward, the world coming to a standstill as she blinked. She had to be seeing things, because... "Cody?"

The word came out too quiet, but Cody seemed to hear, because his face split with a blinding grin. "Howdy, Hustler."

She ran toward him, and his laughter wrapped around her just as surely as his arms when he squeezed her tight and lifted her right off her feet. She kissed him hard, laughing right along with him as he spun her around.

"Does this mean you're happy to see me?" he asked when she pulled back for air.

"Yes!"

He set her down on her feet and wiped away a tear she hadn't realized had fallen. His tone was gentle as he leaned down so none of the bystanders could hear. "Why are you crying?"

Her lips trembled, and she leaned into his strength.

"Because I missed you, and the last time we spoke, I thought maybe you wanted to end things, and—"

He laughed. "No way. It was taking everything in me not to tell you my plan. I wanted to surprise you. It was Lizzy's idea. She said it'd be romantic, but I hate that I made you think for a second that I didn't want to be with you."

"It's okay." Sierra laughed, squeezing him around the waist. "Just promise me we don't have to be apart again."

"I promise," he said. So simply.

And for the first time since she spotted him, reason started to filter in. "Wait, really?" She leaned back to get a better look at his face. "How long are you staying? And how did you manage this, and—"

With a laugh, he pressed a finger to her lips and glanced meaningfully toward her boss, who was watching their happy reunion with a satisfied grin. Gabby was smiling beside him as she wiped away tears, and the kids in the courtyard were gaping open-mouthed.

"Meet our new handyman," her boss declared. With a shake of his head, he added, "You don't want to know how much red tape I had to cut through to make this happen so quickly."

"You…" Sierra's mouth flapped open and closed, and then she spun to face Cody. "Seriously?"

"Seriously."

"B-But your job—"

"JJ should be back on the ranch by now," Cody said. "They'll be fine without me."

"And your family—"

"All but pushed me onto the plane," he admitted with a wry smile. "Turns out I'm not much fun to be around when I'm heartbroken and missing my girlfriend."

She smiled, her hands coming to rest on his chest like she could assure herself this wasn't some dream. "So you're really here."

"I'm here." He leaned down close so it was just the two of them again in their own little world. "I'm here, and I'm not going anywhere." He paused and seemed to rethink that. "Or, let's just say, I'm not going anywhere without you. Where you go, I go."

"So we're on this adventure together, then?" Her voice quivered with hope and excitement that was almost too good to be true.

"Together." He kissed her forehead. "Forever." He kissed the tip of her nose. "And wherever life takes us." He kissed her lips then, and this one was soft and tender.

It was a promise. A vow.

And as Sierra kissed him back, she told him without words that she was in this all the way. Body, heart, and soul. She pulled back just long enough to whisper the words she'd been dying to say. "I love you, Cowboy."

His smile was slow and sweet and made the butterflies in her belly take flight. "I love you, too, Hustler. More than anything in the world."

She let out a shaky breath. "Well...okay then."

"Okay then." He grinned.

And then he kissed her so well, she couldn't have said another word if she'd tried.

EPILOGUE

One month into his new job, and Cody had never been happier.

From where he worked on setting up the exam equipment in this new remote town in the mountains, he could see Sierra kneeling in front of a little girl who was pouting as she held a Band-Aid-clad finger up for Sierra to see.

Cody grinned as he watched his girlfriend work. She was so good with kids. So good with everyone, really. He'd been in awe watching her this past month and admired her more with each passing day.

The woman was fearless when they traveled—never hesitating to try new foods or speak the language even when she was met with laughter when she messed up. She never complained when the conditions were rough and always had a joke or a comforting word when her coworkers struggled.

The woman never ceased to amaze him, and seeing the world with her had brought him more joy this past month than he'd ever known possible.

Of course, that wasn't to say he didn't miss home. But

as his family and friends kept reassuring him whenever they called and texted—which they did often—they'd be there waiting when he and Sierra had another break.

And he'd appreciate the heck out of every second he was in Aspire and surrounded by his family.

His phone dinged with a text.

This village had decent reception, which was a blessing. He frowned down at the message and then hailed Sierra when she stood and the little girl ran off smiling.

"Everything okay?" she asked, her smile so sweet and full, it made him forget for a second what he'd even called her over to say.

"Oh, uh, yeah…probably nothing. But I got a text from Kit asking us to call now if we can, since they're all together."

Her brows knitted. "Okay, yeah. Let's go to my tent. My laptop seems to work better."

They squished into the camera frame as it rang on the other end, Sierra snuggled up in his lap as they waited to see the beloved, familiar faces back home.

JJ's bearded face filled the screen first, so close his nose looked crazy big, and his face was sideways on the screen. He flipped it, and his face turned but then went back to being wrong again.

"Dang it," JJ muttered.

Sierra started to snicker.

"Never can get the hang of these stupid things. Lia, baby, help me out here."

Dahlia pulled him back, taking the iPad out of his hands. "You don't have to be quite so close, babe."

Dahlia's face filled the screen. "Hey, you two. You're looking good. Let me just…" Propping the device on the table, she sat back so Sierra and Cody could see the room behind them. They were sitting in the dining room at the ranch house.

Cody and Sierra exchanged silly grins. "We're all good here," Sierra said for them both.

JJ and Dahlia had been disappointed to come home and find Cody already gone. And Cody had felt bad about not being able to say goodbye to one of his best friends. But they'd all been in constant contact, even if JJ wasn't particularly fond of the technology involved.

"Is there something wrong?" Cody asked. "What's with the SOS?"

"Nothing wrong!" Emma called out from off-screen. "Sorry if we gave you a scare."

Emma walked into view, Lizzy and Daisy following in her wake. Rose was bouncing a fussy Kiara in her arms and waved from the distance. "Hey, guys!"

Cody and Sierra both waved back, grinning when Dex appeared to pull funny faces at his daughter just as Kit turned to shush the twins, who decided now was the perfect time to start a "who can scream the loudest" competition.

"Outside. Go talk to the pigs." Kit pointed to the back door, and the kids ran off laughing.

"Mick, can you keep an eye on them please?" Daisy batted her eyelashes at Levi's eldest daughter, who rolled her eyes but followed the twins out back without any kind of verbal complaint. "Thank you!" Daisy sang, then turned back to the screen with her dazzling grin.

"We just wanted to fill you in on the latest." Lizzy flicked her sunny blonde hair over her shoulder. "Oh, and just as a warning, Chloe and Corbin want to call you later to perform their poem they learned at school."

"Of course. Can't wait." Sierra grinned.

"Tell 'em the news before we lose the connection." Emma nudged her sister.

"Yeah. This is big," Daisy said, her smile easing any remaining worry.

"We found April," Dahlia announced, looking satisfied.

"You did?" Sierra straightened with excitement. "That's great news."

"Yeah. We know where she is, but she still won't answer our calls." Emma frowned.

"But," Nash cut in, "Boone offered to go get her."

JJ nodded, his expression thoughtful. "We all thought it might be best if the sisters don't gang up on her. They might be too intimidating."

"Hey, we don't gang up on anyone." Daisy laughed out the words as Levi pulled her in for a sideways hug and kissed the side of her head.

"I wouldn't say we're intimidating," Lizzy added.

Sierra started to giggle. "No, of course not. Just…"

"Persistent," Emma finished proudly. "We're just persistent."

"Exactly." Daisy nodded.

All the men kept quiet.

"Well, I think sending Boone is a great plan," Sierra said. "And once you get her home, let me know. Cody and I can request a trip back if we need to finalize the inheritance."

One way or the other…

The words went unsaid, but they all knew what she meant.

April was the deciding factor, and no one knew which way she'd lean.

"That's what we were hoping you'd say," Emma sighed.

"We can't wait to see you both," Kit added.

The topic changed to general ranch business, but when the call ended, Cody turned to Sierra with a questioning look. "You're really okay with heading back early?"

"If it means getting the family business squared away, then yeah." She leaned into him. "Even if we travel, family will always come first." She kissed him gently. "I learned that from you."

He tightened his arm around her. "Okay then, I guess we'll be making a trip home a little sooner than we thought."

She smiled as she looped her arms around his neck. "We'll go to *Aspire* soon," she clarified. "But when I'm in your arms...that's where I feel at home, Cowboy. You are my home."

His heart clenched with sheer, unadulterated joy as he leaned in to kiss her.

She was right, of course. This woman was his home now...and she would be until the end of time.

Thank you so much for reading Sierra and Cody's romance. I love these two together. The way they challenge each other is my favorite part of this book.

I'm getting excited for April's story. How will she react when Boone finds her? Can the hot cowboy she remembers from high school persuade her to face her fears and return home for good?

FINDING HOME WITH MY COWBOY

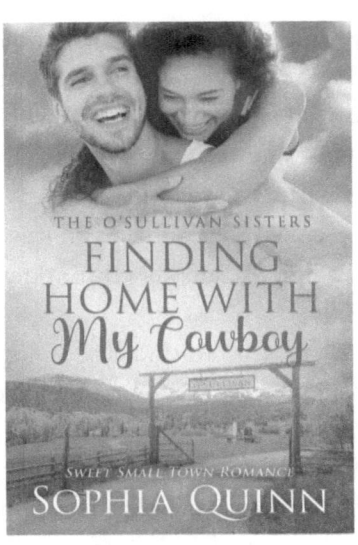

THE O'SULLIVAN SISTERS

FINDING
HOME WITH
My Cowboy

SWEET SMALL TOWN ROMANCE

SOPHIA QUINN

When the place you called home is the last place you want to be...

April O'Sullivan is on the run. The youngest sister in the O'Sullivan clan doesn't know where home is anymore, but it's definitely not with the six half-sisters she never knew existed until just before her father passed away. But now, grieving for the life she lost, she's desperate for answers, and she's not going back to her father's ranch until she finds them.

There's only one problem. April's new family has sent someone to fetch her. And that someone was the bane of her existence in high school. Boone Donahue probably didn't even remember the artsy geek he'd gone to school with, but April can't forget the cocky, big shot quarterback with the charming grin and the Greek god bod. He's the kinda guy who always gets his way—because who could say no to a charmer like Boone? Well, April can. And she will. There's no way she's going to let Boone drag her back to the ranch before she's good and ready. So if that means he's tagging along while she uncovers her family's dirty secrets, so be it.

But when Boone's famous charm makes her smile when she's at her lowest, and when those broad shoulders are there for her to cry on, it's easy to forget that he's an unwanted reminder of home. In fact, some days it starts to feel like maybe....Boone is her home.

AVAILABLE IN JULY 2023

ACKNOWLEDGMENTS

Dear reader,

Sierra is a woman of many layers and working with her was fun. I love her spirit for travel and her heart for those in need. I love how much Cody complements her. Their first meeting—those scenes playing pool—were my favorite to write. They had a great first introduction and it set the tone for the entire book.

Thank you so much for reading. I hope you enjoyed the story and getting to know a little more about Frank. I'm looking forward to shedding some light on this mysterious man and touching on his romance with Loretta. It'll be a strange feeling wrapping up this series, but I'm also excited to finally see the whole family together.

If you enjoyed the book, I'd like to encourage you to leave a review on Amazon and/or Goodreads. Reviews and ratings help to validate the book. They also assist other readers in making a choice over whether to purchase or not. Your honest review is a huge help to everyone.

And speaking of help, no book is complete without a team of people, so I'd like to thank Deborah for this gorgeous cover. It took us a while to find the perfect couple, but you did it! Thank you, Kristin, for being such a wonderful copy-editor, and to my proofreaders who caught those last few mistakes and then helped me promote the book.

Thank you to my lovely readers. Thank you for the beautiful feedback and for enjoying these books enough to read every one of them. I so appreciate your support and encouragement.

And just before I go, I'd like to thank God for his unfailing love. No matter where we end up, or what we choose to do with our lives, His love is constant and I'm so grateful for that fact.

ABOUT THE AUTHOR

Sophia Quinn is the pen-name of writing buddies Maggie Dallen and Melissa Pearl Guyan (Forever Love Publishing Ltd). Between them, they have been writing romance for 10 years and have published over 200 novels. They are having so much fun writing sweet small-town romance together and have a large collection of stories they are looking forward to producing. Get ready for idyllic small towns, characters you can fall in love with and romance that will capture your heart.

www.foreverlovepublishing/sophiaquinn